DANCING WITH DARKNESS

H J REESE

DANCING WITH DARKNESS

THE WILD HUNT
BOOK ONE

H J REESE

Copyright © 2023 by H J Reese.

All rights reserved.

No part of this publication may be reproduced, stored or transmitted in any form or by any means, electronic, mechanical, photocopying, recording, scanning, or otherwise without written permission from the publisher. It is illegal to copy this book, post it to a website, or distribute it by any other means without permission.

This novel is entirely a work of fiction. The names, characters and incidents portrayed in it are the work of the author's imagination. Any resemblance to actual persons, living or dead, events or localities is entirely coincidental.

Cover designed by MiblArt

ISBN: 978-1-7389528-3-0

❀ Created with Vellum

CONTENT WARNINGS

Dancing with Darkness is a fantasy romance novel based around the myth of the Wild Hunt.

Its content warnings include: sex, violence, swearing, and hunting/animal related triggers.

To my littles and J, who will one day know those stories I told at bedtime found their way into a book. (But will never be allowed to read them because of the added sex and the swearing and the general death vibe of the whole damn thing.)

Also, Simon says to—so I did.

Summer Court

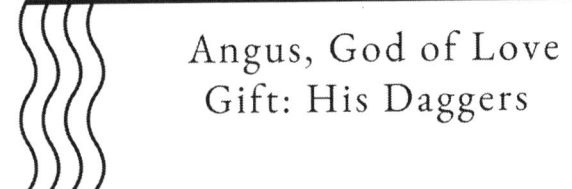

Angus, God of Love
Gift: His Daggers

I am the water
The river runs through me

Autumn Court

Gael, God of Forging
Gift: His Hammer

Hope lights the fire
Fury fans the flames
Courage carries me through

SPRING COURT

Daina, Goddess of Fertility and Air
Gift: The Berserker

With a song on its wings
And life at its feet
Wind guides us all

WINTER COURT

Bruma, Goddess of Ice
Gift: Frost Witch

Frost quiets my mind
Ice hardens my soul
I will persevere

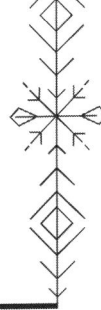

1

"Valentina! Valentina!"

His voice was ragged and shrill; not like when he used to summon me out of the top branches of Summer Court's mango trees in the forest across from our house.

No, now he was screaming.

Everyone was.

I spun my head through the chaos, trying to stay nimble on my feet through the charging crowd. Flashes of knees and bunched silk dresses in white-knuckled fists blinded me as I scrambled through the running fae. They were trying to get away.

Away from what, I still wasn't quite sure.

I found safety from being trampled near a gigantic statue of Angus, our adored God of Love, in the middle of our town's beloved courtyard. The heat of an eternal summer sun sparkled above me as I gripped the back of the statue's calf and hoisted my scrawny self onto its base, trying to get a better view. I stood as tall as I could, pressed up onto my tippy toes on the statue's stone feet. Like I would when Father and I danced during

Summer's festivals. I willed my water magic to calm my racing heart so I could listen for Father's voice again.

But someone, maybe many, bumped into the statue behind me and I flew forward to the rough cobblestone, scraping my knuckles against its surface. I drew in a sharp breath as blood coated my six-year-old hands. I blinked down at them. The pain would have crippled me if I wasn't so used to it.

"Valentina!" came my father's voice again.

I jutted my head up to hear better as a foot came crashing forward into my nose. In their panic, whoever it was had not stopped running. I tucked my head down as more fae ran by, and I did my best to scrunch myself into a tight ball. Blood dripped from my nose to my mouth and I spit it out onto the stone. But against my cheek, the cobblestone below did something it never did in Summer Court.

It turned cold.

I held my hand up, sheltering my eyes from the shining sun, and jerked away from the frost that was creeping, slinking, its way across the courtyard. What does this mean? Where was Father? He would know.

And there, through stomping feet and shrieking fae—I saw him.

Father!

He was packed in tight with a group of others. Seri Wynivere, our neighbor two doors down, was sobbing beside him on the far side of the square.

Father flailed his arms out towards me like he was trying to pull me across the courtyard on an invisible string, screaming my name again and again, beckoning me over and over.

I wiped my sweaty hands down the bright-pink silk now plastered to my legs. Oh! That's how he found me. He must have seen my dress! It was the pretty one I saved for my birthday. Seri helped me sew it. My cake still sat at home, uncut, candles blown out. My wish, sent up to our god, Angus. Did he hear me? Was this happening because of me?

I took off for Father, wiping my bloody nose on the white ruffled sleeve. I'd worry about the stain later. Father was . . . why was everyone so scared? Now and then, in between the screaming, I could hear the Robinswallow River bubbling past as I raced along it down the courtyard.

But then, around the last of the fleeing fae, I saw them, with their long-reaching spears and their precision bows fastened to their backs, soldiers clad in bronze armor inlaid with azure swirls. My feet faltered.

Winter's soldiers.

And though I now understood how the courtyard froze, I did not understand why they were here. In Willowspeak of Summer Court of all places. No one here was particularly wealthy. Most weren't even fae.

I sucked in a breath and dipped around a knee, charging forward. My legs burned; my breath fogged in front of my face as I dodged around a hip.

Father and the others had been pushed back against the raised porch of Ms. Multhorn's house. Her clay flowerpots crunched under the soldiers' boots as they jabbed their spears forward. I slunk up behind, jumped the railing to the porch, climbing as fast as my little legs would go.

"Father!" I yelled, clinging to the baluster with one small dirty hand, and reaching out for him with the other. Reaching through the hostage fae.

No, *not* fae.

I looked at the front of the crowd. Mrs. Greenthrow, who lived a few houses down from Seri, clutched her husband's coat, holding him tightly to her. He was a grumpy old faeless, a fae with no magic, who would shoo us off his grass when us faelings, those younger than eighteen, played too close. We were spotty with our magic and sometimes one of us would accidentally flood it.

But this wasn't the Mr. Greenthrow I knew as my eyes traced the tear marks down his round, wrinkled face.

I looked to the back of the crowd. Being pressed against the vines that ran up the side of the house were Mr. and Mrs. Ravenash. They clung, arms outstretched, encasing one of their young faelings, enclosing her between them so she didn't get trampled. Her name was Lililou, but we called her Lulu for short. They huddled, pressing their foreheads together, defeated. Their son, Roshan, was my best friend. He'd flood Mr. Greenthrow's lawn on purpose.

They were all faeless. Magicless fae on Eadha Island. They could not work the magic of water like fae from Summer Court were supposed to.

I yelped when someone grabbed my hand, and I almost slipped off the railing entirely. It was Father. The crowd jostled him as they pushed away from Winter's spears.

"Valentina, sweet Valentina. You must do it now," he urged. Father's fingers gripped my flesh so tightly I stuffed down the urge to pull free.

The soldiers' eyelashes and eyebrows were as white as the frost that was creeping up the balusters. They moved closer still, shoving and pushing. Then the screaming *really* began, moving, growing into a palpable force I could not get away from.

"Father!" I yelled over the noise.

"Valentina! Ugh!" he cried. "Do it now!"

The panic in his words made my body shake. I knew what he wanted, but there was still so much I did not understand.

But it was Father, and he was asking for help, so I did what he needed. I opened my magic, not my water magic, but my *other* magic.

I took away his pain; pulled it from his body as if it weren't there at all.

I brought it into me.

And as the ice and frost gathered up his calves and spread across his thighs, it was my own body that felt Winter's cold wrath.

A scream bubbled up from my throat and no matter how hard I tried, I couldn't pull out of his grip. Not that it would do me any good now.

He suddenly released my wrist and I fell back off the railing and onto my butt to the hard, alderwood of Ms. Multhorn's porch. I scrambled backward with numb feet and aching legs, wishing to pull away from the pain that rose up, up, up and into my core. I clawed my little fingers into the wood and dragged my limp feet across to the other side of the porch. Backing away more and more, wishing to run and hide in sweet-smelling mango trees.

And right before I stumbled back under the railing and off the porch altogether, I saw Winter's soldiers pull their spears back to a ready stance and turn away. Turn away from the crowd of faeless they just froze to death in the courtyard. My neighbors, my friends—my father.

They all stood still; unmoving, like translucent blue ice sculptures. Their expressions were etched in time, frozen with the agony they felt as they died, all screeching and writhing in pain. Except for one. Except for Father's, whose face was one of comfort, calmed in placated bliss with his gaze locked upwards, lovingly turned towards the ever-burning sun.

That was the last thing I saw before I tumbled off the deck and plunged into the steady flow of the Robinswallow River.

I am the water
The river runs through me

Now that river was carrying me down and away. Away from my home and all that I had ever known. I muttered our mantra over and over through chattering teeth. Wishing that when I blew out my birthday candles, I would have wished to never be able to take another's pain—instead of the stupid faeling-like wish I had made.

I grabbed a large piece of driftwood as it floated by, but the weight of it spun me around and around. My nerve endings snapped to life like a roaring fire and then dulled to an all-consuming numbness that prevented me from moving my legs at all. I leaned my cheek against the wet wood, sucking in deep breaths, as I became helpless in the current. On a rotation around, my eye caught on the armor of a Winter's soldier facing the racing river and *gods*, I wish I hadn't looked. But I did.

Though a bronze helmet hid most of the face, a sky-blue gaze traced my path, followed me, like a lingering chill, down and around the winding river.

2

VALENTINA

FOURTEEN YEARS LATER

B Y ALL ACCOUNTS, it was just a chair. An artless piece of furniture tucked against an emerald-green wall in Daria's Otti Theater. Overshadowed to everyone but me by an enormous, lavish picture frame that reached almost from floor to ceiling.

I leaned against the carved alder doorframe that led to the kitchens downstairs and picked at my chapped hands. They were raw from scrubbing our guest's dinner plates for the last hour. The smell of honey pastries wafted up from the steep stairs I just came out of. It was a smell that usually stole my attention.

And yet—I stared, fixated on the chair.

It was an older chair, one with a low splintered back, used ages ago when the theater was visited by Summer Court only.

But time and use had taken its toll and marked it with scuffed rungs and a broken leg.

A stray hip of a Springfae in the crowded auditorium knocked into it, sending it wobbling in a desperate cry for attention. I sighed and leaned farther against the doorframe because only I saw it.

The rest of the chairs were stained a deep walnut brown, faceted by gold rivets that held the olive plush cushion on the back and seat. Beautifully crafted chairs to match the beautifully decorated performance theater.

Word spread far and wide across Eadha Island about the craftsmanship of the Otti Theater in Elaria of Summer Court. And I wrung my hands together, wishing they would stop shaking, because they weren't talking about this chair.

Not my chair.

I pulled at the side seam of my dress, oh gods when did it get so tight? It constricted my lungs and the corset boning dug into my stomach. But a dress like this was necessary for the company I hoped to keep tonight.

Against better judgment, I scanned the audience. Panic seized me, sharp and strong, as bile rose to my throat. It was a full house.

And worse, it was almost curtain time.

A thud and a growl down the back hallway pulled me from my dread, followed by cursing I recognized. I took off quickly, through sheer crimson curtains, passing dancers getting ready for their sets. Stockings were being pulled on, makeup applied with the wave of a hand, dresses cinched tight to the laughing tune of some of Summer Court's most lovely fae. I ducked behind a lineup of dancers practicing in tandem, dodged their cruel glances and sharp elbows, and tried to slight the watchful eye of Daria, the theater's owner, and my employer. Three steps later, I dipped around the corner, clear of the staff, and frowned at the sight.

"Braeth," I said carefully, drifting towards the giant magog holding my friend by the throat near a tattered side door not meant for the audience's eyes.

I rounded his enormous back, rested my hand on his thick forearm and looked up into his fat, puckered face. "Put Roshan down," I said, low and firm. Which was the only proper way to speak to a magog, a creature as big as an ogre and only slightly more reasonable.

Magogs were large, almost fae-like creatures. That is, if a fae was stung by a thousand hornets and as a result, pockets of its body swelled up in disfigured bumps. Usually even an eye would be askew. They originated from the western Yegevani Mountains in Spring Court and were smarter than their near cousins, ogres.

But just barely.

I am the water
The river runs through me

I concentrated on Summer Court's mantra as I sent my water magic to quell the chasing anxiety. Magogs could sense agitation, and I needed this one to listen to me. I sucked in a deep breath as it soothed my soul.

"'E was sneaking around again, Miss Valentina. I don't like 'em." Braeth's big meaty head dipped from side to side. "I don't like 'em around Miss Daria. This one's tricky."

His fist tensed around Roshan's neck, his forearm flexed stiff under my hand, causing a gurgling sound to escape Roshan.

Daria employed three magogs as guards for Otti Theater.

Though big and dumb, they were impervious to a fae's magic. Which was good because we saw all manner of fae here.

"I promised you a broken bone if I ever saw you flintin' about again. Peepin' on Miss Daria's dancers," Braeth continued.

It was an awkward move, stepping between the two of them, but I didn't have time for this. Roshan sniffled as he got a face-full of my hair. Magogs had bad tempers; Daria counted on it. But I had some place I needed to be.

"Easy there, fella," I said as I craned my neck, trying to catch the gaze of his massive roaming eyes—just like the last time we did this. "Roshan is harmless. Daria is about to go on stage. Alone, with Autumnfae at her toes. I'll take care of poor Roshan here and you go check on her before Sisaria's set."

An ugliness bubbled up in my gut as Braeth's eyebrows furrowed. It felt manipulative to use Daria's name on him like that. But if he was out for blood and powdered bones, might as well make it an Autumnfae's.

It took grumbling, it took steadiness, but eventually the big magog placed—or rather threw—Roshan down and trudged off in the direction I came from. I watched his big lumpy back —set with straggly black hairs escaping his sleeveless overshirt— go as Roshan's dark stare bore into the side of my face.

"I'm not that poor, Val," his scratchy throat tried to spit out.

I raised an eyebrow as he straightened the giant's fist-shaped wrinkles out of his probably stolen, deep-red tunic.

"Well, you're not going to get any richer when Braeth catches you again and decides to smash you to pieces." I moved past him, back out the door our magog caught him trying to sneak in through. "He'll mail you home in a box."

The eternally warm summer air coated my face as the smell of hibiscus, thankfully, overpowered the sweat Braeth left behind. It was always clear here, never a cloud to dampen our days nor hide our starry night sky. I looked up at the silver moon from where it sat high in the sky. Perpetually the same.

"Like that dumb ogre would ever know how to mail anything," Roshan mumbled, sauntering close behind.

I smiled as we walked alongside the large, vine-covered theater wall. Any magog would brandish you a stain on the cobblestone if they heard you refer to them as an ogre, a beast viler than them, resembling more animal than fae. Less civilized. Though said to be less hairy.

"Where's your brothers?" I asked, rounding the east corner, beckoning for him to follow.

Otti Theater was open to all manner of fae from any court on Eadha Island. Anyone willing to travel, and willing to pay. All kinds of performances happened on that same dusty stage I was at minutes ago. Though sometimes things got a bit wild. Clothing got a bit scarce. And all kinds of sounds came from the back rooms behind the theater, down the opposite hallway as my rooms. Where, for even more dimas, Eadha's currency, you could have a dancer for a performance of a different kind. We were Summerfae. Passion was in our nature, fueled by the heat of this ever-burning sun and our ruling god, Angus, the God of Love.

"Supply run to Hawrenthia. I'm in charge until they get back."

I winced, watching as he puffed out his chest and smoothed down his tunic. I knew there were at least two faelings at home younger than him. Their parents and sister were killed in the same raid by Winter Court soldiers that took my father in a different town fourteen years ago. A raid organized by Winter's long-time and current ruler, Lord Aborys.

I wrapped an arm around my friend's waist and guided him onwards, leaning my head on his side. Roshan's brown eyes held a pain I could never ignore, and a fire churned in their depths that spoke to something inside of me. A mutual hatred for Winter Court, a wish for retribution, and a brutal understanding that neither of us were ever going to be worthy of executing it.

"Don't look at me like that," he said. "They are sleeping, and I told the neighbor to watch them."

"The one with the . . ." I reached up and flicked his nose with the tip of my finger.

"The pig snout? Yeah, that one."

I'd never seen her. I wasn't allowed to leave the theater. But I hid, high above the stage, on the large support beams, eating honey pastries and listening to the dancer's gossip. Rumors floated around that her mother had relations with an agriculture god resulting in her only daughter having the nose of a swine. Others said it was because she was always sticking her nose in other people's business. But Roshan coerced it out of her brother that she was cursed as a baby by a god who took offense to her crying at the shores in Hawrenthia, Summer Court's capital.

"Up here." I pointed to a wooden keg under a half-opened window covered in wisteria vines. I caught sight of my broken chair on the other side and my skin flushed cold.

Roshan raised an eyebrow before hoisting himself up, pushing the greenery aside. I leaned in passed my friend and pulled open the wooden shutter farther as Roshan's eyes widened. I refused to look again at the chair just below or the picture frame to its right.

It wasn't a bad vantage point, really. Especially for someone who wasn't supposed to see it at all. Roshan would have had to sell every article he owned—including the stolen ones on his back—to be able to afford an hour in our theater. But there was something in the way Roshan looked at Sisaria, our best dancer and one of my only friends, that made my heart swell.

It wasn't the way the rest of them did, as they fidgeted their hips in their gold-studded chairs, licking dry lips with flicking tongues. Roshan, when he snuck in times before, grew still when she danced, and entirely ceased breathing when she smiled. If I had any idea what love was, I would have thought that was it. So, this way, with him tucked into the vines, Roshan didn't end up a puddle on our theater steps by a magog with three brain cells.

"Leave as soon as Sisaria's set is over. Daria will kill us both if she finds out I'm helping you again. The only thing I want to see is this bald spot on the back of your head running away."

He swatted off my hand as I pulled on a chunk of midnight hair.

"You hear?"

"Yes, Val. Of course. Sisaria. Done. I got it." He looked down at me from the empty mead keg, his eyes shining. "Has she mentioned me?"

I froze. I introduced them once, hid him from Daria under the guise of a Summerfae soldier and Sisaria surprised us both when she brought him up to her room, instead of down to the rooms in the back hallway. Which at the time I found odd, but she said they just talked. Though I found her humming outside in the back hammocks hours later and she would just smile at me when I asked her why. And somehow, I've found myself saving a love-bound Roshan from the magogs ever since.

I knew it wasn't the answer he wanted, but I was fae and I could not lie, so I said, "Sisaria keeps to herself."

Unlike the rest of the dancers in Otti.

I turned and walked, slippered feet on sandy soil, back to the side doorway. Daria would need me soon but with one hand on the carved wooden doorknob, ready to go inside, I found myself hesitating.

This would have been the time a parent, though Roshan was much my own age of twenty years, would threaten their faeling to obey with some warning of siccing a monster of Eadha on them. In an attempt at coercion, they'd say their souls would be stolen, pulled straight from their bodies by the sounding hooves of the Wild Hunt, or by its hounds, led by the Lord of Shadows, who ruled one court over to the south. Be dragged to the bottom depths of the sea by the mermaids in the eastern waters. Or be eaten by those blasted seamutts in the western seas outside of Spring Court. Or darker things inland, things even ancient fae were wary to talk about.

But I wasn't Roshan's guardian, nor was I any proper form of a parental figure. Lord Aborys was responsible for most of that and one day I would rejoice with the rest of them when some brave fae brought down that tyrant.

But fae like Roshan and I would never see anything other than pieces of Elaria that fae more powerful than us would allow. So, no warning came from my lips as I winked at him, closed the side door to the forever warm air of Summer Court, and headed to one of the places I was allowed to be. The splintered, worn chair with the broken leg.

The theater's hazy, thick incense assaulted my senses again, clouding my vision and I leaned into the feeling. Full houses always started me off exhilarated, caused my blood to scream. My body hummed, and I closed my eyes to the feeling, wishing it was enough to quench the anxiety. A stray thought wondered if my mother was a performer and a sour taste permeated my mouth. Once my thoughts trailed to my father, I shook my head, sharp and hard, willing the thoughts to rattle free from my head. Nothing good came from thinking of the past.

Not tonight. No.
Because I had a visitor of my own coming.

VALENTINA

A GENERAL CALM ran through the crowd. With the exception of the Autumnfae hollering at the front, food flying out of their wide mouths in a despicable display of manners. Likely it was their second plate of dinner, too.

Daria was already up on stage, charismatic as ever, when I reached my spot against the east side of the theater auditorium. I glanced out the window to make sure Roshan had settled and wasn't magog meat. Daria was immaculate, as she gave a perfect performance of smooth hand gestures added with a beautiful resounding voice that carried as she started the night off with a song. Her hair sat back high on her head, only to be outdone by the massive, blood-red ballgown that took up most of the stage. But her eye twitched and I knew she was furious at the fur-clad fae in the front row spitting honey mead on the stage at her feet.

But kicking out an Autumnfae, brash and severe as they were, was a good way to call The War of Many to your doorstep. A war that had been brewing for centuries between the courts of Eadha, tempered only by acts of hospitality between them, such as this. Daria could have directed the magogs to throw the three firefae out into the sand where they came from, but instead, she directed that silently furious gaze at me.

Her eyes flicked to the chair, then back up. My pulse quickened; it was time.

Daria's song softly ended and she glided to the side stage as Sisaria twirled front and center. Her waist-long golden hair was pulled back into a massive updo I'd tease her about later, but right now, I couldn't stop the shaking. I ran a trembling finger against the grainy, rough back of the chair at my side.

It wobbled.

"Val, sit down. I can't see Sisaria," Roshan said in annoyance out the window at my back.

His voice startled me, and I sat down more abruptly than I wanted to. The boning of my dress cinched in again. Oh gods, I was going to burn this dress after tonight.

Daria pursed her lips from the side stage at my insubordination and my face flushed. She was the only reason I had a place to sleep at night, and I almost rushed to grab the edge of the picture frame. My mouth dried out. I couldn't have her angry.

The music started and Sisaria did three pirouettes to the other side of the stage, full of a limber grace. She dipped down with the beat of the song, a fast one I'd seen her practicing during late afternoons when most of the theater was just waking up.

I wiped sweat from my brow with the back of my hand.

Roshan's heavy breath on the back of my head made me feel like the walls were closing in, but I couldn't find the words to tell him to shove off so I clung harder to the rubbed-worn bronze picture frame.

The frame was a clunky thing made of bronze metal molded into shapes of fast-moving ships on angry seas and the twirling mermaids below. I smoothed a thumb over the rubbed-worn tail of the largest mermaid, as I did every night we had a show.

The music swelled as the aerial ties fell from the ceiling right into Sisaria's open palms. It was a flawless performance that sent the crowd into a round of cheers. Vile things left the mouths of the Autumnfae, and I prayed to Angus that they wouldn't be heading to the back rooms tonight.

The sweat dripped down my bodice as I fought to choke down my angst. I didn't trust myself to send my water magic out to soothe it. Sisaria turned around the soft lilac silk ties slowly, building suspense with a dazzling smile plastered across her ruby-red lips. Roshan's breath stopped against the back of my head. And *this* was the reason Daria had me do this during her performance. No one dared look away. No one dared look at the kitchen female in the rickety chair, sweat plastered to her forehead clinging to a massive bronze frame.

Sisaria climbed the ties like a ladder into the clouds, spinning them around her slender torso as she went. She was as graceful as a vine up a beam, enthralling the audience in a daze. My gaze snagged on Daria, whose eyes were on me, brimming with intensity, arms tight across her body. I wiped my forehead with the back of my hand again.

Sisaria reached the top as the crescendo peaked.

It was time.

I slammed my eyes shut and released the *other* magic that flowed through my veins and sent it through the conductive surface of the frame I clung onto. I knew Sisaria would release her grip and let gravity spin her down the ties, like a water drop down a windowpane. Near the end she would tug tightly on the ties halting her descent, inches from the dusty floor as my magic, the magic that saw the aching fae of Spring, Summer and Autumn in the audience, start a dance of its own.

It saw the way they favored a foot or rubbed a worn shoulder. It saw the way they grimaced as they stretched a sore calf out. What pain was blind to me before became crystal clear. My magic sought it out because that was its job. It wanted to please, to fix. All sixty-three of them. Even if I wanted to be anywhere but here, in the broken chair, taking the pain from fae who would never know my name.

The hurt shoulder hit me first and I sucked in a breath, feeling the pain radiate down my own. And then the rest hit me all at once. The dull aching pain of Spring soldiers' knees as they traveled the furthest for our performances. Various pains from Summer Court, who came so often, none of it shocked me. Stiff backs and sore hands, mostly. But my calves tightened, and I curled my toes in revolt at what was coming from the skin-peeling, throats-burning, heads-pounding Autumnfae.

The picture frame was a bit of magic and a lot of innovation. A self-preservation tool I designed and built five years ago. Without it, my magic only worked with physical contact. Through an accidental bump here, the brushing of a hand in passing a mead glass there. It was slow work and dragged my night on into eternity. With this invention, I could take it from everyone, albeit excruciating pain, all at once.

I tried to swallow the nausea that rolled through me when a sharp stabbing pain above my left eye had me tilting my head back. This pain I was familiar with. Daria was prone to migraines, usually caused by the stress of the theater on nights Autumnfae made the torturous trek across the Glenora Desert. My lungs caved in as my magic found them seated in the front row, backs to the rest of the warring courts. They'd never know it was me who took their thirst away; my lungs burning like fire to saplings, harsh and thorough. A pained cough escaped me before I sucked in a breath. I wasn't supposed to draw attention.

"Val? What's wrong? Are you okay?" Roshan asked.

"Don't. Speak," I gritted, my voice hoarse. Because I wasn't a particularly good dishwasher, and at best, a mediocre seamstress. I was an okay sparring partner for some dancers whose sets required such moves and props. But this, *this* I was good at.

I was a really good parlor trick.

I was the reason Daria's theater was the busiest and most profitable establishment on the island of Eadha. Rumors moved through the courts like minnows down a stream. It spread that Daria's performances were gifts from the gods. A cure to ailments. A magic in the air that purged them temporarily from their discomfort.

And there I sat, toes curled in, sweat tracing the curves of my spine as all sixty-three fae achieved a state of harmonic bliss.

A whisper of a name on the lips of an enemy caught my attention as the music changed and Sisaria switched to a slower number. My breaths came shallow, and I didn't foresee myself being able to move for the next hour at least, but I craned my neck, leaning into the polished bronze of the frame to try to hear it again. I might as well have been invisible to the Autumnfae as they whispered among themselves. And that was their first mistake, because they never whispered. It caught my attention as I leaned forward, listening for Cillian's name again.

"And what of Cillian?" the skinniest firefae said. The red fox fur around his shoulders looked muddy under our lowered lights and flickering candles.

"He'll be nowhere near Blackwater Junction in three days' time. The equinox is one month away. Lady Fede will have him wrapped up in her skirts until then."

I stilled. Where was Blackwater Junction? An ugly anger shot through me at the mention of General Cillian and Lady Fede, the Lady of his court, Spring Court. But I knew he wasn't with Lady Fede. Because that general was coming to visit me in my rooms tonight. I leaned deeper still, stifling a bellowing cough.

"Val—" Roshan started again.

But instinct—what happened when my concentration was broken—had my palm to his face as I shoved him back through the window he was leaning in on. A grunt and a thud rang out from outside as he landed in the sandy, hard-packed ground of Elaria.

What were these Autumnfae saying about Cillian? And what was in Blackwater Junction?

"General Mohr has made a bargain with the owner of this hedonistic theater to entice Cillian to stay for a few days. It'll allow us to investigate Blackwater," the largest Autumnfae said, bringing his cup to his lips. "There's been a long-lingering magic there. Mohr wants to know more before it begins."

What begins? My mouth dropped open, and I searched for Daria. I found her staring at me from the right wing of the stage, brows furrowed. But I was a gaping fish because my employer had just made a deal against my . . . Cillian. She knew what I heard. She shook her head once, severe and sharp, in a warning. I licked my dry lips.

I knew that look. She'd been giving it to me for over a decade, ever since she took me in when my town and family were ransacked by Winter Court. And this was the price I paid. But now she was asking me to pick sides against the only one outside Elaria I could trust. The only one I brought into *my* bedroom.

I peeled my stiff hand from the picture frame. I didn't dare look at the crowd. Their euphoric expressions at my expense filled me with a sadness that lingered longer than the pain ever did. So, I watched Daria, my boss, and my savior as she came out to the stage to sing the hymn of the God of Love as she took credit for my abilities. She didn't look at me again, despite me searching for a nod from her. A smile, something to acknowledge a job well done.

Halfway into her song—which seemed to go for hours—the front doors whooshed open, blowing out the dozen lit candles across the large mezzanine. Summerfae, in clothes like mine of dark silk and stiff boning, feigned attention on Daria but kept a cautious eye on what the wind carried. I turned as quickly as my stiff neck would allow to see the burly, fur-clad backs of the Autumnfae as they retreated out a backdoor of the theater. Springfae, marked by a telltale strand of silver hair, stayed glued to Daria, because they knew who was coming and they didn't have a reason to fear. My heart thumped in my chest, and I didn't have to look to know General Cillian had come in. I'd recognize the smell of him anywhere.

Daria ended her song early, albeit a little abruptly. I swallowed a smile as the honey pastries I smelled earlier appeared on the tables, acting as a buffer against Cillian's interruption. The smell alone drove my mouth to salivate, and I didn't have to wonder anymore why my dress felt cinched in.

Roshan—who didn't listen to my earlier request to leave and had resumed his position—leaned in through the window, popped one into his mouth and was reaching for another when I scooped it first. I shoved it into my mouth with shaking fingers, hoping it would starve off the nausea. The sweet honey coated my tongue, and I felt my shoulders slacken. This, and Cillian, were the closest to any bliss I'd ever find. I searched for him through the thick incense billowing towards me. My head and shoulder still throbbed in pain.

But he was here, and everything was going to be okay.

A cool breeze continued from the door, blowing my skirts tight around my legs, that smelled purely of Cillian and held the weight of a powerful fae. I searched for the familiar green eyes in a crowd of fae I didn't know. There, just inside the entrance off to the side, came the general of Spring Court's army. His soldiers, flanked on either side, marked by Spring's birch tree insignia, did not pretend to be calm in a foreign court with potential enemies so close. I inhaled the heady smell of narcissus —early spring daffodils—and of Cillian as my eyes met his. My midnight hair blew off my shoulders, tickling my back and the rest of the candles flickered, struggling to stay alit in the wind magic Springfae carried.

The heaviness of his attention made my skin flush for a myriad of different reasons. None of which were fear of being alone in my rooms tonight.

Daria's sickly-sweet voice rang out over the jeers, promising more. Promising satisfaction. But it would not be from me. My part was done.

"Roshan, go home," I said, putting weight on my aching feet as I hobbled to the back hallways, passed dancers getting ready for the next set.

I grabbed a giggling Sisaria and gave her a congratulatory kiss on the cheek. She squeezed my hands. Hers, small and boney, were warm in mine. I contemplated mentioning Roshan, but she drifted away with the rest of the dancers. Her blonde hair bobbed with every move.

I dodged a support beam on weak knees, barely able to see in front of me through the thick incense Daria lit on nights as busy as this when strong wiry hands grabbed me in an embrace. Smooshing my head into an equally strong wiry chest.

"By the gods, Val. That's the closest I've seen Sisaria get without leaving snot marks on the stage." Petri, another dancer and my main sparring partner, tousled my hair.

I looked up into his deep-set brown eyes and pulled his long fingers from my hair. "She's very impressive," I said through clenched teeth because I hadn't seen. I was just a little busy then.

"Are we training tonight?" he shouted as I shifted to pass him.

I pulled his arms off my shoulders, grabbed the wine bottle he held in one hand, and took a deep swig. Sweet summer strawberry wine battled the dry throat from Autumn Court soldiers.

Petri was a valiant sparring partner and, aside from Sisaria, my only friend in the theater. It was those long-reaching arms that made it so hard to spar him—with my shorter stature and even shorter daggers. I preferred fighting up close and personal, and Petri's long reach and lithe body kept me at bay.

Most of the time.

I turned back. "Can't tonight, Petri." My eyes flashed and my lips turned up. "I have a guest."

His eyebrows reached his cropped-short brown hairline. "Oh. That explains why Daria was cursing back here." His face frowned as he rubbed his bicep where I accidentally nicked him yesterday. My ability to take away pain never reached the back where the dancers waited. "She's jealous you're bedding the very fine and very sexy general of Spring."

"She is? Or you are?" I joked as he stole the wine bottle back.

But before he could answer, a wave of chilled air blasted down the corridor, chasing the foggy incense again.

As if pulled by the mention of him, the large body of Cillian darkened the other end of the hallway behind me. He leaned his massive arms on either side of the hallway above his head and narrowed his gaze. Apparently, I'd not stopped to say hi.

"Don't come looking for me unless someone is dead or dying," I whispered to Petri. "Or unless they bring up more of those honey pastries. The ones on those fancy trays." I just *loved* those damn things.

His head bobbed as he nodded vehemently, shoving a nearby gawking dancer out of the way. Because that's what people did in Cillian's presence. They gawked.

I swallowed my anticipation as the next song rang around the theater and Cillian stalked towards us. A muffled crowd erupted in cheers to what was happening on stage, likely a set with much less clothing than before. I hoped Roshan was gone.

My breath caught in my throat as Cillian's stare became voracious. He could steal the air from my lungs if he wanted to. Collapse them in on my body as all Springfae could. But Cillian had a want radiating from his body of a different kind, and a need in his eyes that sent my heart racing. Half of Eadha was afraid of him. A beast so unlike magogs and ogres in every way possible but deadlier than them all.

A fabric, silky soft and light as air, was pressed into my hand. I pulled my eyes away to see Petri—still staring at Cillian—shove a Caterina del Aamod scarf into my hands. My body softened at the thought of us using the shimmering gold and silver ties, which were scarves blessed by Angus to bind two lovers together until both were properly and utterly satisfied. The magic that coursed through it made the scarf lock around both parties until they were perfectly undignified. Until their bones, muscles and very souls were turned into puddles of satisfied goo on the floor, bed, wall, mountainside. Wherever, really.

"We won't be needing this Petri." Cillian had reached us, tugged the Caterina del Aamod scarf out of my hands and placed it carelessly on the dressing table beside us. His hands found their way to my shoulders and pulled me back against him. The heat of him coursed through every fiber of my being as he lowered his mouth to my ear. "I'll make sure she's properly satiated."

I was sure Petri was going to pass out. The slender Summerfae was beside himself, and if my body wasn't weak from earlier, I would have laughed at the absolute mess Cillian had turned him into.

I peeked up at Cillian behind me. His oak-brown hair waved lazily across his forehead as his face framed down into a strong jawline. A smirk graced his curved mouth as he raised a dark eyebrow, gently guiding me to take us to my bedroom. And my feet got right on to it.

Cillian's predatory nature was a heavy thing behind me, a demanding presence that raised goosebumps along my arms. His hand snaked up and around my torso, pulling me closer—if it was possible—to his hard body. I swayed my hips, leaning into him as we walked in tandem, earning a very satisfying groan. Cillian guided me onward towards my room behind the mess of the theater. His impatient hand tightened on my stomach as we reached the entrance.

It had been a month since he last visited. He'd come, claiming he was on diplomacy missions between the courts, though I'd yet to see any peace follow his travels. Autumn's soldiers were attacking weaknesses in Spring's borders and Spring was retaliating in-kind. It irritated Daria, the squabbling of these courts when Winter, the real threat she said, was busy up north.

I turned to face him when we reached my bedroom door. Staring up into his greedy gaze, an uneasiness spread through my chest, remembering the Autumnfae and their venomous whispers. He searched my eyes, as if it would tell him where my thoughts had led me. But instead, I ran a steady finger across his chest and ducked into my room. The secrets I held were for his ears only, and the theater was full of prying eyes, sneaks, and sulkers. After all, that's how I found out this secret to begin with.

And because Cillian held secrets of my own. Ones Daria swore me not to tell.

4

VALENTINA

CILLIAN WAS AT the top of the list of monsters parents scared their faelings with. He was unique, a gift given to his court by Daina, Spring's God of Fertility and Air, though others called him a curse. Others said he was a creature brought up from the Underworld.

He was the Berserker.

Gift or curse or monster? All rumors could have been true.

Petri heard from the eldest fae in Elaria that it hadn't happened in over a hundred years. When the war song called to Cillian so strongly that he transformed into a monster, a cross between a wolf and a bear, who no longer recognized friend from foe. They said, back a few centuries ago, he slaughtered thousands, on his side as well, leaving mangled bodies in his wake.

But right then, that beast kissed up my neck and pressed into me, pinning me between his warm body and the closed bedroom door. I left the lights low and threw up silencing wards, a magic worth its weight in gold in a theater such as this.

His hard mouth lapped at mine, eliciting a moan I was sure even Daria would have heard. His hands ran down to my thighs, lighting a fire on their path as they sifted through my skirts, and lifted. I wrapped my shaky legs around his narrow torso as he turned, walked us over and pressed us down onto my bed.

His pupils were dilated as he bore down on me, and I inhaled the sweet smell of valerian and jasmine, those white flowers that spilled over the walls of Spring Court canyon that I could see from the theater.

"Cillian, I've miss—" I started, desperate to pull him close, hold him longer. I wished to ask him how he was. Was he hurt? Did he need my help?

But he growled and ground his hips into mine, eliciting a whimper from me that he kissed away.

I pushed my hands between us and fought with the buttons of his shirt as his hands worked farther down. And only when I felt him hard and smooth at my center did I pull his lower lip into my teeth as he sank into me.

Slowly, at first, and then all at once.

Cillian groaned, leaned his head back as he picked up the pace, thrusting, until we were both panting with desire. He bunched up my skirts in his hands and held my waist steady as I explored the firm muscles of his taut arms. I sucked his neck until his thrusts became erratic and I knew he was close. I traced my lips against his collarbone and dug my nails into his back. Any marks wouldn't last, and I knew it drove him crazy.

But he was impatient this time as he held me tight, so tight, to him. His possessive hands explored my chest, pulling and kneading until they traced up my collarbone and found my neck. He leaned down with hard thrusts, turned my head to the side and sunk his teeth in. In a claiming nature that reminded me just how much of a beast he was.

That breathlessness, the one I knew as love—the one that

healed this aching loneliness—consumed me and I knew everything was going to be okay.

Cillian was here.

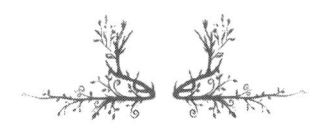

SUMMER MORNING SUNLIGHT, soft and warm, streamed in through the open window above my head. I peeked open an eye. Cillian was *still* here.

I trailed my fingers down Cillian's spine where he lay beside me. Muscles, like mountains on either side, flexed under my touch and goosebumps rose to greet me. He moaned, dozing naked in placated bliss.

"Theloshws," he mumbled into the pillow.

I stilled my hand tracing his back. "Come again?"

"The Lord of Shadows," he repeated, turning his head to face me, watching me through slitted eyes. Cillian's voice was marked with an accent like most Springfae, almost musical.

"I'm Valentina, dear Cillian." I leaned down to nip at his ear, teasing, but my spine grew stiff. "Try to keep your lovers straight."

"What? No." He shot up to his elbows, his mussed hair flopped to his forehead. "Kaderyn, the Lord of The Court of Shadows, has been seen traveling through Autumn, heading this way. No one knows what he wants this time, and he's not inclined to tell anyone. I want you to be careful."

It was hard to think about the fallen leader of the Wild Hunt when I had a beast of my own beside me.

And it was ludicrous.

The idea that the Lord of Shadows and me, a dishwasher from Elaria, might be a part of the same circles, was laughable.

Cillian pushed his wavy hair out of his eyes and the sheer concern drawn on his face had me recoiling. We rarely talked when we were together, his choice, not mine, and I sat up across from him, covering my body with my rose silk sheets.

I bit my lip. "He's probably just trying to get some sunlight. I would too if I lived under that gloomy canopy suspended over his court."

Many rumors passed through the theater on how exactly Kaderyn, the leader of the Wild Hunt, a unit of ghost Hunters responsible for guiding broken souls to the Underworld, turned fae and acquired an entire court on Eadha. Some rumors as condemning as stealing the soul of a god during a Wild Hunt raid. Some were as graceless as fornicating with a tree sprite. My favorite though, was that a warrior fae saved her betrothed by slaying Kaderyn right out of the night sky just as he was about to take her lover's soul. The harbinger of death, others called him. Whatever he was, it had nothing to do with me, with Elaria, or with my broken chair in Otti Theater.

My eyes went to my bag, hanging off a corner post on my bed, the one I kept my daggers in. I was uncertain if they could pierce the skin of the Lord of Shadows if it came down to it. Cillian had the daggers forged for me with Autumnfae bronze, the strongest on Eadha. They were engraved with Cillian's crest on their hilt, a howling wolf's head in an outline of a beast's paw. My chest warmed at the thought of him caring for my well-being. Though I don't know why Cillian felt it was necessary to mark them with his insignia. Likely a power move. Not unlike the strutting peacocking of the Autumnfae earlier. Spilling mead and secrets faster than Sisaria's feet could dance.

"Cillian," I blurted, remembering, "what's in Blackwater Junction?"

His eyes shot to mine and narrowed. "What do *you* know of Blackwater Junction?"

My face heated at his sharpness, his accusation, and my words tumbled out all at once. "I overheard Autumnfae talking last night. General Mohr of Autumn Court is sending soldiers there."

His shoulders stiffened. "Val, you should have told me this last night." He sucked in a breath. "Blackwater Junction is a town on the apex of the three northern courts. It is the last clear passageway from the borders of Autumn to Spring and then up into Winter. Daria offered my soldiers two nights in the back rooms, free of charge. She better not have known about this."

The urge to cry hit me hard. I wanted to go back to cuddling under the covers. "I just wanted you to be prepared."

"There's nothing there." He looked down at his hands. "But if he secures the town, it'll mean stealing it from Lady Fede, which is a declaration of war. And we aren't ready. They are felling trees in Lady of the Woods faster than ever to fuel their kilns. They have all Eadha's metal, and they hoard far too many weapons."

Their ability to pull fire from their fingertips made them the best forgers across the island. The Yegevani Mountains, north of their court was the only source of metals on the island. Said to be a gift from Autumn Court's god, Gael. But something about Cillian's demeanor told me his brain was off trudging along the hillsides of the island and not in the room naked with me anymore. And I longed to go back to our petting.

I brushed a thumb across his stiff jaw, but he pulled away.

"Don't worry your beautiful head about it." He leaned in and kissed the top of my head before rolling out of bed and pulling his pants on. "And don't go telling anyone else's secrets around here. I can take care of myself. You have a gift that would be exploited should anyone ever find out." He shrugged on his shirt. "You'd be a weapon of war."

I sulked, pulling the covers over my suddenly exposed self.

This was going too fast. He was leaving too soon. It would be a month before I saw him again. "Can you send someone else?"

"Blackwater Junction is a merchant town," he continued, eyes forlorn, still not meeting mine. "Not a town of fighters. Valentina, stay out of the dramas of the island." The bed sagged as he sat to put on his boots. "Fae can fight far longer when someone else is carrying their pain for them."

"I would be useful," I whispered, cringing at how it sounded. Weak and entirely too vulnerable. *What was wrong with me?*

But his eyes met mine with a hard rage. "Being a tool for someone else's war is not my idea of being of value."

Lady Fede, ruler of Spring Court, coerced people into doing what she wanted for fear of her general. Once her husband, the original lord of Spring, fell ill hundreds of years ago, she proceeded to rule with a cruel, beautiful fist and Cillian was her tool for this war. A tool Lady Fede manipulated to her best ability. And it was clear it was affecting him deeper than he'd ever tell me.

"Don't tell anyone what you overheard," he reiterated as he kissed my lips, bruised from last night. "Stay in Elaria."

"Cillian . . ." I pleaded and my heart was being wrenched from my body. What was I going to say? Stay here? For me?

He leaned down again to trace my lips with his, but his eyes and thoughts had soared miles away to wherever this Blackwater Junction was. Loneliness morphed itself into despair. I was so sheltered in this theater, I knew maybe five other fae on the entire island of Eadha. I had no idea what was out there. But I cared for the male leaving my bed right now and I didn't know how to tell him. I didn't know how to convince him to stay. And what was worse, something deep in my gut knew nothing I could say would pull Cillian in enough to hold me a little longer.

He grabbed his sword, branded with the same insignia as my daggers, and headed for the door but he stopped and turned, and I swelled with the hope that he was changing his mind. Or at least not leaving me here right now, naked and alone. He rolled his shoulders back once, a move I'd recognize a thousand times over and a slick layer of sweat broke out over my skin. My heart fell, and my palms turned clammy.

"Val, would you . . . do you mind?" he grimaced, flexing his shoulder as he sauntered back to me.

And I did it. I took away his pain, took it into myself.

I laid carefully back down on sheets still smelling of him, clenching an aching shoulder as tears ran down my face.

And with that, he was gone, leaving me in my room. Alone.

Again.

5

VALENTINA

I DIPPED TO the left, narrowly escaping Petri's long-reaching arms and the sword that he wielded in his tight grip. It was three days later, and no amount of training had sated this sadness I had tucked deep in my abdomen. So deep a pit, it threatened to consume me whole.

"So how was it?" he asked as he lunged again, trying for the third time to start idle conversation.

It was a beautiful day. The sun had risen so high that the stones of the courtyard grew too hot if you stayed in one place long enough. The courtyard's four walls stretched seven feet tall on all sides—only Braeth and his tall magog-stature could see over them without aid. But Daria had her magic here too, blocking the courtyard from prying eyes. The clang of bronze on bronze echoed around the walls as Petri and I practiced his swordplay.

"How was what?" I grunted as I slashed a dagger at his impossibly long sword. Something, minutes ago, he was relating to another appendage of himself.

I had put on my favorite dress this morning in hopes of pulling myself out of this loneliness.

It was cut low and shaped tightly, so that it did not shift during our training. It was adorned with gold sequins and a base of deep, blood-red satin and shifts of green so bold they looked black. Summerfae learned young to walk with such grace as not to rustle the adornments like the little metal rings filled with gems that lined the hem along the bottom and the shoulders. We took pride in our clothing. Even when shame filled me with how quick Cillian left this time.

Petri narrowed his gaze and stalked around me. His body, looking for a way to get past my daggers, slender and strong; his eyes, looking for a way to patch my soul. The eternal summer sun sent his body glistening and a bead of sweat dribbled past the mark of Summerfae, a small blue-black tattoo of a raindrop on his shoulder blade.

But I wasn't ready to talk, so I hardened my gaze and lifted my chin. He rolled his eyes and swung his sword once. An attestation to his strength, as the thing was huge, and I danced back again. But he knew my weakness was fighting at a distance. Inside an opponent's arms' reach is where I was best, my small body able to invade an opponent with ease until my daggers could find their mark. So that's what I did.

As Petri took a moment to relate his sword, again, to what was between his legs, I dove under the shining bronze metal. With a foot on his thigh and a knee on his chest, I had a dagger at his throat before he finished blabbing.

His eyes widened once in warning before water sloshed down hard on my head in a steady stream that soaked me instantly and slicked his body and my grip.

I fell hard to the cobblestone at his feet.

"Cheater," I sputtered, pulling strands of my waist-length black hair out of my mouth.

He crouched to the ground beside me, laughing. "We are the water. The river flows through us. Don't forget to use it when there's a blade at *your* neck."

I managed to smile at my friend before squinting into the late morning sky.

Warm breezes pushed the smell of honeysuckles through Elaria like a flock of seagulls from the coast. Farmers' fields, merchant shops, and storefronts, often worked by the faeless, a derogatory term as far as I was concerned, lined the stream that ran around the west side of town and down to the docks of Robinswallow River. Faeless were magicless. For whatever reason, they couldn't wield the magic of any of the gods, couldn't survive most wounds if infected, and as such, couldn't gain respect from most of Eadha's fae. Daria said the only thing they were good at was being the subject of Lord Aborys of Winter Court's raids. He wanted them dead.

Hawrenthia, Summer's capital, hugged the western coastline on the far side of the court.

I raised a hand, blocking the ever-burning sun as the Anduat Mountains stood, grey and barren, before its peaks became shrouded in cloud cover. The sweltering Glenora Desert lay between me and them.

Lazy mornings, soft afternoons, and wild cacophony of nights. This was our theater. This was Elaria. Nothing more.

"Have you ever wanted to see the rest of Eadha, Petri?"

He was silent for so long I looked back to my friend, whose crumpled face sent a pang through my heart. If Cillian had left any parts of it still whole.

"Don't dream of places fae like you and I will never see."

I frowned as claustrophobia, stubbornness and a heat that sent my blood racing reared its ugly head. "I could scale this blasted wall and be gone before Daria lights the incense for curtain call."

He grimaced because he'd have to tell on me. We both knew it. Daria had everyone working for her. She gave fae like Petri jobs and safety in a court hell-bent on ignoring the war. Refusing to retaliate even when fae of our own court went missing or when Winter Court decimated an entire town of faeless. Lord Grigory of Summer Court was probably holding up somewhere in Hawrenthia, eating delicacies off the bodies of his servants, promptly running to his rooms when the topic of the war was brought up. Daria's skin would turn a wonderful shade of red, like the color of a rising sun, whenever anyone brought up our lord. She'd dive into a lecture on how her theater was the only thing keeping the peace at this end of the island. A more prideful lord would have drowned her where she stood. But it wasn't like Lord Grigory ever visited Elaria, the last town near the outskirts of the court. Instead, he built the Glenora Desert to the east as protection from Autumn Court's growing army. But as more and more Autumnfae came to our performances, it was clear the desert had stopped being a deterrent a year ago. Though it was no place I'd ever wanted to be.

Autumnfae soldiers were either finding a pass Cillian hadn't closed off through Spring Court or braving the three-day trek across the desert. They would stay in Elaria for a week to recover before heading back across to whatever it was they did in their court.

"Come on, Val. Daria is just looking out for you. She loves you like a faeling. Whatever her reasoning to want to protect you, I must respect her on that."

But something was burning in me. Something familiar but not in a comfortable way. It pressed me on. "Would you stop me, Petri? If I climbed the wall."

"Come on, love. This is what we do, this is who we are. Grab a bag." He sighed and gestured to the dancers' bags lining the wall.

I sucked in a deep breath. Did the courtyard always feel so suffocating? The rough cobblestone poked through my black, silk slipper shoes. It was far too hot to wear anything heavier in Summer Court, but the heat was suddenly choking me.

I shoved my daggers into the multicolored sequined bag, groaning as a small hole poked through the fabric. Oh, by the gods, why? I'd be the one to stitch it as one of the few fae in the theater who knew how. I groaned. What was I doing?! Confronting my friends and creating more work for myself. I scrubbed at my damp face, trying to get ahold of my thoughts.

Screaming funneled out from the front of the theater and adrenaline had me take off running, throwing the bag over my shoulder. My wet hair sloshed against my shoulders and the metal rings on my dress clanged together with every step. There was no point in stealth now. Petri stayed close on my heels as we flew through quiet corridors lined with tossed clothing and snuffed-out incense sticks.

A second blood-curdling scream rang out as we rounded the corner that led to the auditorium. Petri suddenly wrapped an arm around me, and pulled me to a hard stop as the largest Autumnfae I'd ever seen stood in the center of the room. He was dressed in his orange and brown furs and had a beard braided sharply across his chest, and I didn't breathe at all as his large meaty hand was locked around sweet Sisaria's neck. He had snaked his other hand through her hair, and judging by the look on her face, he was pulling. Hard.

Dancers shrieked around us, but most clung to Daria, who stood tall and defiant in the center of the room. Chairs, those beautifully decorated chairs, were either smashed to pieces or scattered on their sides. Avril, the curly redhead whose show was always after Sisaria's, clung to the stage.

"Tell me, mistress," the Autumnfae spat to Daria. His gravelly voice was low. "Tell me whose head I need to take for giving my plans to my enemy."

"We are a performing theater, General Mohr. Nothing more." Her voice was steady, but I'd been watching her perform for fourteen years. She was scared, and Daria was never scared. Annoyed and frustrated, sure, but never scared. And that told me I should be terrified.

He tightened his grip on Sisaria's hair and the sound of her poor sobbing had me stepping forward. But Daria moved immediately in front of me, blocking my way.

"The Berserker's soldiers confessed they heard of my plans from a worker at Otti Theater. My men tell me what happens in the back rooms of this frivolous pleasure house. I want to know which of your swill blabbed to that *fucking* General Cillian. Which one of you condemned my soldiers? Huh?" His fingertips glowed deep amber red as Sisaria let out a blood-curdling scream and steam rose from her throat.

She clawed at his hand, her water magic raring to stop the burning, desperate for release.

"Don't hurt her!" I stepped forward, pushing past Daria. "It was me."

"Get back here," Daria begged, reaching for me, but I ignored her.

Sisaria's neck was scorched, and I was to blame. "Take me instead. Let her go."

Mohr frowned. "There's no difference between one whore or another. I lost four of my best soldiers this week. There's no reason you shouldn't do the same. Bring four of them with us."

The room erupted in chaos as the dancers scrambled to pull out of the sizzling firefaes' clutches. The soldiers shoved Petri into the wall when he tried to grab a dancer back from them.

"It was her! It was Valentina. Just take *her*."

I spun around from where I was, my heart running wild as I reached for Sisaria, her face panic-stricken. I frowned at the voice. *Avril?* She stood there pointing at me, her red ringlet hair wild, her blue eyes fierce.

Silence hushed over the commotion. Dreadful silence.

"In what world is one female worth the lives of four of my best?" General Mohr asked, unnaturally calm, pulling Sisaria back from my grasp.

But Avril didn't stop. "Because she is a freak! Something is wrong with her. She can take pain away. I don't know how, but I've seen her do it to Daria a hundred times."

My heart dropped like a stone, and I didn't dare move. I couldn't.

"Avril, you stupid sullied fae," Daria huffed out. "General Mohr, ignore her." But her voice was shaking, and her face had turned ashen.

But she hadn't denied it. I swallowed. Fae could not lie.

It was too late. Something had changed in the air. The Autumnfae closest to me grabbed me with calloused hands and faced me towards a furious General Mohr of Autumn Court. I might as well have been underwater because everything suddenly felt so far away as my eyes widened, and a ringing echoed in my head, threatening to pull me under. This was my secret. How could Avril have seen? Daria was so careful on the nights she called me to her.

Mohr tossed Sisaria— wild golden hair flying—into Daria, who caught her with a grunt. The scorch marks puckered her delicate, fair neck. General Mohr stalked to me until his scarred, tanned face became inches from mine.

"Avril," he muttered. "If you deceive a general of Autumn Court, I can assure you, there will be consequences."

"She's Cillian's lover! She can—"

But before Avril could say another word, her eyes shot open wide and she choked and gurgled, spurting out mouthfuls of water. I watched Daria's hand twitch, though her eyes never lingered near the red-haired Summerfae now drowning on dry land in our theater's wrecked auditorium.

Mohr reached out and wrapped his thick, wrinkled hand around my throat. I struggled away, away from those fire fingers, but the other Autumnfae held tight. My nose curled as the smell of Sisaria's burnt flesh still coated his fingers. Could I pull out my daggers before he moved another inch? I could feel the padding of other things in my side bag I had grabbed from the courtyard wall. It must have already held a change of clothes and an extra pair of folded silk slippers. My water magic wasn't nearly as strong as Daria's, and it worried me she wasn't attacking the firefae. I craned my neck to look back at her. Why weren't they fighting? Why weren't we—and that's when I saw a magog's severed head laying on the stage. Severed from his massive, disfigured body. Not Braeth. The nose was wrong and ears too big. But a magog, nonetheless. Bile rose in my mouth.

Mohr leaned in so far that his gold eyes bore through me, cold and impenetrable. I heard him sniff sharply near my ear before he whispered, "Prove it."

This burning inside me I felt in the courtyard, this foreign discomfort running through me, had my mouth opening. "She hates me. She'll say anything." Avril was one of the ones Petri warned me to stay away from.

But I knew this fight would not end until Mohr got what he felt owed to him. Elaria would forever be on his radar now. Thanks to me. Thanks to me for warning Cillian about the raid and Cillian apparently doing the opposite of what I asked.

So, I looked into his golden eyes once more. The ones promising pain. "But it *was* me who told Cillian about your attack." And because I had no good sense with this endless internal burning, my mouth kept going. "Your stupid soldiers talk so gods damned loud—"

That did it.

The last thing I saw was Mohr's face—framed by reddish hair—curling in a fury as something sharp hit the back of my water-soaked head, and I was pitched into darkness.

6

VALENTINA

INSTINCT HAD ME pushing up off the ground before I could figure out where I was. The sudden jolt of movement sent my body spinning and my elbow jammed into something hard at my back, sending pain radiating to my fingertips. My vision faded in and out of darkness as my body grew accustomed to sitting upright, and my blood tried to figure out which way it was going. I was vaguely aware of a jostling, a rocking that bent my body back against a wooden bench. I blinked hard. I had to figure out what was happening. And the heat, oh gods, why was it so hot?

"Oh look, you're finally awake. You're not good at anything, are you?" Avril's snide voice had my head snapping up across to the adjacent bench where she leaned in the corner.

Her normally vibrant summer dress was coated in a fine red dust. I cocked my head; *what was that*?

I ignored her taunting altogether. We'd never had a full conversation before. Sisaria and Petri had warned me often enough. The day she called me the poor dishwasher with an icicle father, I promptly stayed clear of her entirely. "Where are we?" I looked around the small wooden carriage we were in.

The only light sifted in from identical small windows on either side of the cabin. I reached for my bag at my side, searching for my daggers, and felt nothing. I dropped my head in my hands and groaned loudly. My daggers were gone, my head hurt, and I was trapped with Avril, who so ruthlessly betrayed me, and now heading only the gods know where with angry brutal firefae. And why was it so hot? I moved my hand to my chest and tried sucking in a deep breath. Why couldn't I breathe?

I needed air. Now.

I used the bench for stability as I shoved the thick leather curtain aside. And what faced me back sent dread straight into my bones. My hand shook against the smooth rawhide clenched in my grasp because the high simmering sun of the Glenora Desert stared back at me.

Lord Grigory's only reaction to the war was to desecrate a parcel of land, barren and bone-dry between Summer and Autumn. He pulled the water straight from the soil, evaporating it into the skies above. Nothing grew, nothing lived, and nobody survived for long. The Robinswallow River that ran from the west seas deep into Summer Court petered out straight into the desert; fizzling itself into mist and steam as it reached the desert edges. They said the mirages were so real some fae would make it back to Autumn stark raving mad. But I wondered how far off that was from their normal dispositions.

"Close it," Avril snapped, as she shielded her squinting eyes.

I dropped back down to the floor, my head between my knees, as everything hit me all at once. The memory of Sisaria's burning flesh, and Daria drowning Avril, though apparently fine as she now sat before me. I rubbed a sore spot on my head, pulling back as crusted blood flaked off onto my fingertips. The truth settled itself nicely into my gut. They were taking an unholy path through the Glenora Desert.

They were taking us to Autumn Court.

"How long have we been traveling?" I asked, an octave higher than I meant to. I pulled at the edges of my crimson and green dress, wishing it wasn't so tight. Still, that endless fire burned me up from the inside out.

Avril refused to look at me as she sat there, arms crossed, her normally sleek red hair, frizzy and worn, and shrugged like she was mildly inconvenienced. Her mark of Summerfae bobbed on her clavicle where it peeked out from the neck of her dress. "Half a day, maybe."

My skin flushed quickly with a layer of sweat. How was I going to get us out of this? I caused this. I caused the ruthless General Mohr of Autumn Court to set his eyes on Elaria and our theater. I was the reason Avril was out here now. Even if she was the one who gave me up. Fear and that dreadful burning had me up and reaching for the doorknob when a cool, damp hand clamped around my wrist.

"Don't even think about trying to escape," Avril said, and I snapped my gaze up to her as her piercing eyes bore into me. "Their general has promised to let me go if I keep you behaving in here."

Any hope I carried, fell. There was no getting *us* out of this. There was only getting *me* out of this, but this fire inside was making me angry. "Do you really think he'll just grant you a golden carriage ride back across the desert? He and his soldiers have traveled straight across the desert and are now going straight back without so much as a break. What makes you think they will risk their lives a third time bringing you back?"

"You were the one to blab to Cillian. You are the reason we are in this mess."

"Let go of my arm, Avril."

"Or what, dishwasher?"

A fury rose in me far quicker than anything had before, and my fist snapped out before I could give it another thought. Avril dropped forward, clutching her nose as tears welled in her eyes. Before I could think to apologize, a shout rang out, and the carriage jolted to a standstill. Avril and I froze, half locked in each other's arms.

Heavy footfalls headed for the right side of the carriage. Avril shrunk away from me and the door, wiping her nose on her skirts. I crouched down, braced for Mohr's large boney face to open the door, ready to kick out a foot towards his staggering height. I couldn't go to Autumn Court. This was exactly what Cillian warned me about. The latch rang out and it might as well have been a lightning bolt because I sprang into action. I forced the door open the rest of the way and jutted out my slippered heel, searching to connect with General Mohr's massive, red-bearded face.

But whoever it was, was shorter than the general and my heel clipped his forehead instead of the middle of his face like I'd hoped.

He reacted well, grabbing my outstretched leg and rendering my bottom half immobile. In a frenzy, I went straight for the eyes. This unknown heat boiled my blood into unmanageable degrees. I couldn't stop to recognize myself. It was the desert. It had to be.

The dry heat of it hit me hard and the sudden sun blinded me as I lashed out any which way I could at the Autumnfae below me. I pulled at thick, coarse hair and a fur vest. Some of it had to be attached to something important. The Autumnfae shook his head like he was fighting a bee's nest as his arms tried to wrap around my thrashing body.

"That's enough," bellowed Mohr, spitting grit.

My eyes were wild as I tried to track the sound, eventually

stopping to see a bloody-nosed Avril cowering, kneeling beneath his hands. He gripped her far harder than necessary for a traveling caravan stuck in the desert, nothing but sand for miles in any which direction.

Half a dozen soldiers ambled off their horses, huffing and puffing loudly. Their lips were cracked and covered in the same red dust that covered everything. The desert wasn't treating them any better out here. They all eyed me as I perched on the Autumnfae's head.

"She's got a lot of spit in her for a Summerfae, General," the fae below me said from somewhere tied up in my skirts and limbs. He was shorter than Mohr, but larger, broader across his shoulders. And he had no problem holding me up by the forearms as if presenting me as a gift to Mohr.

I was feral—distempered and raging. Acting on emotions I never knew I carried.

My blood coated two knuckles where they split on Avril's nose. My hair hung across half my face and my dress had ridden up and over, and I had no idea if I was properly covered. Or that I even cared. Because that damn heat running rampant in my body overrode everything else. Some small part of me clung to my water magic as it tried to soothe gently, tried to keep me sane.

I am the water.
The river runs to me . . . or was it *through* me?

How could I be forgetting?

Mohr grunted. "Pitch the tents quickly. There's a sandstorm coming."

As a surprise to both of us, Avril and I were given water. Which I guzzled far longer than she, as we sat off to the side in the carriage's shade. The horses were tended to with a startlingly delicate care. Water canteens were poured on their sweat-soaked backs as they nibbled on apple slices. Soldiers would pass us and without a word, drop empty water canteens at our feet. Then they quickly and efficiently set up tents, but not without a lot of yelling and cursing.

Loud, stupid, Autumnfae, I grumbled. Their fire magic was of no use to them in a desecrated desert.

By the near end of it, a large beige canvas tent sat square in the middle and each soldier—I counted six in total—got a tent, each surrounding it. A dozen or so canteens lay in the dust at our feet, much to my confusion. I kicked a few away, but Avril just sat there patiently, picking her nails. I wasn't exactly getting on her good side by repositioning her nose, so I didn't dare talk to her. But there was a comfort in having her here with me. A familiarity, no matter how much I longed for Petri or Sisaria. Or even Roshan—*gods*, he'd know what to do.

Large thick-soled boots I'd come to know as Mohr's came into view, and I peered up into his severe face, half blinded by the scorching sun. It cast his face into shadows.

"Get up." He stalked, with a slight hobble I was trained to notice, to the biggest tent. "Bring the canteens."

The bottles clanged together in our arms as Avril and I awkwardly shuffled to the tent Mohr had disappeared into. I kicked one I couldn't carry across the desert with my foot to the tent entrance.

It was the large tent in the middle, far larger than it looked on the outside. I'd never needed to make magic do my bidding in this form, but it was impressive. Avril, who had lived a life I never took an interest in, didn't seem phased. Her strength at our situation made it easier to pretend I hadn't gotten her into this mess.

I told Cillian what I heard to save him. Avril told a secret that wasn't hers to save herself.

The tent was extensively furnished inside with some tables and chairs and a fur-clad makeshift bed in the corner. A small table off to the side held a black, faded open-top satchel.

Mohr started busying himself over a map that lay on a table in the middle as wind-blown sand pelted into the sides of the tent, causing it to cave in. "Fill those canteens, Summerfae. Every last one of them."

I looked back at the canteen I just punted across the desert sand and my mouth slacked open. It all made sense. That's why we were still alive in his convoy. He was using us for our water magic. And suddenly this desert and this company seemed less dangerous to a Summerfae.

Avril didn't waste any time and got to work quickly. She pulled the plugs out sharply and held a palm over its mouthpiece. When I just watched her, she shot me a glare, daring me to rebel now in Mohr's company.

I sucked in a breath and grabbed a canteen. If this was how we were going to survive, then sure, I'd fill water canteens. I would use my water magic to fill every single water bottle from here to Autumn Court and do it again on our return to Elaria.

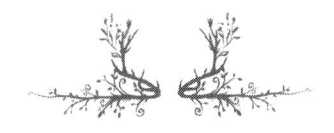

Two hours later, I shoved the plug into the last canteen, finally finished. It took me twice as long to fill the canteens as Avril, but we managed it. Twenty-four various sized vessels, now full to the brim, lined the side wall of the tent.

Avril seemed to have figured out something while filling the canteens because once she was done, I sat there scrunching up my nose as she used her hands to adjust her breasts inside her ruby-red dress. She didn't look at me again as she sauntered slowly around the tent.

"The skins are beautiful," she cooed, throwing lingering gazes at Mohr. She moved her fingers—soft fluttery fingers—against the animal skins that lay draped everywhere. And eventually, his small glances at her turned into outright staring. "So soft and supple."

Mohr's gaze was heavy on Avril now as she meandered towards him, and dipped a finger in whatever he was drinking from his cup on the table.

"You've never come to Otti Theater, General Mohr." She raised her wet finger to her lips, and sucked on it as her eyes shuttered closed with a desire I had to assume was forced. "I can show you what you've been missing."

I was never a dancer—as much as I loved the music—and I was never the one to go to the back rooms with the paying customers. But her confidence captivated even me, as I stood there feeling like a baked potato. Though it took concentration to smooth out my scrunched nose, because trying to seduce a miserable, massive Autumnfae was not my idea of a 'good plan'.

Mohr stilled before her. His eyes were calculating, sharp and distrusting. I wondered if she saw what I saw. But it didn't stop his hand from tracing up the side of her body and, as out of place as I felt, a new hope sparked inside. I was five feet from the entrance to the tent, water-filled canteens lay at my feet, and I knew where the carriage was.

I glanced quickly to the entrance. Could I leave Avril here? Her vibrant hair matched that of Mohr's, and I wondered how well she'd fit in with Autumn Court.

She leaned her head back, moaning at his touch and I shrugged; she'd be fine. It wasn't often, especially during the war, where fae crossed the court lines for love but it could happen.

I thought of Cillian, of Spring Court, and me of Summer. I would have made it work. If he asked me to, I would have moved to Spring to be with him. But he never asked and would change the subject when I asked him to stay even five more minutes in Summer.

Mohr's hand slid into Avril's red hair, and she leaned into his touch. I thought I should turn away but I heard her breathing hitch and a yelp leave her lips as Mohr's fist closed near the base of her skull, pulling sharply, before he stared at my retreating body. "We are going to play a game."

"I'm not really in the mood, thanks," I said without thinking. The words seemed to bubble up from this ever-churning fire.

But Avril was panicking; both her hands were trying to clasp over just one of his through her hair.

"What is the boiling point of water, Summerfae?" He leaned in close to her face and I took a step forward, out of instinct.

Unless Avril had some kick-ass water abilities I didn't know about, we weren't getting out of this. We were both Summerfae, sure, but not nearly as old as Daria or trained as Mohr. Magic aged with us. Getting more potent and stronger. Young fae were rarely ever leaders in armies for this reason.

"Better question," Mohr continued. "What is the boiling point of Summer blood?"

Avril convulsed under his grip, screaming over the raging sandstorm outside.

"Stop," I shouted as I took a step closer. My own body, still heated from the desert.

He sent a pointed look my way, those gold emotionless eyes tracking me as I searched for something to use. "Take away my pain and I won't melt her from the inside out. You do have the ability to take away pain, don't you? Show me what you can do."

I froze. He must not have forgotten about what Avril had told him. I swallowed. "I told you, she hates me. She would say anything to get rid of me."

"And I think you're evading my question." He had to raise his voice over Avril's screaming.

She was scratching at anything she could reach, leaving tracks of her nails on his muscular forearm. Streams of water snaked down her body, dripping into puddles at her feet, soaking into the muted furs. She laid a pale hand on his broad chest, and I could see her trying her best to shove water down his throat, but he batted it away, not so much as flinching.

"You know my soldiers would come back spouting rumors. 'So gods damn loud' is what I think you called them, yes? Well, they'd say a performance at Otti Theater would heal their aches. And I never took mind to their stories; never put much weight into the idea that a female could heal.

"And it's incredibly ironic to me that after all these years of trying every pain relief tonic on Eadha, that you'd fall into my lap because of Cillian." He looked Avril over from toe to head, lifting her like she was a small animal, inspecting her. "I don't know how long she has. She's fairly young. I give her maybe four minutes."

Oh gods, I pulled my hands through my hair. I couldn't think. This raging heat scorched through my body and clouded my judgment. Apart from his limp, he looked fine. What pain could he possibly have? "What pain?" I screamed, finally asking. "Stop this. You're a monster."

Avril was being burned alive and I was throwing whatever I could now. Whatever was near me, I hurled at him. I tried my water magic, but even it was failing me, sputtering to droplets on my silk shoes. Filling the canteens must have tired me out.

His grip on her hair shifted, losing traction as her body was flooding the tent and I took it as a chance to pounce. I closed the distance between us and struck out, sneaking under his arm, and latched onto his back. He tried to reach for me, but I dodged his fingers, and his massive arms wouldn't allow his elbow to bend backward that way. With one foot on the back of his calf and the other on the table his drink was on, I climbed up his body and locked my arm around his tree-trunk neck. And pulled tight. I kept my leg around his torso, locking his free arm down at his side. But he was large, and I struggled to lock my feet together around him.

Avril's eyes were wild as she frantically tried to pull out of his grasp. The light in her blue eyes started to fade as steam rose from her skin.

My stomach dropped, I was not working fast enough. "Okay, okay! Stop hurting her. I'll do it. Let her go." I'd taken too long trying to come up with a plan against a mad general. There was no way to save her but this.

"Her life is depending on it," he ground out, his throat bobbing against my forearm.

My fury vanished as I clung onto his back. There was no avoiding this. But once I did this, once I showed him the power of what I could do, there was no going back. And the more who knew, the more I could be manipulated. Just as I was when I was six. Just as I was now. I placed my hand against his scruffy forearm and cringed when I felt the gouges of Avril's nail marks.

Mohr had no visible ailments, so I couldn't prepare for it.

And I was blindsided. Shooting pain radiated down my spine and I stiffened against his body. It felt like a knife was hilt deep in my upper back, dragging, lingering across the nerve endings. My muscles tensed in surprise, in opposition to what I knew better to do for spine pain.

I was vaguely aware of Avril dropping to the floor as she

scrambled away on hands and knees in a pool of her own water, her feet failing to make traction against the slick skins.

Mohr sighed heavily under my arms as his muscles relaxed. His meaty hands now clung me, his new lifeline, selfishly, to his back in a sandy desert with both of us so far from home.

When it was over, when my back was so stiff with pain I didn't dare breathe a deep breath, Mohr peeled me off of him and carried me bridal style to the makeshift bed. His normally emotionless eyes were full of shimmering golden awe as he stared down at me. And it was worse, so much worse, having him look at me like that than the way he did before. But my body was locked up tight and I couldn't cower from his gaze.

Why did it have to be the spine? What I would have given for it to have been a big toe. And with a furrow of his brow, Mohr dropped me unceremoniously to the pile of furs. I moaned, curling in fetal position with my face pressed into the soft bedding.

Avril watched from where she was, heaving, leaning over herself on the floor, eyes wide. Probably just as surprised I saved her as I was.

The wind whipped sharply, caving in the far side of the tent. The storm was converging in on us. We stared at each other with raw fear and hopelessness before something flew at her, hitting her in the ribs. I blinked as she lifted the canteen Mohr tossed at her.

"I promised you I would let you go back to your court. You're free to go." He tossed a hand towards the tent entrance where a mountain of sand had already gathered.

"There's a desert storm raging out there," she spat out. Her burned throat clipped the words short. My own breathing turned short and shallow. It was a death sentence. "I won't make it back," she added.

Mohr took two gigantic steps to her, picked her up and

tossed her, like he did the canteen, towards the entrance of the tent. All I could do was move my eyes, shift my gaze but inside I was screaming. Screaming at this firefae and his cruelty with my spine locked stiff in agony.

"You won't survive if you stay," he growled. "Get out before I take back my canteen."

Avril's eyes narrowed as she looked once to the space between us. She grunted, pushed to her feet, and was gone. And that's when a canteen of water had been measured to be worth more than my life.

7

VALENTINA

"WHAT ARE YOU?" Mohr asked for the sixth time. I sat, tied to a chair in the center of the tent, heaving at the blood-boiling fury I felt towards the half dozen Autumnfae surrounding me.

An hour after Avril left me, I could move again. The stabbing pain in my upper spine, taken from Mohr, became manageable. I had managed to close my eyes for maybe an hour after that before the bristling Autumnfae soldiers made their way into the tent. They eyed me with an attention I couldn't fathom giving another living creature. It was a calculated look, all done in a three second once-over. Each fae's eyes grazed my body, weighed its worth like a tradable or usable tool rather than a living, breathing being on Eadha Island.

I wanted to vomit.

Once their assessment was done, they each pretended I simply . . . wasn't there; pretended there wasn't a scared Summerfae tied and folded in on herself on another damn chair. And that degrading evaluation, that I wasn't worth a single second glance, fueled the anger simmering inside.

Mohr led a meeting, basic things about supplies, and pointed occasionally to the map, showing the route we would take across the desert and into Autumn Court. I wondered how far Avril would make it. If she would alert Lord Grigory at my capture. Or better yet, Cillian. But my heart sank at the thought. Lord Grigory was not getting involved in The War of Many. Ever the diplomatic court, he never instigated a negotiation, never fought back against attacks. Not the least when I narrowly escaped Lord Aborys of Winter Court's attack when he froze the faeless of Willowspeak.

And not now, being taken by Autumn Court—just a dishwasher from Elaria—who admitted to betraying the court to the east. And Cillian, who was also working on the defensive, keeping Lady Fede from launching a full-blown attack against Autumn's advances because he was afraid of what he would turn into on the battlefield. I was lost in thought, or spiraling in hopelessness, when I heard my name again.

"Valentina?" he said. My name on Mohr's tongue was menacing, and it snapped me back to the present. He knew about my ability to take another's pain and that sent my body prickling with anticipation.

How stupid I was to be upset at the indifference of the other soldiers. This was so much worse. So, I said nothing.

"Is she a spy for Spring Court?" one soldier asked, the one who I tried to kick in the face leaving the carriage.

"She's going to help us win the war," Mohr said with reverence, eyes dancing. "Valentina, I'll ask again. What do you know of Spring Court's plans? Are they planning an attack? What has Cillian told you?"

I dropped my head. The heat was building, and I had an ugly feeling it wasn't because of the desert heat. My blood pounded with the need to move, to fight, to scream, to do *something*. An uncomfortable magic sang across my parched skin. What were they doing to me? The fuming anger had me struggling to leash in my tongue, and I bit down on it sharply. So, I again said nothing as I wrestled to regain *Valentina's* thoughts —not whoever's were taking control.

The backhand of a soldier slapped my head to the side so hard my teeth bit through the flesh of my cheek. "He asked you a question. What do you know?"

I stilled; my head lolled to the side. All control gone. "What I know? I know how to sew with the finest silks in Eadha. I know how to befriend pink, speckled canaries from Spring's Canyon." I paused, spitting out blood onto a thrown fur rug. "The trick is thistle seeds."

The soldier's fist shot out again, clattering my teeth together as my head whipped to the other side.

I saw stars; hateful, pain-filled stars. The fury burned harder as something coursed through me. "Wait, wait, wait!" I spat out before a third fist came down.

He took a step back, not any more amused.

Hate seared inside me, deep and heavy, dulling the pain of my face and I gave into the anger. "I know your court will fall. I know better fae will take your place, and I know I will smile up from my grave as I see you laid in yours."

Full absolute hatred fueled Mohr's face as his soldiers looked at him, expecting. I braced for the next hit, but no amount of preparedness could be made for the sheer pain that split across my gut. The force of Mohr's fist to my stomach knocked the chair back and my head ricocheted off the floor.

"Get out. Everyone out." Mohr leaned down, his breath hot and sour in my ear as he said, "I know you're not a spy. No one would trust a seductress with secrets. You may be Cillian's whore, but you're mine now, Valentina."

And if I ever, at any point, thought I was going to get out of this unscathed, it was at this moment I realized how wrong I was. How far into the other side of this island I'd trenched. There was no coming back from Mohr and his cruel, unfeeling eyes and his hot, sticky hands as he dragged out pain of my own.

I was alone with a monster.

8

VALENTINA

SHORTLY AFTER DAWN, Mohr shook me awake where I lay on the one linen throw that lined my crude bed. The furs proved too hot in the desert heat and something about them was off. Something had me piling them high in the bed's corner. Away from me entirely.

Mohr pointed to the canteens at the mouth of the tent. He had distributed them last night after the meeting—and my beating. The fact that they were back now had me wheezing. "Fill the canteens."

I swallowed. I couldn't feel my water magic anywhere inside me. "And if I can't?"

His golden eyes flew to mine. "There are a thousand ways I can get you to do what I want." He seemed to think this over for a moment before reaching out and grabbing me by my forearm, dragging and throwing me into the canteens.

I crashed into them, sending them flying and curled in on myself as tears streamed down my cheeks.

"I hate you."

"I imagine so. But you will fill our canteens and keep the pain out of my spine. You won't talk back to me in front of my soldiers. If you fail to do any of it, I'll add more uses to your list. And, trust me, you'll hate me even more when I'm done. Fill the canteens."

I took one of the leather-bound vessels in a shaky grip. Red clay flaked off to the dust-covered floor. Falling, like my hopes of surviving this desert. I put my skin-broken and bruised hand over its mouth, searching deep for the power to make water flow from my body like a stream's edge over river rocks.

Nothing. I could feel the emptiness—that dragging emptiness—where my water magic once flowed deep and strong. It left me at the same time Avril did. Slowly it depleted from me, and then all at once, gone for good. So now, holding this canteen with my traitorous hands, I was angry that my water magic left me like Avril. I rubbed a dirty hand down my face.

Mohr's scrutiny flushed my skin.

"I can't."

"What?" he barked.

"I said, I can't," I screamed, the rage building. This unknown feeling took over again. I could feel my blood rushing through my body and the anger seemed to flow with it. I was taking heaving breaths now, unable to control much of anything.

"I'll go back and burn down that entire fucking town. I'll drag that little blonde one to my Fortress in the camps and let them do what they will to her."

I screamed loud and strong, matching his fury as I launched the canteen at his head. He narrowly caught it as his eyes and stance moved wide, bumping into the table that kept the black leather satchel. Its contents clattered to the floor in a pile of strong-smelling herbs and broken jars. It was a medicine bag.

And his surprise filled me with an ugly joy that had me

bracing for a fight. Which seemed like the only logical thing my mind could focus on.

He looked at the canteen, at me, and back at the canteen. His confusion startled me from where I now stood, fists curled. "Does your lord know you're a traitor to your court?"

"I am Summerfae." *I am the water. The river*—I shook my head, trying to think through the anger to remember my mantra.

Mohr turned the canteen over and all fight left me at once as hand-shaped scorch marks were burned into the sides of the beige-skinned canteen. Small, once-Summerfae handprints. What was happening? My mind was reeling, searching for explanations.

I didn't notice Mohr until he was beside me, placing the burnt canteen back into my hands. I had no idea how I used fire magic, but his proximity had fueled my anger again. I wanted him away, far away, but instead he brushed a fingertip across my cheek, wiping away a tear as we stared down at my hands. My fingertips, once the color of freshly cut maple wood, now were alit with soft flames. And I forgot to breathe because I was on fire and nothing hurt.

It was powerful and intense in a way water magic wasn't. I stared at the flames for what felt like an eternity before Mohr laid his hand inches above mine. Stealing the fire from my fingertips; taking my power once more. I crumpled to the ground again, watching my fingers turn back to their normal color. But Mohr didn't leave. Why wouldn't he just leave?

He knelt beside me, wincing, and undid the buttons on his black-sleeved tunic he kept under his furs, pushing it up to his forearm. He grabbed my hand—fire: gone, water: long gone, just confusion now in its place. His skin was dry under my fingertips, and I was glad my stomach was empty, or I'd have been sick all over these damn canteens at his touch. And when

I didn't immediately take his pain away, his grip bore into mine.

I let go of the floodgates that held back my magic. But it was too quick, and I was far too exhausted. The blinding pain down my neck locked me up, and I toppled over.

He stood over me, looking down at my broken figure. "I don't know what you are, Valentina of, supposed, Elaria. But you're mine now."

His pain had lodged itself nicely into my upper spine as I sunk into a pile of empty canteens I couldn't fill. He left the tent with a last order to clean up the mess of the medicine bag that, he stated, he no longer needed.

For a while, it was all I could do to remember to breathe.

But eventually, I started sobbing, loud and unyielding. And even then, no tears would come.

We spent the next full day traveling the desert. Mohr stopped the convoy to come to me three times to take away his pain. By this time, I had the nerve to ask him what it was.

"It's back," he said, voice harsh, through the cabin door. He was covered in red dust so thick I couldn't rightly tell him from a different soldier except for his limp and his voice.

He looked like the desert was swallowing him whole.

And gods knew he felt like it as I generously and involuntarily took that pain, too. He threw a bag of food onto the seat next to me. More of the hard sour bread I'd had for breakfast and a handful of almonds. This morning there had been some cherry jelly from Elaria they must have picked up while I was knocked out back at Otti Theater. The sticky tang of Elaria-grown cherries comforted me to no end, and I had licked the small jar clean. As such, there wasn't any in this bag.

"No more jam?"

"You'll eat what I give you. When I give it," he said. "Why does the pain keep returning?"

"It's not permanent," I mumbled, sifting through the items. "What is its cause?"

"A god's sword," he mumbled as he rolled his shoulder before leaning his large head on the doorframe. "Stabbed me in the spine between the upper vertebrae. Through seamutt-skin furs, through armor plating." Like the trunk of a tree, the spine was our lifeline. Strong and deeply rooted in the earth. "I've tried every type of pain relief available on Eadha. It'll never heal."

I blew out a sigh and looked back at the knot in the maplewood of the wagon. Figures a god somewhere wanted him dead. Our gods had weapons forged in the outer reaches of the Otherworld and gave them to each of the courts. They all did different things, and I wasn't privy to what they each did. Except for Cillian. My heart hurt just thinking of him.

"How much farther?" I asked instead.

"Half a day."

When I didn't immediately move to take away his pain, he slapped his massive hand on the bench next to me. And when it was done, when I took his pain away, he locked the cabin door, gave it a smack on the side, letting the drivers know to carry on. I wished the desert *would* swallow him whole, pull him under to its sandy depths. It sure was trying.

Sometime later, when I had regained my strength, I tried to eat the food. But the bread stayed hard in my dry mouth and the almonds did the opposite of quenching me. Like the desert air, they seemed to pull the moisture out entirely. Figures they'd keep all liquids for themselves.

I was shoving the food back in the bag when we jostled to a stop again—way too soon for half a day's travels. The door thrust open and in came the dust. I sheltered my face from its pelting as soldiers began heaving in boxes and tent structures at my feet. I lifted them quickly, huddling on the bench. When they were done, and the caravan was stuffed full, there was another smack on the side and away the horses went again. I shimmied beside a box of tent poles and a bag I prayed was different food and reached for the leather curtain blocking the window. Shoving it aside, I saw why all this was put with me. They were leaving behind the other carriage, its doors left open to the brutality of the desert.

The wind whipped through both sides. And there in front lay a prone horse and what looked like a body. Already, in the ten feet we'd traveled, the sand had covered the soldier's feet.

I didn't know what I was expecting. That Autumnfae would stop and bury their dead in a desert designed to kill them? And none of this was right. None of this had to happen if the courts would stop fighting. I sat back, huddled into my spot because I knew I wasn't lucky enough for that to be General Mohr we were leaving for the desert to claim.

9

KADERYN

Lord of The Court of Shadows
Fallen Leader of the Wild Hunt

"If you don't stay tucked in my hood, next time I'm going to leave you in a satchel on the horse."

Teal, the one-foot-tall, blue-skinned pixie fussed about beside my ear in the darkness of my coat's hood.

"I've been cooped up here for ages
In small cramped-in places.
How long 'til we're out of this court?
Oh, don't scoff at me.
I know what the plan is
Avoid Autumnfae's gazes
But it's unwise to be forgetting the port," Teal seethed.

"My shadows are not stuck in Autumn's seaport, Teal. And

you can come out once we've reached the safety of the trees on the other side of this fucking town." I kept my voice low and swirled my shadows around me.

Last thing I needed was attention. I didn't think Autumnfae would challenge me in their court without their general around. And I tried not to think of whatever poor fae he was out terrorizing so I turned back to Teal and said, "Though I don't think there is enough meat on you to grab the attention of the firefae. I can't say they wouldn't kill you for sport. A journey to the port would take us two days off reaching my shadows. I'm not risking it."

We'd stopped to rest Malvasia, my mare, just outside Iradown Tavern. I looked up now to its glowing sign as some Autumnfae soldiers reluctantly moved out of my way. Hopefully we'd get out of here unscathed. Nothing was more important than regaining my shadows.

Nothing.

10

VALENTINA

Slowly, ever so slowly, the wind whipping the carriage ceased its attack. Until all at once, it was gone entirely. The jostling increased, and I struggled to stay on top of the boxes that threatened to topple me over.

I had raided what I could from the food stash, some dried pears, and a tangy dried berry we didn't have in Summer Court. I'd found the linen blanket from my stay in Mohr's tent and shoved it into my food satchel. In my rummaging, I found Mohr's medicine bag. A well-crafted black leather coated the outside, worn out at its edges. I didn't touch it, still remembering being forced to pile its contents back in on itself back at the tent. There was no sign of my multicolored bag that held my daggers. I only hoped that they'd appreciate their own exemplarily forging and not have thrown them out into the desert.

Propped up on the cabin bench, I leaned over a crushed box, stepping on a contraption I didn't care to recognize, and looked out the window. It looked like we were traveling on the back of a porcupine. Most of the trees could find their leaves laying at their roots, having lost them completely. They stood tall and abrupt with thick trunks and golden leaf litter shaped like arrowheads below. I'd never seen this tree before. In Summer we had maples and oaks inland and willows by the shorelines and almost every fruit tree Eadha had to offer. But I'd never seen Autumn's fallen leaves before.

As we traveled, I made a nest on top of the mess in the disheveled cabin and glued myself to the window, watching the flaming colors go by. We passed some trees that still had leaves; bold reds and soft oranges, that fluttered, almost danced, to the ground like the maple keys back home. A deer ran out from the bushes and when the caravan—starved and dehydrated as we were—didn't stop, I knew our destination must have been close.

The sun stretched low in the sky as a welcome chill air blew in from the cracks in the carriage and it jolted to a stop. I peeked out the window as the last rays of the sun, rosy red like everything else in Autumn Court, shone on the hobbled street we stopped on. I could see well-oiled wood, glistening black in the setting sun, and framed small shops along the street. It was too dark to see their signs properly except for the one with its sign aglow by a gutter of fire beneath it. *Iradown Tavern*, it read in bold lettering of glimmering bronze.

A soldier I only recognized by his dust-covered furs dropped to his knees at its entrance, shouting praises to Autumn Court's god and curses to the desert. He was followed by a few more of my caravan who met others by the entrance doors. They greeted each other in shouts and claps on the back before walking inside.

Panic started to set in. I was so thirsty I couldn't think straight and every second that passed they were leaving me here, trapped in this carriage.

"Hey," I shouted, smashing a fist into the door.

But Autumnfae were loud.

So loud.

One more Autumnfae went into the tavern. My hands were shaking as adrenaline, one last bout of energy coursed through me, and I kicked at the door, sending it rattling. But my black lace slippers were meant for soft Summer floors, dusty stages, and warm courtyards. Not kicking in doors in Autumn Court. A court built by fae of fury and fire. So, I did it again, and again, as hard as I could.

His big, lumbering back and telltale limp gave Mohr away. He turned back to look at the cabin and my mouth clamped shut. I was going to burn from the inside out before I begged that monster for anything. A shorter but broader soldier, covered in dust—his beard caked together in hardened clay—turned to look. It was the one I tried attacking when we first entered the desert. He stopped, and I laid a hand against the now cool glass in a plea. Desperate to endure an Autumn Court tavern than stay cooped up, with my insides tying together, in the carriage's cabin. Mohr muttered something to him, surprisingly low enough that I couldn't hear before the soldier walked my way.

I heard the clanging of the latch as he unlocked the door, but it didn't open. Sand had gathered in its cracks and the heat had expanded the wood. I watched as he tried again, and it hefted open with a grunt. Everything had gotten so chaotic inside that I hadn't realized how much the door was holding everything together. And I should have thought it through, but the contents of the wagon rained down at his feet; me included.

I toppled out, too weak to brace myself as the chill air slapped me wide awake. But I looked up from the feet of the large Autumnfae and I said something I refused to say to Mohr. "Please. I'm so thirsty."

He stared at me with the same contempt they did in the tent in the desert, but I was out of options, so I stared back.

"Get up. You cause me any trouble in there, and I'll tie you to the back of the horses for the rest of the trip."

I nodded, hobbling to my feet. More Autumnfae attention was the last thing I needed. He hooked his arms on the bags and boxes that fell out with me and threw them unceremoniously back into the cabin before shutting the door quickly and hard enough that it jammed itself without needing the lock.

I looked over the carriage. It was missing the entire back bench, presumably lost to the desert. The wind had peppered the sides of it so hard that small stones stuck into its wood. The Autumnfae grabbed my arm with a scorching grip and shoved me towards the tavern. It took concentration not to recoil at his touch.

Some Autumnfae males stood around outside, belching and staring. The chilly air blew my red and green skirts around my legs and the uneven cobblestone was bumpy under my feet. I didn't exactly blend in. But whatever the soldier's ranking was who ushered me in through the wooden double doors edged in bronze inlay, made the rest stay quiet.

And, like expected, inside was deafening. So roaring loud that I found myself huddled in the crook of the soldier's side. They shouted to talk; they bellowed instead of laughed; they were full of raw emotion and unbridled manners. And as a fire stoked to life in my belly, I was terrified I was turning into one of them.

"In here," the soldier said, moving us to a booth seat close to the stage at the far end of the tavern.

Tall dancers were doing a type of dance I'd never seen in the same furs I'd grown accustomed to seeing from Autumn, but much more scantily dressed. The dancers seemed to be the reason for much of the hollering and suddenly the behavior in

Otti Theater with the soldiers in the front row became clear. This must be what they did. This must be how they enjoyed performances.

A black-haired Autumnfae female came to the table with a tray in her hand. Her midriff and thighs were on full display. Her golden eyes looked from the soldier to me. What was I supposed to order? My cheeks heated at the thought of a Summerfae asking for water.

"Mayken," she said, but it came out as more of a question.

"Get us a pitcher of water and two glasses of Typhina. Cold." He scratched at his beard and flakes of clay fell onto the greasy slick table.

I swiped a finger against the table and grimaced when my finger came back coated in a sticky vile-smelling oil. Ah, that was how they kept their furniture from soaking up all the drinks they spill.

"What's Typhina?" I cleared my scratchy throat.

Mayken didn't grace me with an answer or choose to acknowledge me at all. So, I settled into the booth, trying to avoid the golden eyes watching me from everywhere else. Mohr sat alone in the front row at a massive table, pulling apart the carcass of a roasted bird. He chewed in between mouthfuls of a dark amber liquid that he swished in his mouth from cheek to cheek before gulping down. And like a mouse in a cathouse, I leaned into the shadows against the wall of the booth, wishing they'd swallow me whole.

The waitress came minutes later, golden eyes still not leaving me alone. And the fire inside surged as I met her gaze. She narrowed her eyes. "Here," she said, putting down a thick, glass water pitcher, an empty glass, and two glasses of a deep ruby-red liquid in front of Mayken.

"Another glass, Gena," he said as he poured the water into the empty glass and passed whatever Typhina was to me.

She scrunched her nose at me before slamming another glass on the table and walking away.

I was really good at making friends.

Mayken filled it, but before it was halfway full, I dove for it, two hands on either side of the heavy glass, gulping it down.

"Small sips or you'll retch everywhere," Mayken said, pushing my water glass back to the table. He sipped his. "Drink the juice. It'll replenish you."

I looked at it, condensation dripped down it and beaded on the oiled table. We didn't have this Typhina drink in Elaria. "You first," I challenged.

He gaffed and shifted in his seat, no doubt uncomfortable with my company. "I liked it better when you didn't have so much to say."

"Quiet and complacent is how you like your females?" The fire inside me churned, built up again. "You think *I* talk too much? You males come to Elaria from all over for a good time and have such a *need* to flaunt your plights and victories that all it takes is some well-meaning questions and careful touches and you all fall apart just the same." Anything I knew of the island was from the rumors the dancers gossiped to each other about from their previous night's guests.

He stilled before grabbing his glass and taking a mouthful. I took a small gulp of my own and grimaced; my cheeks puckered in, and I recoiled. The sour liquid swirled in my mouth, not because it was agreeable, but because I was looking for the courage to swallow it. I briefly considered the repercussions should I spit it out. It couldn't possibly ruin the table anymore.

Mayken gave a hearty laugh. His chest bumped into the table with every bellow, sending the drinks sloshing. I glared at him, swallowing the mouthful, and steadied my blissful water glass against a shaking table.

"You'll recover quicker with that coursing through your bloodstream. It gives back what the desert took."

I ignored him. I wanted out of this court and away from this fire magic.

A large body blocked the entrance to the booth, and we both looked up—way up, to Mohr's disapproving face. "That's enough," he growled. "Get up."

Before I could move, he grabbed me roughly and dragged me from the booth. I raked my nails across the wooden bench trying to stop the monster from getting me again. Thick tarry oil lodged underneath my nails. We pulled at each other until we made it back to his table at the front, and he shoved me into a seat beside him with heavy hands on my shoulders. And anytime I tried to flee, his grip bore down.

Dozens of Autumnfae at my back was not my idea of relaxing so I focused on the dancing in front of me. The music was harsher, not in a bad way, just more intense. But the dancing was different entirely. We danced like the soft caress of water flowing on rocky shores. Autumnfae dances seemed sharp and there was a sense of urgency, like flames licking a night's sky.

The Autumnfae females were beautiful, even when they regarded me with disdain or curiosity. I supposed few Summerfae ever found themselves on this side of the desert. And my blue eyes immediately distinguished me as different. As all Autumnfae, no matter their skin or hair color, had golden eyes. Just as all Summerfae were born with a water drop tattoo on our collarbone. Mine, perhaps, a little different. And Springfae were marked by a streak of silver in their hair. A nod to their god, the God of Fertility and Air and her supposedly silver hair. Winterfae, though diverse as they were, all had white eyelashes and eyebrows.

Mohr moved a hand to my hip and dug his fingers in. If I

pulled away, his fingers grew hot, like bites from fire ants on my skin. Tears filled my eyes and, I sent up a prayer to Angus, to protect me in this forsaken court. To not forget about me; whatever it was I was becoming. Loneliness plundered deep in my soul and, I tried to rein in my fear, wishing the song would never end instead. Wished I never had to go back to the carriage.

Mohr moved his head near mine, his breath became hot on my neck, and I grimaced. "You'll only talk to those I say you can talk to. Get too friendly and I'll take it all awa—"

But before he could say anymore, an explosion from the front of the tavern near the door shook the floor and toppled our glasses. The nauseating smell of rotten eggs followed it.

Chaos exploded as the once cheerful, hollering Autumnfae all went on the defensive, swords drawn and fingers aflame. Mohr stood, hand wrapped in my thick black hair, and pulled me across the chair and to the floor. He pushed through the crowd, his forearm swinging people aside, dragging me behind like a discarded dishrag. I struggled to stay on my feet but fell to my knees. The worn wood sunk splinters into my skin and the puddles of amber liquid soaked into my dress.

I gripped his hand with both of mine, trying to release the pressure against my scalp as he finally came to a stop on the edge of the commotion. Black inky swirls mixed slowly with billowing grey smoke from whatever exploded before us. My eyes tried to sift through the mess. And then I saw him.

Sitting on a partially broken bench facing the onslaught of the crowd, the smoke relieved itself to show the first Shadowfae I'd ever seen. Clad in thick black fabric with deep pockets and onyx buckles, and a black cloak overtop, this male sat unfazed. Unfazed that most of his booth was now in pieces at his feet. Unfazed that he had thirty angry Autumnfae, swords drawn, surrounding him. And unfazed that there was a glinting blue-green spark coming out of the side of his hood. His feet hooked together at the ankles as his arms rested across his chest.

"You're a long way from home, Kaderyn," General Mohr snarled out above me.

Kaderyn, I moved the name over my tongue. *Where have I heard that before?* My lips parted slightly as recognition settled uneasily in. Not just any Shadowfae, The Lord of Shadows—the ex-leader of the Wild Hunt. I tried to catch my breath as I knelt between the Lord of Shadow Court and General Mohr.

"Kill him, General! He covered me in *fucking* ale," one of Mohr's soldiers rumbled out, peppering the air with spit. I recognized him from our caravan, the one who backhanded me when I was tied to the chair.

Inky tendrils of shadows swirled between the Lord of Shadows' hands, quicker and quicker until a black sword appeared from it, thick and strong. He jabbed it down, piercing the greasy wood floor with a thud that shushed the crowd again. "Easy now."

"No one's seen you for ages. Still searching for your lost shadows?" Mohr mocked.

Kaderyn stood suddenly and thrust his sword to the throat of the soldier from the caravans, backing him up against the wall. "You tell me if I need them." His voice was deep and husky, calm in a way I'd never heard before.

A heaviness ran through the tavern. Patrons backed up or shifted their feet, rethinking their role in what was about to happen. I didn't think Autumnfae would ever back down from a fight, but I had a feeling some of them wanted to.

Kaderyn continued, "It was a slight mishap, no one died. And I should remind you, your soldiers came at me first."

The Lord of Shadows' silver eyes looked down to me at Mohr's feet. Those same shiny eyes flicked to Mohr's hand, and to his knuckles scraping my scalp. "Why is it you hide behind a . . . what court *are* you?" His eyes narrowed, assessing me.

"You're in Autumn Court, Kaderyn," Mohr warned, and I grimaced as his hand pulled me back in a show of possession.

Kaderyn's face grew hard. His features became severe as he pushed the sword farther into the soldier's throat. Blood slowly trickled down his skin in a fine line.

"By the gods, General!" the soldier shrieked, pleading, as his hands patted the wall at his back, looking for a crack big enough to sink into.

A pair of eyes—larger than any fae's—peered out from beside Kaderyn's head, beneath his cloak hood, watching me. Small blue hands slipped out from the shadows and clung onto the edge of his shoulder. I blinked twice, trying to figure out what creature would be hiding in the hood of the scariest fae on Eadha.

"What do you want?" Mohr said.

"I suppose a bargain," Kaderyn answered as he withdrew his sword from the soldier's neck, and it disappeared again in the smoke and shadows it came from. He sat back down on the broken bench with his arms splayed against the back of the seat.

Mohr grunted. "You and your gods' damn games. Isn't that what got you into your mess?"

Kade laughed but ignored him. "It looks like you've had a harrowing trip, General. From the Summer Court, no doubt. Nasty desert Lord Grigory made. But Lord Ohrem has welcomed me into his court and as such, I am your guest. I don't take threats lightly and they can and will be reciprocated." He paused, considering something. "Unless you choose to trade the female at your feet for your soldiers' necks at my sword."

I froze on the spot, staring at those silver eyes which were now so careful not to meet mine. Kaderyn rested his hands in his coat pockets. A picture of peace but we all knew better.

The general froze once before letting out a loose chuckle. "She's just a seductress from a theater in Elaria. Spoils of war and such."

I glanced a wary look up at Mohr. I wasn't a seductress in the least. And it worried me he thought as much. I sucked in a deep breath. No matter what happened in the next few minutes, I had to get away from Mohr for good. Before he made good on his deal and found another use for me.

"As I can see. Which is why it would be nothing to trade your males' lives for such a fae."

General Mohr went deathly still behind me. So still that goosebumps traced up my neck at the tension he was creating. "You want my whore?" he chuckled. "Is this what I hear?"

Oh, no.

Kaderyn sniffed sharply. "You let her go until I'm through with her and I spare your unit to die another day." Kaderyn looked bored by this point as he grabbed a glass of black inky liquid, pulled out pieces of what could have been shards from the destroyed table and chugged it in one go, before tossing the glass into the heap of splintered wood at his feet.

"Why?" Mohr asked, but he had lost his confidence and edge and it showed.

Kaderyn laughed and the beautiful sound echoed deep into my bones. "As you said, I like my games."

The heat was building against my hairline as Mohr's fingers curled tight. The air became sweltering again, I couldn't breathe. Kaderyn was making Mohr choose between me or his soldiers. And no matter what abilities I had, Mohr would have a mutiny on his hands if he chose me over them. Especially ones who had just gone and come back over the Glenora Desert for him, leaving their friends behind in its dusty clutches.

Yet still, Mohr hesitated.

Those silver eyes flickered, watching, before Kaderyn

drawled, "General, I'd make a decision quickly. I might be known for my games, but I'm not known for my patience." Inky blackness rolled out again as the hilt of a sword materialized. Tendrils crept from his body at steady, slow intervals, licking the air.

The soldiers grew restless. Here was their commander, hesitating for the life of a Summerfae. Regardless of what he really used me for, it was not going unnoticed.

And in the second it took the general to look around quickly at the reactions of his brothers, the Lord of Shadows was up, reaching out a hand for me. I looked from his hand to his eyes, but he just watched the general like an unmoving wall.

Mohr's hands loosened slightly on my hair, and I took full advantage. I gasped and dove forward, grabbing Kaderyn's solid, strong hand with both of mine. He pulled me to my feet with a guided hand under my elbow and angled his body between Mohr and me. It was a lesser of two evils at this point as my scalp was singed from Mohr's fire fingers.

But this close to him and his smell overwhelmed me. Like camp smoke and soft flowers I didn't know the name of. Kaderyn was rumored to be a ghost, but everything about him was solid and warm and strong. But all thoughts of him were gone as I glanced at Mohr's face. Such unbridled anger, so gods damn angry.

"Well, that's about enough fun for today," Kaderyn said as he gently laid a guiding hand on my back and moved us to the door. "We will be on our way, as promised."

I glanced back at him. Though he walked with a swagger, unfazed at the situation, his one hand rested on my back and the other one sat firmly on the materializing hilt of his shadowsword.

11

KADERYN

A COUPLE DOZEN Autumnfae at my back and my thoughts couldn't clear from the fae before me. If only Teal would stop chattering in my ear long enough for me to get a clear reading of what her deal was. The water droplet on her chest, though weirdly marked as it was, told me she was from Summer. Which made sense with her navy-blue eyes—scared as they were—staring up at me from that fucking general's feet. But the heat, the fury rolling off her, was purely Autumnfae.

I led us out into the dark night. The cool sting of Autumn air mingled with the heat of a magical desert, clashing like warring swords. Half the street was covered in fine sand, blown in from the west from the Glenora Desert. We'd entered Iradown as a band of Autumnfae were sweeping it up and taking it to a storefront three buildings down named The Flaming Gaffer. Likely to turn it into the blown glass that Teal just accidentally blew up all over their tavern.

So much for stealth.

Speaking of the blue-skinned pixie on my shoulder. . . "Teal?" I said, trying to keep the annoyance from my voice.

I felt her move beside my left ear, her soft breath blowing against it. She poked her little oblong head out from under my hood.

I watched the female's eyes before us go wide upon seeing Teal.

"So sorry, Kaderyn
It slipped from my fingers
Like driftwood through winding rivers.
I dare say it won't happen again."

Teal was speed-rhyming.

She knew I was agitated as we headed for my horse where she was tied up outside to the left of the tavern. It was a risk coming to this court at all. But we'd had to. Saving a fae from General Mohr had *not* been part of the plan.

"Wait, my bag," the female said, pulling out of my guiding hands and taking a large step back.

I focused in on her. The light from the torches along the street lit her aglow. Her eyes were wide and bloodshot—her hair, a mess of knots and dried clay. I grimaced. There was no need to ask where she'd just come from.

Teal's small blue hand patted my cheek urgently, and I groaned. Teal wasn't going to let me walk away from this fae. I cursed my bad fucking luck. We didn't need this. We stopped only for a drink and to rest Malvasia. I contemplated telling the fae I saved to be happy to have her life and forget about her bag, but Teal's buzzing in my ear made me reconsider.

"Where is it?" I growled.

"It might be in the carriage we came in on."

Might? I groaned.

But she continued, "Please, it's . . . it's important."

"Where?" I said again, no nicer.

She looked around quickly, head darting like a raven's, before trotting on light feet around to the back of the tavern. I followed. My large steps took twice that of hers, and Teal flittered around my head, leaving trails of blue pixie sparks in her wake.

A row of exhausted horses panted against the rails they were tied to. Two lay down on the ground completely. The desert was unforgiving to all creatures.

The female took a wide berth around the main cabin of the wagon and went for the driver's seat. Her fingers danced along its edges as she tried to pry up the storage compartment.

I looked around once, waiting for her to lift the worn wooden top, eager to get out of this sand and fire town. I narrowly got us out of that fucking tavern and I didn't need Autumnfae to see us stealing from their caravan.

Teal had gone over and was trying, unsuccessfully, to pry up the chair with her. But Teal was ten full pounds of pure Spring pixie, measuring no taller than twelve-inches high. Her abilities did not ride on the strength of her arms. But before my little companion could possibly do anything else to compromise us, I stalked over and smashed a fist to the side of the seat. Chunks of clay fell to our feet as Teal and the female stared at me, wide-eyed.

"Get what you need. Quickly."

She grabbed a colorful bag and hopped down, stumbling from the wagon. I beckoned Teal back to my shoulder, and we walked back to my horse. Autumn Court was no safe place for a pixie. We needed to get going before Mohr regained his composure; before he reined in his seething soldiers.

Malvasia's brown ear twitched upon seeing us. She pulled at the ties holding her still in this ugly fucking town. Time to go.

"Take care," I said over my shoulder to the fae I saved.

"Wh—What?"

"I bargained for you to go free." I mounted Malvasia as the fae gaped at me with maddening, deep-blue eyes. I didn't have time for this. My shadows were calling. "But I do suggest you leave Autumn Court quickly. General Mohr did not want to give you up easily."

"I thought you bargai—"

"I bargained for them to let you go until I was through with you. I don't imagine we have much of a use for each other. You're free to go. But go quickly as I suppose the general will clue in fairly shortly once his pride reins itself back in and his soldiers calm down."

She took a deep breath and swung her bag over her shoulder as she looked up for guidance to the north mountain face of the Anduat Mountains. Teal and I watched on. She'd never seen a pixie before, and the way she looked at the mountains told me it, too, was a new venture.

Oh no.

"Safe travels," she mumbled before taking five steps towards the Anduat Mountains.

Fuck. My next breath caught in my throat and the words came out too quickly. "The Anduat Mountains are in the Courtless territory. And not to mention, there's an ogre roaming them. You'll find his victims' bones before you reach the tree line and your head missing from its body before you reach the mountain's base."

I watched as she looked down at her shaking hands. I could smell the tar beneath her nails from where I sat atop Malvasia.

"I won't survive the desert again," she said as her eyes pierced me still, their navy blue echoing a home I was desperate to get back to.

Teal whimpered from where she sat beside my ear. From the

edge of my vision, I could see her saucer-sized eyes go wide. For *fuck's* sake.

"You are—" she started.

"Teal, no," I interrupted, but she stuck out her tongue at me and blew a raspberry.

"You are cordially invited
Until properly sided
Once Spring Court's marked boundaries are clear.
Autumn is no place for Summer
You've already suffered
Through tribulations, I can tell were severe.
And that vile ogre won't care
If you've got sand in your hair
He'll gobble you down all the same."

I rubbed a hand down my face.
"You're heading north through Spring? Over the desert?" she asked as I glared at the pixie's face, who seemed pretty pleased with herself from where she sat on my shoulder.
"You can stay with us until we've cleared the Glenora and I'll direct you to Summer Court from there."
This entire trip was becoming one headache after another. We had to make it to the edge of the Lady of the Woods forest before first light, and this fae didn't look able to stay on a horse if I tied her to it.
"Follow me." I hopped off and fixed Malvasia's reins in my hands. I was going to have to buy her a horse, unless she was hiding money in that distracting red and green dress.
She walked closer beside us, and I had a vague idea she was saying something about how grateful she was, but I was too

busy thinking of how to get us out of this mess. My eyes lingered to her arms as she brushed them up and down with her hands.

And a coat. I was going to have to buy her a coat.

Teal was definitely on dish duty tonight.

"Tell me your name," I said, frowning.

Those big blue eyes looked up at me and my stomach dropped, like a frothing sea was threatening to pull me under. "Valentina," she said before pausing. "Valentina from Summer Court."

"This is Teal." I nodded to the pixie on my shoulder. But I was getting impatient and Teal's wings in my ear were pissing me off. We needed to be done with Autumn Court.

It cost me way too much dimas for a horse and the Autumnfae selling them took too much pride in separating me from my currency.

So, I stole his coat when his back was turned.

"It'll be a little big, but it's warmer than your . . ."

I stopped because I was suddenly very aware of her dress and the parts of her it was not covering. I rubbed at my eyes; this whole mess was fucking ridiculous.

"Put it on." I thrust it into her hands and trotted Malvasia on ahead. It was dark and traveling by night was not ideal, but we needed space between us and Mohr.

Teal left my shoulder minutes after Valentina had her hood up, having found a new spot tucked under the large, burly, stolen Autumnfae coat made of thick fox fur. Fur, that I wasn't sure was strictly an animal. I could hear her asking Teal if it was just us traveling, and I cleared my throat when Teal wanted to delve into more information than our new companion needed to know.

I'd spent hundreds of years stuck on this fucking island, separated from my Hunters in the Wild Hunt. Half my shadows were gone, split across Eadha in locked chests of iron I couldn't touch. And for a really long time, way too long, there was no way for me to get them out.

I unconsciously patted my left back pocket.

Until now.

And I wasn't going to let a lost fae from Summer Court distract me from returning to my rightful place in the Wild Hunt. As if in answer, a large gust of wind blew the yew tree branches together, clattering like bones of the dead. It blew the hood from Valentina's face, exposing a squealing Teal chattering away in her ear. Valentina's curious eyes swooped up to mine. They held me captive as the voices of the dead moaned longingly at me from below the ground. Voices of souls stuck, trapped in limbo, no better off than me.

I clicked my heels once into Malvasia's side, breaking eye contact with Valentina. I couldn't and I wouldn't get caught up in the plights of the island.

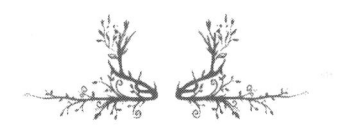

A FEW HOURS LATER, only guided by the light of the moon through Autumn Court's outer borders of a rolling forest, we stopped to rest the horses. And I was sure she had woven her hands into the horse's mane to keep from falling off completely. We tucked our backs against the roots of a massive, uprooted yew tree. It would protect from the wind and any attacks from behind us.

I was riding through the court on good faith with Lord Ohrem on an invitation to visit over a century ago. I'd found loopholes with their hospitality and bargaining rules early on, becoming fae. To survive, I had to. I unrolled the packs from Malvasia's side and worked at setting up the tent.

Teal flitted from Valentina's shoulder and got started pulling the kettle and herbs out of the pack. It was long after I had the tent up—with the use of a bit of shadow magic to help—and a roaring fire going, that I realized Valentina was still on her horse.

I surprised even myself when I let out a laugh. "You're stuck, aren't you?"

Her face scrunched up. "Don't laugh at me. I've only ridden a few times when I was little."

I sauntered over and lifted her off. "You're still little." Her body was hidden under the massive coat, but she wobbled in my arms, and I sobered up quickly. "Go get food from the brown pack by the tent."

She wrapped her hands in the giant coat and her voice was a whisper. "Do you have a water canteen?"

I pursed my lips and narrowed my eyes. *A Summerfae* asking for water? I frowned. I was under the impression she could make it from thin air. I nodded to the fire. "Over by Teal. She'll have some tea ready shortly."

She left my arms quickly, almost abruptly. Curiosity had me watching her go. My eyes shot to black, inky swirls trailing along behind her black-slippered feet. I blinked before calling my shadows to me sharply and they retreated to me, swirling about as anxiously as I felt. What *exactly* did my shadows think they were doing? I brushed a hand through my shoulder-length hair. I needed to focus.

We settled in not too long after. Teal was telling Valentina stories of Spring Court, though it beats me why. Vile backstabbing court as they were.

I had sent a perimeter of shadows low to the ground, trickling in a wide circle around us for protection. If someone was going to come close, I was going to know about it. So it surprised me when Valentina shushed an ever-talking Teal, looked up from the fruit she was picking at, and looked out into the night.

I took another bite of dried jerk beef, pulling it hard between my teeth.

"Lord of Shadows?" she whispered.

"Mmhm."

She dropped the fruit and balled her hands into fists. "Someone's coming."

"Yep." I took another bite of jerky. This one was too salty; I was going to have to cut back on the brine next time.

The fur coat fell to her feet as she shot up, her face panic-stricken, and she slowly backed up towards the fire, grabbing a pair of daggers from the damn colorful sequined bag we had to save in Iradown.

This move sparked something in me. Something I worked hard to stuff down every day since I turned fae. The thrill of the Hunt; the desire to chase down prey. Chasing through the lands the souls destined for the Underworld, or those who don't know any better and run at the sight of my hounds, horses, and Hunters.

Valentina shimmied on her feet, unsure and cautious, like a deer ready to bolt.

I dropped the jerky, trying to rip my focus from the prey drive innately built into me. My voice was gravel as I pushed magic into it, commanding her. "Sit. Down."

But she directed a gaze—full of that fire and fury I was sure marked her as Autumnfae—at me. "Why don't you get up and *do* something."

What?

She lifted her daggers and dropped a foot back to a ready stance. Scared as she was, prey she was not.

Just then, a massive, ground-shaking growl snarled out from my left as I brushed brine salt off my fingers. "I don't have to *do* anything."

I watched as an Autumnfae, clad in his court's disgusting furs, held his hands up and walked into the clearing. Fear shone through his golden eyes. But he was getting no pity from me. Not before, and not now. Not when Jairek Sanguis of the Courtless shoved him forward, closer to us, with a massive palm at his back.

Valentina was breathing heavily beside me now, and Teal had her little arm outstretched flittering through the air, aimed at the one who tried to sneak up on us.

"Welcome back, Jairek," I said, standing to greet our other companion, who nodded to me from behind his captive.

The Autumnfae bristled and curled his nose. "You're not on your lands, Shadow swine."

"Autumnfae forgets its hospitality laws," Teal seethed.
"Guests may not be harmed by the hosting clause.
Guests can not provoke an attack
Or the host can retaliate back."

"Hospitality rules don't apply during the War of Many," the Autumnfae said, spitting on the ground.

I pursed my lips. "I have no interest in the War of Many, if I'm being honest. You four courts could slaughter each other all you want, as long as Shadows and the Courtless are left out of it. But you are right about one thing." I paused. "Jairek?"

Jair tensed and wrapped his hands around the Autumnfae's neck.

The Autumnfae panicked, trying to stop Jair's big hands from getting a firm grip, as he tried to look back at who caught him sneaking. "You're a loyal dog, aren't you?"

Jair leaned forward towards his ear in what looked like an intimate gesture, but I knew better. "More feline, actually," Jair ground out.

Jair's forearms flexed, and he turned his hands sharply, snapping the Autumnfae's neck. He crumpled into a heap on the ground. Out of the corner of my eye, I saw Valentina cover her mouth with the back of her dagger-clad hand. If she was going to hurl, I hoped she'd have good enough sense to do it away from the tent.

I walked up to Jairek and placed a hand on his shoulder. "Good timing, friend."

"He'd been trailing you for a while," Jair said, rolling his shoulders. "And I, him."

I looked down at the dead Autumnfae at Jairek's bare feet. "There's a pair of shoes inside the tent. I'll take care of this."

12

VALENTINA

I'D MADE A TERRIBLE MISTAKE.

When faced with the options of surviving under Mohr's controlling thumb versus leaving with the Lord of Shadow Court and his big-eyed pixie, I thought I'd made the right choice. But now, sitting huddled in on myself inside the large tent, hours after this new fae joined us, by killing an Autumnfae in its own court no less, I wasn't so sure. My palms heated the cold bronze of my daggers. I wasn't putting them down now that I had them.

It was freezing, and I wished to be out by the fire, but something was off about the fur coat Kaderyn had given me. I left it crumbled by the doorway, trying to block the chill of Autumn's air from coming in. The tent was a soft black, almost muted with ties of gold holding it together. Kaderyn apparently had magic to make the inside far bigger than the outside—like Mohr did in the desert. Meaning he was prepared.

I'd never left Elaria. I never needed to know how to work that type of magic or have water magic work that way for me. It dawned on me how unprepared I was to be traveling north through Spring Court. I only hoped that once I met another Springfae, they would let Cillian know I was there.

The floor was lined with onyx and moon-colored cloth that was thinner than a proper rug. I felt the thick roots of the yew trees that lined the sky above us.

I could hear the pixie chattering—with her treble voice and methodical rhyming, it wasn't easy to call it 'talking.' She'd spent a great deal of time going on about Spring Court and its desserts. Which I'd spent a great deal of time listening to. A couple times when I'd asked about their travels, a sharp warning from Kaderyn had her puffing up her chest. Her cheeks would turn red, like it was a struggle to keep her mouth shut. By the third time he shushed her, and I thought she was going to turn purple, I offered a change in topic, which she dove into with vigor.

From my position in the tent, it took a while to pick out Kaderyn's voice from Jairek's. Kaderyn's words were clipped, impatient almost, which I heard towards me quite often. Jairek's voice was more melodic, lower, and often Kaderyn would laugh without inhibition in response to whatever he'd say. *How long have these three traveled together?*

I leaned down, scrunching some of the silver-trimmed blankets under my head against the tent wall nearest the outside fire and almost immediately fell asleep. I'd been in a moving caravan, being thrown into its sides the last time I attempted to sleep. This seemed more peaceful, even with the cawing of a bird overhead. It was so loud it must have been in the trees above.

I pulled my knees up to my chest, but something dark around my feet caught my attention. I shot up to see inky black tendrils of shadows lazily dancing around my ankles and slippered feet. My heart thumped rapidly as I kicked at the transparent smoke, willing it to get off me. They, like living things, fluttered away back under the tent edge and for a still moment, all became silent outside. I held my breath.

"Kaderyn?" Jairek asked.

"Sorry, what was that?" Kaderyn cleared his throat, and I turned my head to hear better.

"Deryn says it's not enough. She was clear. We need the coast."

"It's too dangerous for you. We need to keep to the borders. I don't know how long Lord Ohrem will . . . behave with us in his court."

"The hell with me. If this doesn't work, the Courtless is no better off."

I didn't dare breathe. What were they planning in Autumn Court?

"Kaderyn?" Teal squeaked.
"Your shadows have gone off lurking.
What is it about the Summerfae that has them searching?"

"Quiet, Teal," he snapped.

It became silent again for a moment, except for the sparks of the fire as it cast shadows against the tent.

But much softer he said, "I saw them, too."

I waited ten minutes before laying my head back down. It seems whatever they were discussing was done with. I thought about the last secret I was told not to tell from eavesdropping. No good would come from me prying into information that wasn't for me. So, I pretended to sleep as the tent flap opened, rushing cold firewood air in.

Whoever it was, paused before stepping over the fur coat that I shoved in the crevice. The tent flap fell back in place, shutting out the sting of the cold. I heard shuffling at the other end of the tent and squinted through the darkness. Kaderyn was kneeling by the makeshift beds, stripping off his thick black shirts, unlatching the buckles as he went.

And I should have closed my eyes. I should have pulled the linen cloths right up and over my head. But his swirling black shadows danced across the thick muscles in his back, riding up the curves of his strong shoulder blades and down his muscular arms. The veins in his forearms flexed ridged before his body stiffened and I slammed my eyes shut just as he had turned his head all the way around to me.

I slowly slunk the linen up over my face. I wasn't getting caught up in this fae's problems.

I had my own to worry about.

I WOKE before first light to the soft sound of snoring, and it took me a moment to reorient myself. Kaderyn was asleep, spread out across the entire bed, sheets crumpled up around him like lazy lapdogs. Teal lay curled into his neck, wrapped in his midnight-black hair, mouth slack and snoring softly. No sign of Jairek. I rubbed sand from my dry, crusted eyes.

My stomach rumbled. I had given up on food once the Autumnfae died by the fire. I crawled to the tent door. Teal's snoring masked my scuffles, and I only looked back to realize there were more blankets on me than I had started with. At least four, soft midnight linen blankets lay bunched where I had been laying. I glanced quickly at Kaderyn, lying shirtless. He obviously didn't have an aversion to the cold like I did. I rubbed my feet quickly at the reminder of what Lord Aborys did to my father. And what I did to survive that horror.

I tiptoed out of the tent into the dark, crisp early morning. The air outside was a mixture of fall humid air and a sandy desert breeze, each blow of air passing through each other as if fighting for control. We were still tracing the side of the desert, after all. I was stuffing the side of the tent closed, using the gross fur coat as a weight against the door, when I heard a voice.

"Hello."

I spun so fast I fell back onto my hands before thrusting my daggers out.

Jairek lounged against a fallen log near the nearly burnt-out fire. His arms were above his head, resting on the rotting wood as his mouth curved into a smile, watching my every move. His clothes, though clean, were wrinkled, like he'd slept out here all night.

I mumbled something unintelligible, but a hardiness in my chest had me keeping his gaze.

He reached over beside him and grabbed something out of a black buckled satchel. "Here." He thrust out his hand towards me. "It's jerky. They can hear your stomach growling in Iradown."

But did I trust him enough to put my daggers away? I shoved one in my sequined bag. Happy when it must have hit my spare shoes, as it didn't go right through this time. But I held the other at my side as I side-stepped towards him.

He broke off a piece, tossed it in his mouth before leaning farther to pass it to me.

There was something about him, something strong. Something brave and it made me breathe deep, chasing fear through my body and out through my toes. I shoved the other dagger in my bag and grabbed the broken chunk of jerky before sitting down beside him. He had no streaks of silver to indicate he was from Spring, no water droplet on his clavicle for Summer Court, and his large round eyes were a deep chestnut brown, unlike Autumnfae's gold. Nor were his eyelashes white, signifying Winterfae.

"Where are you from?" I asked.

His eyebrows rose a fraction before answering, and I wondered if maybe it was rude of me to ask. "The Courtless. Teal tells me you're from Summer."

His eyes flicked down to my crude watermark tattoo by my collarbone. The one I did myself when my natural water drop birthmark did not come in. It was the reason it was puckered around the edges and why the lines were shaky.

Any other moment and I would have been hightailing it away from him. *The Courtless?!* Because that would make him a Shifterfae. And his comment last night before he—I swallowed —before he snapped the Autumnfae's neck bounced around my head. 'More feline, actually,' he'd said. I *never* heard rumors about Shifterfae. They never left their court. Was it rude to ask what he shifted into?

I shoved the jerky in my mouth before I said something stupid and my mouth watered, trying to compete with the salt. But at least there wasn't a layer of sand I had to eat through on this compared to back in the Glenora Desert. My belly longed to bite into sweet pears, heated by the Summer sun or a ripe peach, and let the juice run down my fingers.

Jairek placed a wooden water canteen at my feet with that slight, confident smile.

"You don't travel on a horse." I meant it as a question, but it came out like an accusation.

"I do not." And he raised a laughing eyebrow at me. Begging me to ask it.

"That Autumnfae—"

"Would have done far worse to Jairek," Kaderyn's voice rang

out behind me, and I swiveled quickly to see him fully dressed, linens piled in his hands. "Time to pack up. Jair, head up the desert to the tree line. Only come in for water."

I frowned, turning back to Jairek. "Not food?"

He gave me a toothy smile in response before lifting to his feet and stretching his thick arms above his head, yawning.

Kaderyn, fully dressed and ready to go, ignored me entirely.

The sun was slowly gracing us with her presence as her morning glow filtered through the fat scarlet leaves. I laid my hand down and splayed my fingers out against a fallen leaf at my feet. And it was a testament to the size of Autumn's trees that my fingertips were the only part to touch the cold damp earth as the leaf was so large. The vein of the leaf melded with my skin. And I couldn't get over the beauty of . . . well . . . Autumn. Betrayal had me holding still. I didn't want to find this court pretty.

Slowly, ever so slowly, black vines of shadows traced the roots of the ground and danced between my fingers, clashing against the ruby leaf litter. I pulled my hand back to my chest and turned my gaze up to meet the silver ones staring back at me with an unreadable expression.

"Time to go," the Lord of Shadows said, pulling the last strap on Malvasia's saddle.

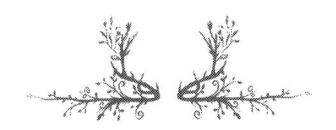

MY MARE and I worked out an agreement early on that morning. I'd leave the reins loose as long as she continued to follow Malvasia as we trailed the edges of a blooming forest. Nothing could get me to loosen my grip on her mane, though, and she gave me that forgiveness.

"It's a bit like Spring
This court that we're in.
A season imprisoned
in constant transition."

Teal lay at my hands against the mare's neck, chewing on what looked like an inedible orange. She'd stop occasionally to spit large white seeds out through her pointed teeth. Teeth I tried not to stare at.

"But I don't care for their food
Or their constant bad moods."

"Or that Typhina brew, erm, drink, I mean." My cheeks heated. Was her rhyming contagious?

Kaderyn snickered from where he sat on Malvasia, riding alongside us. "All pixies speak in rhyme," he explained. "Had I known they were so talkative, I might have chosen just Malvasia as a riding companion."

Teal flew off the mare's neck so fast blue sparks tickled my hands. Her pair of translucent wings, two on each side, and as long as my forearm, reflected soft light like the blue morpho butterflies back home. But she was seething, and her massive black eyes were focused on Kaderyn as she darted for a brown satchel by his knee. Kaderyn seemed to take great pleasure in working up the small pixie.

"And who'd be the map maker?" she spit, pulling out a crumpled swath of beige linen.

I squinted and tilted my head to make out crude smudge lines across some parts of its surface that weren't balled tight in her small hands.

"Who'd be the dishwasher?
Or the tea strainer?"

With each declaration, her face turned from a deep blue to a dark purple.

Kaderyn was outright laughing now, his chest lifting and falling as his long black hair fell into his face, tracing his broad shoulders.

"You're making a map of the island?" I asked, trying to distract the exploding pixie.

Her gigantic eyes shifted to me, suddenly hopeful.
"Don't listen to Kaderyn's jest."

She came over and laid the crude linen across my mare's neck and sat between me and it with no care for personal space. I shimmied my hands to grab the soft edges of the map with my thumbs. Careful to keep my palms wrapped tightly in horsehair.

"I am a useful part of the company's quest.
I'm marking the path we take to the chests—"

"Teal," Kaderyn warned, laughing no more.
But she puffed out her blue belly, stuck out her pink tongue and blew the Lord of Shadows, the ex-leader of the Wild Hunt, a rueful raspberry. A long one. One full of spit.

"It's all right. It's best if I don't know," I said, thinking back to secrets I told to Cillian. "How much longer to the edge of Lady of the Woods?" Once I was over the desert, we would part ways.

Kaderyn opened his mouth to answer but darted to face the forest to our right and pulled Malvasia to a standstill. My mare followed suit rather quickly, and I had to squeeze my thighs to stay on top of her.

"Teal, with me." Kaderyn's shadows grew, swirling faster around him.

My heart beat wildly in my chest. "What is it?" But I heard it, hooves moving fast towards us and a heat brewing in my belly. "Is it Jairek?"

Kaderyn pulled up his black hood and Teal shot to it in a flow of blue sparks, map still crumpled in her little hands. No wonder it was in the condition it was.

Malvasia stood still, ears twitching but otherwise unmoving. My anxiety was traveling through my shaking legs, unnerving my mare.

We bumped into Malvasia twice before Kaderyn swore and grabbed the reins that lay loose on my horse's neck. "Keep silent"—silver eyes pinned me still—"both of you."

It surprised me how well they blended into the woods. How their fur and feather cloaks melded between tree trunks and ashen leaves. I may have heard the group of Autumnfae before I saw them, but by the time I saw them they were on top of us, and I risked falling off the horse to pull the fur hood low on my face. Whatever good that would do. I fought every instinct I had to not jump off the horse and take off running.

The Autumnfae that led was as large as Mohr but he wore a shoulder cape of white feathers speckled with soft brown spots. Each feather reached from the nape of his neck down his broad shoulders and brushed the saddle he rode on. Feathers of a massive bird.

Kaderyn's shadows grew thicker, shading us in a translucent smoke circle that seemed to dare them to enter.

"Lord Kaderyn. My soldiers tell me you've been traveling my court under the guise of an invitation," the male said, his eyes narrowing through the smoke.

"And you've come all this way to greet me personally? I am flattered, Lord Ohrem. Unless, that is, you've rescinded it?"

I watched Kaderyn's hand tuck down by his side where the shadows were thicker, more solid. A faint outline of the hilt of a sword appeared. I looked back at the speaker. Lord Ohrem never visited Otti Theater. I would have remembered those feathers. But the others, at least two of them, I recognized. I tucked my face in farther as shadows licked my torso.

Lord Ohrem gave a pensive look as he said, "An invitation extended almost a century ago."

Kaderyn said nothing.

And I bet it pained Teal quite a bit to do the same.

"Nevertheless, I'll extend the invitation farther, come to our auctions at the Fortress."

Kaderyn sucked in a breath. "I could have sworn the auctions weren't until the fourth of the month."

A small voice chirped from inside his hood.

"Kaderyn, I've conferred
It's the third."

Lord Ohrem showed no surprise if he saw a blue-skinned pixie in Kaderyn's hood.

Kaderyn's head tilted to the side as his shadows slowed. "An invitation to such a place often requires a price."

Lord Ohrem grunted. "Kaderyn, your presence has pulled me from my monthly hunt," he warned. "I can't say I'm happy about it. So, yes, guests of auctions are required to provide an act of good faith."

"Go on."

"I have a malcontent general who is destroying a tavern south of here. Something about being slighted by yourself over a dark-haired female from Summer Court."

My heart was stuttering wildly, and I scrambled to think of a way out of this. I couldn't go back to Mohr. I *wouldn't*.

"Auction her off tomorrow at twilight or I'll personally hunt down that shifter that's tailing you. You're not the only hunter on Eadha, Harbinger, and I will maintain control over my court," Lord Ohrem said.

Kaderyn glared at me, tightening his grip on the reins in his hand.

I was going to throw up or pass out because since they rode up, that anger was back. My fear of Mohr was the only explanation I had. I scrunched my hands into fists, refusing to see if the fire was back.

The lords in front of me continued to talk at length about court proceedings I tuned out entirely because neither seemed particularly distressed they had just discussed auctioning off a female or hunting another fae of Eadha. What exactly *was* Jairek?

After some time, the Autumnfae rode away, back the way they came; a few of them with bows drawn, returning to their hunt.

But the fire inside was still burning. "Give me the reins back. I'll make my way from here."

"Afraid we are going to have a slight detour in our plans," Kaderyn said, not meeting my eyes.

"I refuse to be auctioned off like an object."

"More of an artifact, it seems. It's the coldest month of the year. Winter is reigning and Autumn will hold auctions every month in honor of Gael, Autumn's god, in preparation for the long year ahead. Until it's their time again." He narrowed his eyes. "Why has Mohr deemed you of value to him?"

I wasn't going to tell him a thing. "I won't be going to the Fortress."

"Congratulations, we've both lost that chance to choose.

Come on." He clicked his heels into Malvasia's side and both horses started at a brisk walk in through the forest Lord Ohrem left by.

I tried to slow my breathing, but the trees were closing in. The leaves were cherry red—like a fire I couldn't escape.

"Teal, go find Jairek. Tell him what's happened and tell him to lie low until we're done."

Teal shot out from under his hood and was gone before I blinked. But this was getting too real. Going too far. The weight of my Summer Court bag was heavy at my side with what it contained.

"I'm *not* going to the Fortress," I said again, vaguely aware of shadows swirling around my feet.

His moon-silver eyes looked down at them, then back up to me.

In a standoff, both waiting for the other to act, I launched off my horse and fell to the soft purple heather growing below. We'd been riding for a while and the feeling of my thighs back to their normal gait startled me in a pleasant way, and I took off running.

We'd been traveling parallel to the desert, far enough in that Autumn Court's wind kept the Glenora at bay. And now I was heading straight towards the blowing squall of an unnatural desert because I'd rather die buried in a sand dune than become Mohr's puppet again.

Kaderyn swore behind me and I picked up my pace, shedding the foreign coat, dropping it back to the earth it came from. The green shifts of my dress melded to my legs as I leapt over the last few protruding tree roots before the meadow, then the desert beyond.

Something strong but silent coiled around my left leg and tugged me back. I hit the ground rolling, thankful I was past the biggest of the gnarling roots. Grabbing my daggers out of my bag as I did, I rolled up and spread my stance wide, panting hard. Kaderyn stalked towards me, black shadows twirling around, swirling, as pissed off as he looked. A black tendril retreated from my left leg back into the mesh of shadows around him. His eyes flicked to my bronze daggers.

"I don't have time for this," he snarled.

"I'm not going back to Mohr." I blew a strand of hair from my face. "I'd rather die."

"Ohrem wants you back, or my friend skinned alive. I have places to be, and things to be doing," he growled. "None of which includes running from an angry firefae for a female that has done nothing but cause me to lose dimas and slow my pace because she can't. Ride. A horse."

"Well then, I guess we've both lost the chance to choose *not* to do this." I steadied my grip and was oddly optimistic he wouldn't draw his sword. I tried to ignore what he said about Jairek being skinned alive. The very thought sent my stomach to lodge into my throat. What did that mean?

But the sword materialized slowly, almost menacingly, in his left hand. *Damn.* I sucked in a breath. I was going to have to get close, just like training with Petri. The difference being, his swordplay was for a set of dance moves on a stage, and this now, was for my life.

He moved closer almost lazily, and I dove to the side, slashing across where his thigh was. Exactly step three of practicing with Petri. He moved his massive leg in time, but I danced back, scared of his shadowsword. And my eyes must have shown it because an unreadable expression peeked through his normal look of annoyance I was getting used to seeing. The hefty black sword disappeared in the same swirling shadows, the same way as it did back in Iradown Tavern. Once there, then gone altogether.

I straightened, confused. But he took advantage and

charged at me. I snapped back in time to dodge his reaching hands and slash the dagger through the air towards his neck. But I was used to pulling back, and he seemed used to getting daggers to the throat. He grabbed my hand and held it still. I pulled with a grunt, but his fingers wrapped around my wrist.

"Please let me go," I begged.

"You won't survive the desert," he roared—short-tempered and furious—as he leaned over me.

I looked him dead in the eye, both of us breathing heavily. His captivating silver eyes searched mine as I whispered into the tense cold air between us, "I won't survive General Mohr."

Whatever he was questioning had him silent and still as he stared down at me. But I made the same move as I had with Mohr in the desert tent that day I was captured. One slippered foot on a bent thigh, pushing off to twist the other around to the back of the Shadow Lord and brought the other dagger to his neck. But he was quick, and he held my hand away from forcing pressure.

"You fight like it's a dance," he grunted as I pushed in.

It was hard to ignore how his body heated mine as my back grew goosebumps to Autumn's chill, and an intoxicating smell being this close to his neck consumed me. His hair tickled my face, and the shadows swirled around us—blended and moved—forming in front of both our faces into an outline of a band of horses, cantering in place, manes flying wildly. My mouth dropped open.

A large black horse led the pack, followed by five others. All mounted by shadow figures charging their horses onward. A break in the shadows, a small shadowless dot, shown from a buckle on a boot of a rider near the front of the projection. Like the shadow shows Sisaria would put on in Otti Theater when I was a faeling and too young to know what really went on there. It was magnificent, and I was mesmerized.

And it was all a distraction.

My world turned upside down as he flipped me over him like taking off a coat and I fell into the heather-covered ground with a thud. It drove the air from my lungs, and I was busy gasping for breath instead of clinging onto my daggers. He still held my wrists from where I lay under him, his body weight pinning me down. I squirmed under him, gasping like a fish out of water.

"Shhh . . . take slow breaths. Calm yourself."

I focused on the shadows—the betraying shadow show—as they slowly twirled around his head. I refused to meet his eyes and wished I was back at the theater when he leaned up with one of my daggers in his hand.

His weight pressed his hips into mine as he inspected it, turning it over and back again. Suddenly, his face drew down into a frown before he jabbed my dagger into the dirt beside my head and I let out a squeak, curling into myself like a faeling, laying in the soft heather ground.

His weight lifted off of me and so was gone the heat. But I sucked in a large breath and couldn't stop heaving. I would not beat a Hunter in the Wild Hunt, regardless of if he'd been turned fae or not. I turned my head to the dagger sticking out of the soft flora-covered ground.

Cillian's etched insignia stared back at me.

I fluttered my eyes closed, exhausted. I wasn't getting out of going to the Fortress.

I wasn't getting out of being given back to Mohr.

13

VALENTINA

But I wasn't going easily and Kaderyn knew that.

Which was why, three hours later, I found myself tied to my mare, hands bound, deep in the fire's belly of Autumn's colossal forest. The sun was setting, casting the trees into massive black giants sprawling overtop of us.

Kaderyn led my mare, reins loosely tossed over his forearm, from where he sat on Malvasia. Teal had joined us an hour after our standoff and now busied herself chittering into Kaderyn's ear about things I couldn't hear through his thick, dark hood. He'd occasionally grunt in response.

The leaves littered the ground in oranges and reds, turning the game trails to fire-colored river streams. Squirrels busied themselves bringing nuts into the tall oak trees and screamed at us when they felt we were too close. Which was all the time. The leaves skittered across the ground on a western breeze. The sound, like a parent shushing a faeling before bed. We startled a deer from the trees to our left from where it stood drinking from a river. It lifted its tawny head, ears twisting before taking off into the thicker tree branches. The sound of leather squeaking against itself had my eyes back to Kaderyn as his fists tightened against Malvasia's reins.

A steady, soft pattering started in the distance. A peaceful lulling that, mixed with my mare's steady gait, calmed my nerves. I found myself pouting. I didn't want to like this court. I didn't want to find peace in Autumn's beauty. I wanted to hate it as much as I hated Mohr. But it was a different type of beauty than back home.

On early evenings such as this, I would find myself above the stage in the rafters, watching the dancers practice, getting ready for the night's show. My tongue would be coated in honey from the pastries I missed and my belly warm from strawberry wine. I'd lick my fingers clean as Daria called my name from below, beckoning me to take her pain early or start on the dishes. Depending on the night.

The pattering continued louder and demanded recognition. Cold wet drops fell to my hands, and I craned my neck to look up into the forest canopy. Sure enough, a fat raindrop splashed against my cheek. The warm fox-colored furs that Kaderyn crudely threw on my shoulders once placing me on the horse, kept the rest of me dry as the skies opened up.

The rain was the first water I'd felt since before the desert and I thought I'd be glad, but Autumn was not Summer and the rain was not warm. I shimmied a foot one at a time up, so I was sitting cross-legged on the saddle. Each foot tucked under the thick heavy furs. It was a balancing act to stay upright but being tied to the saddle helped.

Kaderyn led us off the trail under a few massive oak branches, its trunk as wide as I was tall, before dismounting. Kaderyn quickly went to work getting the tent set up, but this time, shadows did that work as he helped Teal build a fire. I watched the shadows work, moving like real hands, grabbing poles and cloth, and fastening it all together. And I'm not sure why he would ever have done it manually with magic like that.

Only once the fire was billowing, winning against the scattered drops that made it through the thick canopy, and the tent was erected, did he come to me. My feet, uncovered from the furs, were wet and freezing and I swallowed down my panic. The last time my feet were freezing, I was six . . . and the Winter lord was showing his ruthlessness.

Kaderyn's rough hands pulled sharply at the ties, and I clenched my stomach muscles to keep my balance. He looked at me curiously before lifting me off. I tumbled off the mare, half falling into his arms and took off for the fire but my feet were no better on the cold, wet ground. I needed them warm. Now.

I stumbled to the fire with my hands still tied at my waist and Kaderyn close behind. I dropped to my butt, slamming my eyes shut to the past—to what I was made to do back then, and stuck my toes so close to the fire that the embers licked my face.

Sticky warm hands pried at the ties on my wrists, and I opened my eyes to see the small nimble fingers of Teal as she tried to work the knots out.

"Get the tea, Teal," Kaderyn commanded as he kneeled down and resumed untying the hemp rope.

I turned away when his gaze reached mine. I might as well have been alone again. He wasn't on my side.

The rope left my skin raw, and though it would heal by tomorrow, I rubbed my wrists out of reflex. I could never take my own pain away. Where would the pain go? It had to go somewhere.

I watched Teal's wings flap furiously as she carried a bronze kettle as big as her over to two mugs where they sat on a fallen log covered in rich, green moss. Steam rose from the spout to combat the rain. She returned the kettle to beside the fire where a pile of red-hot coals waited. I watched her as she looked from the mug to me and back again, with big eyes wide and full of worry. She picked up one matte-black, clay mug and flew over to me, offering it out.

"Tea?" she said, almost as a peace offering.

And I was glad there were no pixies in Summer because they were adorable, and I couldn't find it in me to be mad at one.

"That's kind of you," I said, my voice weak from under-use. I thought about asking what it was, worried I was getting myself into another situation like that sour drink with Mayken. So, I waited for one of them to drink it first.

Teal flew back over to the other cup, pulled a small identical clay mug—a mini mug, the perfect pixie size—out from wherever pixies kept such things, and scooped out a little mugful of the steaming purple tea from the larger one's open mouth.

I smiled as her big eyes and wide smile cheered me to try it from afar. I pressed my lips to the mug and the sweet floral smell wafted over my senses, warming and soothing. I savored the first sip as it passed my tongue, lighting up my taste buds. "What is this?" I asked. It was delicious.

I winced as my shaking hands tipped the mug too far and the heat of the tea burned the roof of my mouth. But it was still divine. Like the melons Daria brought in once in a while from the sea's edge of Summer Court, near Spring's southern cliffside. The orange fleshy ones I was forgetting the name of.

Kaderyn sat down beside me with a grunt, a steaming mug in his hand. Teal flew over and balanced herself on his bent knee, watching me in earnest.

"It's called Nightale Tea. It's made from the roots of the marshmallow plant, dried chanterelles and a type of purple moss that grows only on east-facing tree trunks in Gillies Forest. Steeped for exactly how long Teal says to," he said as he frowned into his mug. "Nothing that will hurt you."

Shadows danced overhead, tying a tarp farther up into the

trees at a slant to stop the rainfall and simultaneously let the smoke rise. I watched them because they, too, were fascinating.

Kaderyn sniffed sharply, and I looked back to the ex-leader of the Wild Hunt, a monster of Eadha, as he sipped his earthy tea beside me with a cute blue-skinned pixie perched on his knee. I knew he was solid enough. He'd been dragging me up and down the damn horse all day, but something about him was off. Something that was not quite fae.

"Are you of the shadows?" I whispered, almost not wanting to know.

His silver eyes met mine, guarded, and I wondered what he could possibly fear in me. I'd almost hyperventilated a few minutes ago trying to keep my feet warm.

"No, Valentina," he finally said as the shadows above us finished their task and quickened into a large swirling tornado around us. It picked up the shadows of the trees, pulling them in. It sucked in the shadows of the boulders, the grass blades, and the anthills as the last of the sun dipped behind the horizon. Swirling, menacing, twirling around us in inky blackness. Like chaos materialized. I looked back to him, still staring at me. "No, the shadows are of me."

And they exploded, covering us in pitch-black darkness, blotting out the roaring fire inches from my toes. The only sense of surrounding was his silver eyes as they pierced mine, holding me hostage. The shadows consumed me with an intoxicating smell of warm vanilla and wood smoke. But there was a promise in the darkness—a safety in its clutches. *Maybe the fire couldn't find me here.*

"Thanks for leaving a lantern on for me," came a laughing, deep voice from the darkness. A voice I knew from earlier.

The shadows retreated into Kaderyn in one swift move. I looked around to see the golden-haired Shifterfae across the fire. Shoeless.

Kaderyn nodded to the tent, and Jairek beamed a wide smile before heading off. He came out a moment later with bulky shoes stuffed on his feet and left them untied. His muscles flexed as he gracefully sat down on the other side of me. Still in the same clothes I'd last seen him in.

"I hear we have a detour," he said, flopping out a bag between us. He pulled out chunks of bread and offered me one before throwing one to Kaderyn.

My mouth watered as I took it, but I noticed the unmistakable rumble in my chest. Something that had me breathing deeper when Jairek was around.

Teal fluttered to Jairek's broad shoulder and pressed her arms affectionately around his face.

"You should feed your new friend more, Kaderyn," he said through large bites of bread.

Kaderyn grunted. "She's feisty at full strength."

But he leaned across me, and I bristled back at the closeness. He dug in the bag that Jairek dropped, pulled out a pomegranate, and something he took by the handful. He handed me the ruby, thick-skinned fruit, and my mouth watered.

I did not hesitate to dig my fingertips in, popping juicy red seeds that dripped down my fingers until I pried it apart, placing the other at my side on an upturned golden leaf. I grated my teeth against the seeds and scooped them out with my tongue. If only I had a dripper of honey to soak them in. It was my first taste of home in over a week.

Kaderyn got up from the fire as Teal's gigantic eyes watched my every move, grimacing.

"Do you want some?" I offered as the staring became uncomfortable.

"Fruit is not supposed to bleed
When you feed," she said as her nose curled.

"I left a surprise for you, Teal," Jairek interrupted, nudging his head into hers with a swollen cheek full of bread. "Over by the edge of the clearing."

She perked up immediately, stashed a sloshing mini mug back from what invisible place she pulled it from and flew to the edge Jairek gestured at. Kaderyn came back with a corked bottle, draped himself across the leaf-littered ground, and took a swig. The smell of oranges and vanilla wafted over.

I turned to Jairek and gave a small smile. "I appreciate the food."

"It's in Kaderyn's pack all the time. Just ask him for it when you're hungry."

I glanced at the Lord of Shadows who was still as death, glaring at the Shifterfae beside me. A squelching sound came from where Teal had flitted to. Something about it made my hair stand up on edge.

Kaderyn's voice distracted me. "Are you warm?"

I felt my face turn up at the thoughtfulness of the question. "I am," I sighed. Because I finally was.

"Good, because Jairek will get that coat tomorrow," Kaderyn said with a nod to my shoulders.

Tears threatened to rise as I balled my hands into fists. I wanted to cry or punch him, but neither would do me any good so I chugged the rest of the mug, threw the skin of the pomegranate in the fire and chuffed off the coat.

The coat fell to my now-warm feet as the brisk air found my bare skin immediately. I moved around the stupid Shadowfae, past the fire, and headed for the tent. Tomorrow was something else entirely, and I swallowed down a scream.

I fell asleep near the tent wall like before, but this time, I pulled all the blankets from the bed. Damn Kaderyn.

I woke at one point to the sound of heavy breathing on the other side of the tent. Breathing tinged with a growl. I searched the bed for Kaderyn, who lay half naked as before. Blanketless. Teal was softly snoring across his hair on a small pillow I hadn't noticed before. I perked my ears to the outside, trying to distinguish whatever it was out there. It was sleeping, that was clear, so it wasn't a threat. But it was big.

I was going to have to find out what Jairek Sanguis of the Courtless could shift into before the day was over.

14

VALENTINA

It took over a day of traveling to reach the far coastline. In typical Autumnfae fashion, I could hear the Fortress before it came into sight. *So damn loud.* And maybe that was a testament to their strength, that they didn't fear who came upon them.

Brave or stupid, I didn't know which one.

The Fortress was solid-red fire brick, reinforced at the corners with glimmering bronze metal. The metal of Autumnfae. The metal they traded with the rest of the island. At least, when things were peaceful and fae weren't going missing.

Jairek had left us early that next morning. With the fur coat.

Wrapped around my shoulders were three layers of soft, spun linen, inky black like most of The Shadow Lord's things. He'd draped them on my shoulders and one across my head shortly before tying my hands back together and me, back to the horse. And in that moment, I despised him almost as much as Mohr. Because he didn't listen to any amount of protesting or pleading.

Teal whispered in his ear again before she darted out to the back of Malvasia, arms crossed as she perched on the brown horse's rear. Occasionally getting flicked with a tail, which she preferred over talking to Kaderyn one second more. I was going to miss the feisty little pixie with her animated limbs, expressive eyes, and nonstop rhyming.

Fear raked me through as we got closer to the Fortress because I was burning again. I was shaking as a fire spread through my chest with every trot forward. Mohr was here.

"Teal, back to my hood," Kaderyn said as the horse's footfalls sounded off worn cobblestone.

We had reached the main road that would point us onward.

Being consumed by an internal fire, I tried one more time. "You can't do this, please."

"Calm yourself, Valentina." Kaderyn's voice was liquid smooth, and I wanted to bite something on him.

"I'd rather die than go back to him," I spit.

He glanced back at me. "You will find yourself doing neither. Now stay calm."

Teal tore from his hood and came so close to my face I went cross-eyed. She spread her arms wide and hugged my dirt-ridden cheeks. I'd imagine being hugged by a starfish was much the same.

"What is he planning, Teal? Where's Jairek?"

But she just pulled back her face and gave me a desperate look. "Erm—"

"Teal. Hood. Now," Kaderyn demanded.

She zipped from me, shooting into the side of his hood in a puff of blue sparks.

"Damn you, Kaderyn," I mumbled, but he ignored me.

And he continued to ignore me as I threw every insult I could think of at him. Every colorful derogatory name I'd ever heard at Otti Theater. The fire flamed through me, and I shook free of the linen blankets. The heat of the unknown fire sparked a fight inside me and I wanted to burn the world down with this anger. *Why hadn't Cillian found me yet?* It'd been well over a week since I was taken. Since I'd traveled a burning desert into a flaming court.

Shirtless, sweaty Autumnfae sparred in a clearing to the left of the Fortress. I could see the east sea from here. It roared as waves crashed along a rock-strewn shore. I longed to find myself beneath its familiar waters.

Farther along, a row of massive docks jutted out as waves broke against its edges. Autumnfae's docks withstood the rage of the sea with their kilned brick and metals, and I became increasingly worried that they weren't as stupid as I thought.

They turned to watch us come up to the Fortress and the way they looked at us gave me a feeling they didn't get many visitors.

I couldn't fathom why.

Kaderyn led us to the stables and dismounted. To the stable fae, a large faeling—my best guess around sixteen years—with a sporadic beard haphazardly braided, he said, "Both horses are to be in the same condition you see now. If not better."

The faeling had tried to puff out his chest. "Oh, making demands are you—"

Kaderyn's shadows flickered out from him once and the faeling stumbled back.

Much less confident the faeling said, "How long do you think you will be?"

Kaderyn looked up at me. "As quick as possible."

Kaderyn untied me from the horse and lifted me off. His gaze moved down to the ropes on my wrist before he grabbed it and raised it up. I looked at what he saw, and there, scorch marks had turned the rope black. Not enough to burn through it, but enough to try.

I ripped my hands away. It was no good explaining this to him. My loss of water magic and the gut-churning fire magic that randomly chose to burn through me. I walked on towards the Fortress surrounded by Autumnfae.

Their skin varied, as dark as smoky quartz to as light as freshly chopped ashwood. But their telltale golden eyes—as golden as the metal they forged—all looked at me the same. And they all looked me over as I walked to the doors of the Fortress, followed by Kaderyn. All looked me over in an emotionless span of three seconds and either turned away or turned up their nose.

I squared my shoulders. Damn them all.

Above the open door, molded in bronze metal and burgundy brick, was the mantra of Autumn Court.

Hope lights the fire
Fury fans the flames
Courage carries us through

The double doors were open, and the cool ocean breeze billowed into the grand hall, fanning the flames of a massive fire roaring in the fireplace carved into the opposite wall. Autumnfae flocked in and out with food and drink nestled in their hands.

But as I lifted my foot to step through the threshold of the Fortress, Kaderyn's thick arms wrapped around my waist in a strange bear-like hold and hoisted me off the ground. I yelped as he side-stepped the rug at the Fortress's entrance and set me down on its other side, inside the large hall.

"What was that for?" I yelled as I pulled my dress back into its rightful position from where it had ridden up.

I ground my teeth together as Kaderyn ignored me entirely.

"Kaderyn! How great of you to accept my invitation to our

monthly auctions," Lord Ohrem shouted over the loud thumping music—like Kaderyn had much of a say in the matter. "You're just in time for the feast."

He shoved out a massive oil-soaked chair from a table surrounded by burly Autumnfae. The cape of long white feathers lay draped on the chair's back. A few lone females, clad in the same small fur outfits I saw in Iradown, bustled around filling thick glass mugs as big as Teal with a foamy amber liquid.

"Save the small talk, Lord Ohrem. I want to be off your soil as much as you want me to be. When does this thing start?"

I slowly glanced at Kaderyn, who, I was sure, just signed his death sentence. But Lord Ohrem's smile just widened.

"Yes, yes. But first a feast and a dance, then the auction begins." His golden eyes raked me over as he clapped Kaderyn on the shoulder. Hard. "She's a pretty little thing, Kaderyn. You'll be on your way by night's end. Have a seat and enjoy yourselves."

I looked back out the doors to the sea—to freedom—but Kaderyn's strong hand clamped on my forearm and coaxed me in on farther.

We found a table that kept our backs to an outside wall and Kaderyn pulled me down to sit. Rich food appeared on the tables shortly after—smoked salmon, roasted birds, cauldrons of soup with sticky ladles and creamy mashed purple yams.

The table held many curving bronze vases of orange chrysanthemums and large sunflowers bigger than Teal. Gold candlelight flickered from flames on three candelabras evenly placed across the oil-soaked table. Kaderyn didn't hesitate to dig into the large roasted turkey and spoon vegetables onto both our plates. He tossed a few loaves of bread in the bag at his side, not caring who saw.

I grimaced at the table. I longed for figs and warm, sun-heated tomatoes, not boiled mashed roots. I picked at the yams and roasted potatoes until finally a dessert of apples and cinnamon appeared. That's when I looked deep into Kaderyn's —a ruthless Hunter in the Wild Hunt's—eyes as I scooped his dish into mine and took a large mouthful.

He narrowed his eyes as I licked the spoon clean. He could have his dessert when he was long gone away from me.

"Come dance, female!" came the voice of a large burly male. But instead of furs, he wore layers of shirts all dyed a deep brown. And before I could say no, he had me up and walking to the center of the other dancing fae. I was terrified to look up into his face. I knew he wasn't Mohr by the stature alone, but I wanted nothing more to do with Autumnfae.

"Don't look so scared," he said as he twirled me and pulled me back again. But he kept an arm's length between us, and I appreciated it enough to steal a glance.

He looked pleasant, smiled even, as his gold eyes glittered off the light of the roaring fire. I caught sight of the sprawling tattoos that marked his chest and climbed up his neck. Some looked like drawings of things I recognized, a bow, and a deer curved back. Others looked like lines scattered, as if someone threw sticks on his skin and where they lay, tattoos appeared. His brown hair was messy, but I picked out a few braids on either side of his head. And though he was twice my size, no malice came from him as I'd come to expect from Autumnfae.

He sang along to the music as we danced. A clomping of metal-tipped boots on the wooden stage floor echoed through the drumming around us.

"I won't hurt ya," he said as he backed away for a brief moment to do some type of dancing I did not recognize. He laughed a hearty bellow as he did some moves his large body looked silly doing.

"There are Autumnfae females here who would enjoy

dancing with you more than I. No offense," I added quickly, shouting over the steady thumping of the beat.

He made a few quick foolish moves again that brought an involuntary smile to my lips before he came back to grab my hands again. "There are," he agreed, before sending me into a twirl. "But dancing with them would not piss off the Hunter at your side."

He leaned down and kissed the top of my hand in a surprisingly gentle gesture. I looked to Kaderyn through the throngs of firefae, whose silver eyes flicked from my hand to my face.

I turned back to the Autumnfae, who was howling into the music now and leaned into his ear. I didn't have a voice that could carry over this drumming. "I don't think dancing with me affects him at all."

"Is that why he keeps shadows around your wrist then?" he asked, pulling my hand up in between our faces. And sure enough, there was a string of shadows linked around my wrist like a bracelet. He continued, "Ah, don't worry yourself, Valentina. I'm just having a little fun."

He did a few more dance moves that looked like a crane or a fish out of water and my belly hurt from laughing so hard.

"I've been demoted, forced to stay at the Fortress while others get to go off and have some fun," he said, huffing.

But my feet stilled the small shuffling I was doing, and I sobered up. *What fun was he talking about? Capturing me in Otti Theater? Harassing whatever town Cillian had to go save?*

"Aye, I've heard of your travels, and I don't blame ya for that anger you're shooting me now. Though it's far too strong for any fae who prays to Angus."

I frowned. He knew an awful lot about me.

He did another ridiculous clapping move and shoved another male out of the way when he'd encroached on our space.

"I don't know how anything gets done with all the rage you Autumnfae carry," I mumbled, watching the other male get up and whip around to my dancing partner with fists closed.

He took one look at who it was and straightened his shirt and abruptly turned away.

He shrugged. Or was it a new dance move? I wasn't sure. "Smash things, mostly," he said before thrusting a pointed finger in the air. "But anger breeds action. And action brings change."

"You're done here," came Kaderyn's voice from above my head.

I turned quickly and bumped into his solid chest.

The Autumnfae laughed hard with his head thrown back. "Oh, maybe with Valentina, here. But, for the rest of it, I'm just getting started."

And with that, he grabbed a bowl off the nearest table and threw something that looked like an acorn in his mouth and moved on through the crowd, continuing on his ridiculous dance moves.

We watched him go, as every second made the moment between us awkward. We were Shadows and Summer standing in the middle of a sea of Autumn; most of whom were all gyrating to the drum's heavy beat.

"Here," Kaderyn groaned as he pulled me to his chest.

My throat locked up as one of his hands stayed in one of mine and the other went to my back. I looked away as we swayed to the music.

"Don't worry, it'll be over soon."

I whipped my head towards his. "For you, maybe. This time tomorrow, you'll be across this court while I'll be here. Stuck with a monster."

"And you think you're better off in my company?"

"You must not know Mohr at all," I mumbled to my toes. It didn't matter if Kaderyn heard. He didn't care.

He grabbed my chin and thrust it up to look at him. His jaw flexed as the shadows licked around us, snapping like whips in the air. "He'll hurt you, won't he?"

Tears welled in my eyes, threatened to spill, and clouded my vision. And when they finally overflowed—because being trapped with Mohr was so monumentally worse than being alone again in a dusty theater—I slammed them shut.

Kaderyn's hand held me still; I couldn't turn my face away. A long moment stretched as I stayed captured by shadows with my eyes closed to the world.

But then a soft, warm breath warmed the tears trailing down my face. I opened my eyes to see Kaderyn's face now inches from mine. Time stood still as he leaned down and brushed his lips—barely harder than a feather—against mine. Tingling jolted from my head to my toes at such a delicate move from a deadly Hunter.

"Attention! The auction will soon be underway. Bring your . . . gifts into the backrooms to get ready," Lord Ohrem's voice rang out as the music stopped dead.

Kaderyn abruptly pulled away but held my wrist in his hand. I frowned at him as he cleared his throat. "That's you. Let's go."

A female fae who I had seen serving food, the one with hair much the same color as mine but far curlier, came up to us. She introduced herself as Terna and her golden eyes grazed over us both like it was a sight she'd seen all too often before. She gestured for us to follow her, leading us through the tables and chairs, with that same tar-like smell back at Iradown Tavern.

The room she brought us to was small and had many narrow dressing tables with mirrors fastened to them with bronze clips. Small stools sat before them. Piles of clothes lay along the far wall. It wasn't the neatest place I'd ever seen.

Understanding dawned on me, hard. It was where the females were made to be presentable before the auction. Where they were traded like parcels or cattle. I shot my eyes to Terna, but the female Autumnfae looked back, expressionless.

"Here's her bag. I don't know if you need it."

We both turned to look at Kaderyn holding out my shimmering multicolored bag from Summer Court. I gasped and grabbed for it, but by just feeling the outside, I knew my daggers were gone.

"I'll hang on to them, Valentina," Kaderyn said, raising an eyebrow. Then he turned to Terna. "Keep an eye on her. She's a runner."

I rung my bag in my hands. I was going to kill him.

But Terna just gave a sharp nod as Kaderyn left, closing the large door behind him. Like she'd heard all this before.

And I wanted to go back; go back to choking on patchouli incense above the rafters in the theater. I missed the smell of settled dust in its walls. I missed Petri's teasing and Sisaria's warmness. And I knew Daria would be falling apart. How was she going to explain why their performances were no longer working to ease the audience's pains? And did Avril make it back?

Was Cillian on his way?

Kaderyn was here making death swords from shadows and working spatial magic with tents in minutes. My magic was limited to silencing wards, and aesthetics, makeup, and hair. But even those had limits.

I tossed my Summer bag against the wall. It was useless without my daggers.

"I can see the knots in your hair from here," Terna said, golden eyes scrutinizing me. "Can you fix it, or do I need to?"

It came out as a simple enough question, but the fire burning inside me wanted her to be condescending so I could hate her. I ran a hand a few inches above my waist-length hair, willing it smooth and tangle-free with my fae glamour. It needed a wash and a real brush. Magic could only hide so much for so long. My palm heated over the tangled mess, and I snapped my hand closed, a little worried I'd light it on fire. I did the same over my face, fixing my makeup to what I knew how to do.

Terna turned back from what she was doing to look at me. "I guess, but you still look Summerfae."

"I *am* Summerfae."

I was expecting heat back, I was expecting a fight. But her eyes did something I hadn't ever seen golden eyes do. They showed compassion. Or pity, and really, I wasn't expecting either. So I ran a hand over my eyes, mimicking her golden ones staring back at me.

She grabbed a dark paste and a small makeup brush. "That's better but we don't keep our lips pink," she said.

And I watched in the bronze-tipped mirror as she painted them deep red, like blood draining from a carcass.

Her throat made a weird sound before she said, "I thought you'd be clammy, like touching a sea slug."

My eyebrows drew in and she—apparently done—pulled away, golden eyes smiling. "You've never seen a Summerfae before?" I asked.

"Mostly Springfae. Summer usually stays out of the soldiers' way." And her eyes met mine with an asking, a curiosity about what I did to earn Autumn Court's attention.

My heart thumped wildly and the fire inside quickened. Opening my mouth is what got me here. I wasn't making that mistake again.

She continued, "When the fae go missing every few years,

Spring blames Autumn. And Autumn, well, we blame everyone. Is this why they've taken you? You know about the missing fae?"

"I know very little about much of the island," I confessed.

She sighed and gave me an outfit similar to hers to change into. The edges of the fur top and skirt tickled my stomach and thighs.

I tugged at the skirt, barely reaching over my backside. If only it covered more skin.

Terna used her magic to tidy up the room, throwing clothing in hampers and tidying makeup around the tables. Things whirled past my head as she asked, "Did you get enough to eat?"

The apple dessert was delicious but wasn't nearly filling enough. Even if I had stolen Kaderyn's, too. Something about the way she asked had me wondering if she thought I wouldn't be eating for a while. So, I shook my head.

She smiled a warm smile and nodded. "I'll be right back."

"Wait." I halted her. I didn't understand; she wasn't faeless but she was being treated as if she was. "Why do you live like this? Why do you let them rule you like this?"

In Summer, males and females were equal. Daria was the most powerful fae in Elaria, after all.

A look in her eye made me throw up silencing wards, a magic I was familiar with.

"Not long ago, we were confined to the caves in the northern mountains." She straightened her back as she took small steps toward me. Golden eyes flickering with fire. "In that short amount of time, we've risen from under their boots to being the jewelry that adorns them. Soon, beside them." Her mouth moved beside my ear in a faint whisper. "Then, when it's done. When it's finally quiet, their ashes will line our roadways." She pulled away, her eyes dulling back to their emotionless gold. "The auction is about to start. Don't do anything stupid," she warned, but there was a smile on her lips.

I watched her go, silently gaping at her. The latch locked shut with a click. I wasn't expecting to like an Autumnfae. But she was just as trapped as I was. Difference was, she had a plan.

I looked at myself in the mirror. For all purposes, I looked perfectly Autumnfae. Even down to the fire heating my fingertips. In the corner of my vision, I saw something out of place in a room full of muddy browns, dulled reds, and golden metal. My shimmering Summer Court bag lay against the far wall where I had thrown it.

Guilt pulled at my fingertips for throwing the only thing I had left of Summer Court. I grabbed it quickly, hugging it to my chest. Still daggerless. But I remembered the second pair of shoes I saw from before and shoved my hand inside. The ones on my feet were now dirty with clay and caked with dirt with rips in the sides from tripping on tree roots. Summer Court slippers had hard soles for stage work, but they couldn't keep up with Autumn's forests.

But my hand instead touched something silky soft, like drawing my hand through running water. I wrapped my hand around the fabric and pulled, letting the bag drop to the floor because I *knew* what fabric felt like water and was lighter than air.

The Caterina del Aamod tie.

Its weightless silk danced through my fingers and fluttered against my skin like butterfly wings.

My brain stuttered to a stop, trying to decipher when . . . how . . . it got in the bag. *Oh.* When the screaming started in the courtyard with Petri, I must have grabbed the wrong bag off the wall.

So, I stood there, impersonating an Autumnfae, holding a

pleasure scarf in a foreign court about to be auctioned away. No more rights than livestock.

My eyes prickled with tears. *Why did the God of Love hate me so much? Why had he abandoned me?* I considered hiding it in a bag of Autumn Court furs. The gold of the ties might blend in for a while, but in the wrong hands these scarfs would not make Autumn Court's females' lives any better. And I didn't want to do that to Terna.

I looked up at the metal-veined support beams above me, looking for a way out of this mess or for a god's advice as the latch unclipped from the door and Kaderyn walked in.

"Okay . . . it won't be long now. Wow, you look—"

His words stuttered to a halt because in a moment of panic and self-preservation, I wrapped one end of the golden ties around his left wrist—

And fused the other end around mine.

Teal peeked out of the darkness beside his head. Her small blue hands leaned on his broad shoulder as she blinked down at the scarf, then up to my face. And as one, we all looked down at the scarf and what I'd just done.

Kaderyn sucked in a breath and a fury washed across his face as shadows exploded around his body, flicking through the air like lightning bolts.

And I couldn't pull away from it all. Because I, being so smart, leashed myself to him with a pleasure scarf.

"By my hounds, female, you're destined to ruin my days."

"Is that . . ." Teal squeaked. But we didn't have time for Teal to get out a full rhyme.

So I helped her.

I swallowed. "A Caterina del Aamod tie."

"I'm going to damn Angus straight to the fucking Underworld, I swear," Kaderyn said, fuming.

"I told you; I won't go back to him."

The shadows licked against my skin. Kaderyn grabbed me under the chin, holding me still, silver eyes piercing mine so close our noses almost touched. "Valentina, I have Jairek, a Shifterfae, hiding in a room brimming with *fucking* Autumn-fae, who take great pride in hunting his kind, risking his life to outbid anyone's offer on you."

I blinked at him.

"It doesn't matter now." Kaderyn dropped his hand from my chin and ran it quickly down his face. Obviously pissed I was still standing there when he was done.

"My teeth can chew through bone and sinew
Let me at that fabric between you two," Teal said,
curling her upper lip to show needle-like teeth.

I chewed my own lip and shifted my feet.

"It's a scarf blessed by the gods, Teal. Very few things will be able to get through this," Kaderyn answered.

"What about your shadowsword?" I asked. Kaderyn was, at one time, the leader of the Wild Hunt. He was godlike, wasn't he? Surely his sword could help.

He stepped closer, his chest bumping into mine. "If you thought my sword could cut through a god's scarf, then you wouldn't have leashed me with it, would you?"

I parted my lips. Not to tell him I hadn't really planned it through at all, but I felt I needed to defend myself, nonetheless.

"Don't. Say. A word. Not now, and not the entire fucking time we're out there." He gathered the excess ties between our hands and stuffed it up into his obsidian-black shirt sleeve. "Teal, tuck back in, please."

He grabbed my hand roughly and tried to cover the rest of the golden ties with his large hand. He turned towards the door, but his angry silver eyes stilled on mine. "Change your eyes back," he demanded.

It took a moment to realize what he said. I'd forgotten I'd changed them to gold with Terna. I brushed a hand quickly across my eyes using my glamour.

"There," he said. "I want to cut off your arm a little bit less now. Let's go."

Minutes later, we were walking out onto a raised maple wood stage. Golden medal marbled through it like veins on a leaf, filling cracks no doubt put there by the angry fae before us. It looked like a lot of patchwork had been done.

It took a few seconds but the crowd of Autumnfae males hushed—much to my surprise—and I didn't know they had the ability to do so. The only sound was the creak of a door opening and shutting.

"I do regret to inform you my gift to the legion is apparently not through with me." Kaderyn held up the magic scarf for all to see. Most chuckled, some yelled profanities. "An insatiable lust this one has and dutifully it would be wrong of me to leave her"—his eyes bore down on me with an unreadable look—"unsatisfied."

It was such an uproarious laughter that I thought we were going to be all right. But Lord Ohrem blocked our path off the stage. "You aren't leaving my court without an offering. It will not make my general happy letting her go." Fury, endless fury, rolled off him. "I hear him causing a stir at the back, even now."

"Last I checked, General Mohr can't break a Caterina del Aamod tie either," Kaderyn said as shadows swirled inky pools at our feet.

"Gael has been hanging around—"

"Ten thousand dimas says we leave now," Kaderyn interrupted, offering a tithe.

"Thirty-four thousand dimas," countered Lord Ohrem.

Kaderyn turned his head slowly, moon-lined eyes piercing me through as he ground his teeth together. Thirty-four thousand dimas was an insane amount of currency.

A commotion was starting at the back of the room and the fire sizzled my skin. *Was it Jairek getting caught? Was Mohr coming up here?*

Oh gods, I needed us to leave. I shifted on my feet beside him.

Kaderyn pulled out a large black pouch and threw it unceremoniously to Lord Ohrem. "There's thirty-two thousand. I think it should suffice to"—he stomped a large heavy boot on the melded stage—"fix this floor properly. I can have the rest delivered when I arrive back in my court if you're so desperate for dimas, Lord Ohrem."

Lord Ohrem let out a belly laugh that seemed to calm the rest of the Autumnfae. "It will do. Safe travels."

And it came out as a warning, not a wish.

Kaderyn grunted back before pulling me off the stage. We were out of the Fortress and into Autumn's night in minutes and back to the horses as quick as I could keep up with him, the soles of my slippers worn far too thin. But I had grabbed my bag and could change my shoes whenever the Lord of Shadows decided to stop making me run.

He tossed a coin to the stable faeling, then, in the same motion and intensity, tossed me onto Malvasia. But I hadn't thought this through. He climbed on behind me and I froze at the unexpected closeness.

His liquid-smooth voice was rough in my ear. "Unless you'd rather run alongside?"

And, really, what was my other option?

"Is Jairek okay?" I asked, ignoring his suggestion as his arm wrapped around me to hold the reins, guiding us out of the grueling Fortress grounds, leading my mare behind us.

Kaderyn's shadows moved slow, too slow. Not like when he was relaxing around the campfire where they, curious things, would come out and flutter up my limbs. No, right now, every lick of the shadows was deliberate and measured. And they kept far away from me.

"Jair took off out the side door once he saw me on stage," Kaderyn explained. "Mohr was the reason for the commotion afterward. A shorter Autumnfae seemed to hold him back."

Bile rose in my throat and dread surged through my veins. I had just pulled more fae into my mess with Mohr.

"You're eventually going to have to tell me why he wants you so bad."

But we were both keeping secrets, so I looked over my shoulder at him, up into his moon-silver eyes. "Are you traveling the island for your shadows?"

He gently patted my thigh with the hand I had tied with the gold-and-silver god's scarf. "No, Valentina. *We* are traveling the island for my shadows."

15

KADERYN

Any progress we made across the Autumn grasses had been dampened by a command to return to the Fortress. Dampened our trek and our spirits. Valentina's, most of all.

So I let her sleep against my chest, shivering in Autumn Court's attire as Malvasia guided us back through the forest until I was certain she, herself, was sleepwalking. I found us covering from prying eyes and Autumn's chill in a small clearing under the canopy of a large maple tree who still kept her leaves and was blocked on the sides by evergreens.

I sent out a trail of shadows, searching for Jairek. Being tied to a Summerfae was making me increasingly dependent on his help and I worried if I was going to be able to get us all out of this alive.

I dropped to my knees and sifted through the leaf litter with one hand for the worm-strewn dirt, the humus, below. Valentina sat half-asleep on the mare and my arm reached up awkwardly because of the ties. But I needed to stop the incessant chattering of the dead first. I thought I would have had time to do this later but with these fucking ties leashing me to her, things got more uncertain.

I shoved my hand into the cold moist ground, connecting me to the spirits of the dead. The ones trapped here like me. The ones I couldn't lead to the Underworld. They weren't trapped in any physical space but lingered in the earth all the same. I shot a string of shadows down, linking them to me, one by one. All thousands of them.

And I wasn't kind when I told them to, absolutely, unequivocally, fuck off.

I jostled Valentina when I was done. Not any kinder. "Hey. Wake up. We're going to camp here for the rest of the night."

She startled quickly, but her eyes were puffy and shadow-marked underneath. And how fucking desperate did she have to be to have just done what she did. I tried to soften my tone.

We set up camp in the most awkward fashion possible. It took concentration I didn't have to hold on to my patience. If I pulled too far setting up the tent, she would yelp and fall into me. If she tried to help Teal with the tea or firewood, I was stuck waiting for her to finish with barely an arm's length of Caterina del Aamod ties between us. My shadows moved, molasses slow, as I focused on them instead of ripping either of our arms off.

By the time my shadows led Jairek to us, we were sitting around the fire, though Valentina was, again, almost in it. I thought for a captive of Autumn Court she'd have more of an aversion to all things fire-like. But it was the cold that seemed to cause her the most distress as she rubbed warmth into her toes.

Must be a Summerfae thing.

Valentina sucked in a breath as Jairek strode out of the forest, his normal cheery self no worse for wear. He was in the same beige and white Courtless clothes that were able to appear and disappear at his will. But he was shoeless, and I was prepared. I greeted him with a grunt and tossed a stolen pair of Autumnfae boots to him.

And Valentina must have been feeling brave because she asked, "Why do you never have shoes?"

Jair gave a small laugh and plopped down beside us, exhausted. "I haven't been able to find a pair that can withstand shifting." He grabbed a loaf of bread I had stolen earlier. "And the clothes are for your benefit," he said with a wink to her.

And I thought she'd turn away, blushing, or with a shyness I'd seen other fae females do over the years, but she just stared at him. There was a bravery to her when Jairek was around, I was seeing it now.

I threw bits of pine boughs on the fire, watching it sizzle as her body beside me grew more and more still. My mouth curled at the corners. *Oh, by my hounds, she was going to ask him.*

"And what is it exactly you shift into?" she asked, and I all but burst out laughing. She abruptly turned to me; navy-blue eyes wide. "What? Is that rude? I'm sorry."

Jair stretched out against the open grasses, beaming, and I rubbed an eye with the heel of my hand. "Are all Summerfae as sheltered as you?" I asked.

She straightened her back, frowning. "Are all Shadowfae as grumpy as you?"

I raised an eyebrow as Jairek let out a loud laugh.

She was daring, indeed.

"Do I want to know why you two are tied together by a cloth reeking of the gods?" Jair asked, still with his shoulders shaking.

And Teal told him. She flew to his chest, curling her legs together like she was telling a riveting fairytale—and not about one more goddamn thing that has gone wrong on this journey. When she was done, Jair turned to me, but I didn't meet his eyes. I was desperate to get my shadows back, and I finally had a way to touch the iron key lost in the river between Autumn and Winter.

I subconsciously touched the Faebric pouch I kept in my back pocket. It was a magical cloth—not unlike the fucking scarf that now tied me to Valentina—that allowed fae to touch iron. It was made of indigo and silver threads given to me by a faeless friend back home near The Court of Shadows.

Iron burned fae skin. A lesson I learned the hard way the first time I tried to get my shadows back.

"Does she know where we're headed?" He stared at me in the way only Jair could.

His attempt at keeping me honest was astounding. And I really wished it was just me and the fucking horse.

"First thing's first. We're out of food. I had planned to be closer to the court lines by now. Lest Autumn finds us hunting in their woods."

And I didn't want to ask Jair to go out hunting, not after I made him risk his life at the Fortress. Even if it was his choice, those hallways were probably the last place he wanted to go.

Teal flew to my shoulder, sloshing her tea as Jair rose, dusted off his hands before saying, "I'm on it."

Jair came back an hour later with an elk draped over the back of his shoulders, and a massive bite taken out of its back haunches. Valentina stared at the gaping hole as we cut it up. He said something along the lines of, "I couldn't resist" and she turned away.

With the exception of Jairek, it had taken me a few months to learn the difference between a Shifterfae and a regular animal. They smelled different. Behaved different. And this one I was sticking to be spit-roasted was pure animal.

By the time we finished eating, at least three of us were yawning and the fourth, Teal, was asleep, snoring in my hood. I sighed. Dishes then bed.

"Any chance you want to fill this with water for dishes?" I placed a large gold pot, one kept in the satchel on Malvasia's side, in front of Valentina then busied myself with folding up our empty seed bags and mesh fruit carriers. We were going to have to stop at the next town north of here. Out of the corner of my eye, I saw Valentina staring at the pot.

"I hear running water. Maybe we can use the river?" she said quickly.

I pursed my lips and tried not to grumble. There were things I couldn't do with less than half my shadows—or I could do, but not without consequences elsewhere. Valentina must be tired. Or maybe there was something more to those scorched ropes I had tied around her wrists. But she couldn't be Autumnfae. Not with eyes so blue . . .

So, I gathered our dirty dishes and put them in the pot, and we started the trek, following the light babble of a stream. Jair stayed behind to watch the horses.

A few minutes into the trees, Teal gave a loud snort, shouted something about maps and went back to breathing steadily, heavy in my hood.

Valentina laughed, delicate and soft and in my tired state I had trouble looking away from her mouth that I so stupidly almost kissed before. "So, how exactly did you three come to travel together?" she asked.

I held up a branch to let her pass through the narrow gaming trail we were following. "Two decades ago, I saved a blue-skinned pixie from an ogre den."

"In the Anduat Mountains?" she asked, gasping.

"No, just one ogre lives in those mountains."

She frowned. "Petri always said ogres live in large groups."

And I hadn't a clue who Petri was, but I answered, nonetheless. "Not Skulhad. He prefers to live alone. And the Anduats provide lots of work for a hungry ogre."

She stilled at my side as the ground got soft and steep. "How do you know?"

I helped her down the soft, fertile, black dirt beside a rushing river I couldn't name. "Because I was the one who put him there."

We weren't supposed to be this far into Autumn Court.

But she was staring at me for more information, so I sighed. "Autumn hunts Shifterfae like animals and, back then, the King of the Courtless had gone missing. Things were crumbling. Skulhad deters the Autumnfae from crossing the mountains into the Courtless territory."

Her voice rose. "The Courtless has a king? Not a lord?"

"It did." I looked away, towards the black stream ahead of us. This part wasn't my story to tell. "Come on, let's get this washed and get some sleep."

We would only have a few hours' sleep before the late morning sun had us up and moving again. We were a long way off from retrieving my key.

I WOKE A FEW HOURS LATER, uncomfortable and hot. Teal's little arm lay splayed across my cheek. She was snoring away. A thin strip of drool traced from her mouth to the satin pillow I brought for her from back home. I used one finger and gently rolled her the other way. She snorted once, licked her pointed teeth, and fell back into a slumber.

I shifted, trying to get comfortable with the shirt's buckles digging into my back, when I noticed another hand lying across my chest. A small sun-kissed hand with a golden tie around its wrist lay relaxed against my thick linen shirt. A shirt I couldn't strip off because of Angus's pleasure scarf.

At best, I could have gotten it down to just one arm, but we were so exhausted I collapsed to the makeshift bed once we were done washing the dishes. Tomorrow I wouldn't be making that mistake if I found myself still attached to her. But some part of me knew I wasn't getting out of this anytime soon. Not nicely at least.

There was one who would know how to do it, and I thought back to the day I met Jair. But deep resentment settled in my bones at the thought of asking that fucking trickster god. And by the time my anger settled down and my shadows stopped swirling, I'd come to the conclusion that I'd cut my own arm off before I asked Adrian, the son of a sea god, for help.

The irony of being leashed by a pleasure scarf in Valentina's moment of desperation was not lost on me. I didn't know what she endured in Mohr's company, but she'd yet to hold eye contact with me for more than mere seconds since I found her in that tavern just outside the desert. Her body was hers and I'd keep it that way.

But I didn't have time to think about her small warm body against mine or her navy-blue eyes, the same color of the seas back home in the Underworld. Or what her curiosity was doing to me. The way she inspected the leaves, the way she watched the vermin run up and down the trees.

Her affectionate smiles towards Teal . . .

I plucked her hand off my chest with a thumb and a forefinger and dropped it down between us. I needed *none* of this. I needed to get my shadows back and return to my rightful place in the Wild Hunt. I needed to ride with my Hunters through the lands of this island and purge the souls trapped from within.

I did not need this waterless Summerfae who could burn ropes black and coerce my shadows to follow her. Whatever was happening on the island, I couldn't possibly give a fuck.

But maybe I'd get her warmer boots in the next town.

Maybe, I could do that.

THREE DAYS of being attached to this seemingly faeless from Summer, and I had to adjust my pace, lower my stride, considerably.

It had been two days since we both went opposite ways around an old oak trunk, stilling our walk to a standstill. I was ready to pitch the tent right then and there on the east side of its antler-chipped bark, rather than walk the three feet around to her side. She must have seen my resolve since she unraveled herself and the ties from the trunk and returned to my side with a sigh.

We were riding northwest through Autumn Court's forests when the hail came down half a day after that. Teal had three leaf dresses on, tucked into my hood, and was bitterly snapping off about the frigid air. I wrapped the edges of my cloak over Valentina, who was the most ill-dressed of us all. I suspected the Autumnfae felt nothing with all that fire burning inside them. I didn't think they could feel frost, compassion, or guilt.

Jair led the way on the mare, guiding us to the only town that might allow us in without a fight, in just his pale taupe-and-white linen clothes, and heavy Autumn boots partially untied, shoved on his feet. He blinked sharply when the hail hit his face, but otherwise stayed in good spirits.

We'd stayed in the cover of the thicker trunks for most of

our trek, but a field now lay between us and the lanterns of Kyrrahalyn. I bent down and pulled one of Valentina's small slippered feet, the lace edge rough, into my hand.

Startled, she looked back at me before flicking her eyes forward.

I leaned farther over her, blocking as much of the hail as I could, and tried to bring warmth back to her toes. I alternated, warming a foot at a time until we could make it to the shelter of the town.

16

VALENTINA

I huddled back against Kaderyn, closeness be damned, the hail was leaving welts against my arms. The cold air sent pins and needles through the foot he wasn't warming, and I thought for sure I was going to lose some toes or my mind at the memories the chill brought back.

The lights of the town were in sight when an ashen smell filtered through the last of the trees, billowing into us like a force combating the rain. I scrunched my nose. The wind and rain carried a smell I'd never been exposed to, and it longed to cling in my hair.

"The Yegevani Mine," Jair said, noticing my reaction as he leaned back on his mare. "Responsible for those daggers you carry."

I tucked my bag in closer to my side. All metal on Eadha was Autumn-forged. Everyone knew that. But being so close to an area responsible for their weapons of war caught me in the throat. "All of Eadha's metals come from one mine?"

Jair nodded as chunks of ice fell from his hair. "One fae,

too. Some say Marcus was gifted a hammer from Gael, Autumn's god. Which is how he can work so quickly."

I swallowed and wished Cillian was on his way. I ignored that deep, gut-wrenching pull whenever I thought of him. I didn't know anymore how long it'd been since I was taken, and I was sure he'd come if he'd known.

Jair sighed and said, "I'll start negotiating our stay," as he took off for the large wooden gate of a town I didn't know.

I prayed they had a roaring fire. Firefae be damned, I was sticking my feet in it.

By the time we reached the gate, Jairek had negotiated with the guard to let us in. And I wanted to cry both in relief of shelter and because I was terrified to be near Autumnfae again. But as we trotted down the town's entrance, the blood-boiling heat—the one I recognized when Autumnfae were around—never came.

The open-air market stalls were wrapped up tightly and their products were hidden behind locked boarded shutters. Either they sealed up for the storm or the company that was headed their way. The guard led us on to a bend in the road before giving Jair directions and walking back the way we came.

I sought his eyes as he passed. Golden. But there was no fire-roaring anger behind them.

"This town's called Kyrrahalyn," Kaderyn said. "We're stopping here until the storm passes and not a minute later. We're behind for time."

"Are you going to tell me where we're going?"

"Somewhere colder. We'll have to get you a coat." He looked down at me, moon-silver eyes unreadable. "And some boots."

"Is that where your shadows are?" I asked as Jair grabbed the reins from Kaderyn, tying Malvasia to a covered horse stall. The smell of warmed oats wafted up from the trough near it.

Kaderyn grunted back, and I sighed as he lifted me down inside a covered barn. Loud music and warm smells fanned out through a door to the left.

Jairek pulled bags off Malvasia, lightening the weight to let her rest while Kaderyn worked on the saddle.

I stretched my arm out so I could be near her head, giving it a rub.

When they were done, Kaderyn said, "Let's get some food, restock, and not overstay our welcome."

The stable locked onto a small inn called The Dented Spoon Inn, where everyone seemed to be during harsh storms such as this. The 'P' in the sign above the door was that of a large bronze spoon replacing that of the letter. Loud, happy talking wafted out the door—and promptly stopped as we walked in.

Golden eyes stared, or tried not to stare, from every which direction. And still, the burning anger never came.

We got a large booth facing the stables. I was learning it was to keep an ear on Malvasia and the other mare. And when the menu came, I knew better than to order the Typhina drink. Even if I had felt better after it.

Kaderyn and Jairek ordered meat and some colorful root vegetables covered in gravy. Teal did the same, but it came raw, bleeding through on a dented metal plate. She had savage tastes for such an adorable small creature wearing dried flower petals and leaves for clothes. A thick orange soup was placed on the table before me, smelling divine, with a hard loaf of bread beside its dented bronze bowl. The utensils looked like someone used them to dig a garden in a rock bed—worn and bent out of shape.

The soup, though, was even better than it smelled, and I found myself sighing into my bronze-hammered spoon. I tried dipping the bread into it, but no amount of soaking would get the hard-crusted edges soft so I abandoned it altogether. Which, as I was also learning, would make it fair game for the others at my table to take. Kaderyn, nestled close beside me because of the ties, grabbed the loaf and pressed it into the gravy on his plate before chewing off pieces and doing it again. I wondered what food they had in The Court of Shadows. What could possibly grow under that rumbling purple canopy of swirling smoke?

Movement out the window to the stables caught our attention. The way things were going, someone was bound to steal the horses.

Three small faelings huddled inside the doorway, giggling, and jumping out of the onslaught of hail. One small blonde female thrust a bronze metal sieve into the biggest faeling's brown hands. He jutted his arm out into the storm beyond the safety of the doorway, a massive smile plastered on his face. But he squinted his eyes shut and braced himself. Ping! Ping!

The weight of the hail landing in the sieve ricocheted his arm down. At one point, he yelped and withdrew his arm and the bowl from the storm. The three of them giggled into the sieve at their catch. The smallest male, whose joints bulged out from his skinny limbs, pulled out a large chunk of ice, admired it with shining golden eyes, then plopped it into his mouth.

But something startled them as they started scrambling over each other, trying to flee. Our server, the one with short bangs cropped an inch down her forehead, came into view. She pulled the bowl out of the faelings' hands and scolded them with words I couldn't hear. But her hands were gentle as she guided them back through the stables. Her golden eyes flicked up to mine through the dirty windowpane. No blood-rushing fire came.

Why couldn't I feel the rush of heat like I did in Iradown and the Fortress? Was it Mohr that caused fire to run through me? A thought hit me. The last time I took pain away was for Mohr in the carriage in the desert. This was the longest I'd ever gone not taking someone else's pain into me. Did that have something to do with it?

I looked around at the table. Kaderyn was grimacing into the dented bronze mug. Jairek was gnawing on a large chunk of meat. And I could still feel that silent resolve in my chest. It puffed with confidence that I knew wasn't my own. I could sense Jairek was different, so why couldn't I feel the Autumnfae surrounding me?

I scrutinized my hands, no flaming fingertips. But no water magic either. It didn't stop me from pushing, searching for any of it. The heat of fire or the calming steadiness of water magic.

Jairek, Teal, and Kaderyn started on about sending for more dimas and Kaderyn said something about better alcohol. But something was happening.

A slow seductive caress against my bare skin sent goosebumps to rise. Swirling, curling inky smooth shadows wrapped around my hands and legs. They danced across my bare thighs, avoided any fur entirely, and dipped across the small space to join Kaderyn's ever-present shadows. They touched, swirled together before his voice above the table cut off abruptly and his face snapped to mine.

I slammed closed my fists, and the shadows went with it. He looked at my hands under the table as his shadows quickened around our feet. My face heated as I avoided his stare, finding Teal's bloody face as she chomped on a chunk of bone, big eyes completely oblivious. But I knew Kaderyn could tell I wasn't breathing.

Because I had just worked shadow magic.

"Do you want another glass?" our server asked, dented sieve jammed under her arm.

I searched her again but still felt nothing. But there was a familiarity to her, the shape of her nose, her deep golden freckles, and the corners of her eyes tipped up like—I realized I was staring.

"No," I blurted quickly. "I don't think my stomach much cares for Autumn drinks."

Her eyes moved to my collarbone, and I bristled under her scrutiny. "We have water, glacier-fed from the Kenevik Narrows. Its purity might even rival Summer's waters."

Before I could answer, Jairek interrupted, "Does it flow to your wells, or do you travel there to harvest it?"

She squinted at us. "Are you asking if the Narrows are clear of Autumnfae?"

"And Winter," Kaderyn added, stabbing a chunk of meat with a bent fork.

She shrugged. "For the most part. Kyrrahalyn acts as a holding town for the metals extracted from the mines." She nodded her head outside—in the same direction Jairek had said the mines were. There was never any gossip at Otti Theater about the mines in the Yegevani Mountains. "Lord Ohrem comes up at the end of the month to transport it down to the Fortress. And Winter?" she said, pausing. "Does whatever it wants."

She avoided our gazes and moved to collect the empty plates from the table, but Kaderyn grabbed the plate she held, holding her still.

Shadows swirled around his hand, demanding her attention, and sparkling golden eyes flicked and narrowed to his. "And yet, here the town stays. Safe. A town full of faeless near the passage to Winter. You can see why I have questions."

My mind whirled. Faeless? Could that be why I felt no fire magic? No magic flowed through them at all. I hadn't been around faeless since I was a faeling in Willowspeak, and even then, our next-door neighbor—between Seri's house and

Father's—was the strongest, oldest fae in the town. The faeless in Elaria stayed away from Otti Theater and I had never questioned why.

This fae before us now was so full of vigor I had a hard time believing she was faeless.

"We serve good food," she snapped, jutting out her chin.

I frowned at her. My hometown was raided by Winter. Lord Aborys murdered thousands of my neighbors. My father included. Winter didn't care about the food.

Kaderyn held her stare and the plate for an uncomfortably long minute before her face shot to mine. And the words tumbled out all at once. "She's dressed in the Fortress's attire. I can tell you've been recently. A female lives and works there with hair dark like mine. But ringlets."

"Terna?" I asked, and everyone at the table looked at me.

The server's face crumpled. "Is she okay?"

I opened my mouth to tell her everything. About Terna and her kindness in trying to get me food, but Jairek held up a hand. "Why does Winter Court let a town of faeless live so close to its borders? Your food is good, but I promise you, they don't give a shit," he said.

Her desperate eyes didn't leave mine. "We bribe them. Helle, the lord's daughter and leader of his army, comes before Lord Ohrem's collection days. We give her some metal, and in turn, they don't bother us. How is my sister?"

"Lord Ohrem knows you do this?" Kaderyn asked.

Her scowl shot to him. "What do you think? He's been murdering faeless since before most of us can remember. The faeless across Eadha have been hiding out in larger cities to avoid the slaughter. But we're Autumn and we aren't hiding."

It was full of a palpable malice that didn't need magic behind it. Ah, there was the Autumnfae anger I'd come to recognize.

She asked again, "How. Is. My Sister."

"She looked healthy," I blurted before Jairek or Kaderyn could make this situation worse. I thought back, trying to get my words precise because she was rightly miserable. "She was... determined."

The server's eyes flashed golden, and her face hardened like Terna's did. I thought back to what Terna said about lining the roadways with the worst of the Autumnfae brutality.

"Strong," I added.

It seemed to resonate with her because her nostrils flared and she said, "My name's Jassa. Do you need a room for the night?"

"It was made clear that that was not an option," Jairek said.

"The Dented Spoon is my father's inn, but I make the decisions here. Plus, that storm isn't letting up well until dawn."

She collected up the rest of the plates, ignoring Kade's miserable growling. Kaderyn was kind enough to let go of the one he was holding hostage.

But before she turned away she spoke again, "I'll get the rooms ready. I hope two will suffice. There will be a merchant open across the street tomorrow at first light." She nodded to my clothes. Or lack thereof. "She won't survive the Narrows in that."

"Any chance there's a discount for foreigners?" Jairek said as he flicked his golden hair out of his face, charisma beaming from him.

"Oh no. He'll likely charge you double," Jassa answered with a sharp smile and a wink.

Kaderyn turned to me, grumbling.

"Least I got us a place for the night." I grimaced, as the exhaustion hit me hard. Autumn food was heavy, and it was lulling me to sleep.

Jairek saved me from Kaderyn's wrath. "I'll see what the

kitchen is willing to let go of for our travels tomorrow. You two go get the rooms secured before your foul mood has Jassa changing her mind."

He smiled before getting up from the table. His big, imposing body unfurled from the booth. By the back of him, Jairek could blend easily into Summer or Autumn Court. As long as he was around other massive males. But his eyes were brown instead of Autumn's golden and there was no watermark on his collarbone. But I watched as the Autumn faeless eyed him carefully, and I had a feeling even faeless could tell he was something else entirely.

Kaderyn got up from the booth and his shadows swirled every which way a foot from his body. Chairs hissed and tables screeched as the patrons abruptly got up from their places and moved away from him. He was the leader of the Wild Hunt after all, and fae, or apparently faeless, were not the type to forget. Teal shot to his hood as silver eyes waited for me to follow out of the booth. Apparently, it was time to go.

If Kaderyn cared how everyone else perceived him, he didn't show it as we weaved through the small spaces between the tables to the front of the inn.

A faeling of about seventeen, almost old enough not to be called a faeling, with a pencil rested against her pointed ear, directed us to where Jassa had organized our rooms for the night. She led us down a hallway and up some stairs before stopping in front of two doors across from each other.

"These are yours for the night," she said. "Jassa said if you need anything to best just wait for dawn to come around, rather than to go looking." She flashed us a cheery smile that contradicted her words before disappearing back the way we came.

We watched her go as I yawned. "Are we safe here?"

"From the hail? Sure." Kaderyn thumped the door open with the heel of his hand and dragged us in before closing it.

My heart skipped a beat as understanding dawned on me. Of course, we were going to have to share a room! I mentally slapped myself and tried to shove down all regret at tying myself to him. But Teal would be here and it wouldn't be as awkward as I feared.

Teal gave a wide yawn before stretching out her little blue arms.

"Well, goodnight my dear friends
This is where my night ends.
I'll be next door sketching the map."

"Teal, for the love of the hounds, Oir—" Kaderyn started.

"Oir's map twas shredded!
And I'm rightfully indebted
To your service as loyal crewmate.
You saved me from ogres
Now, do please move over!" She shoved at his shoulder that was blocking the door.
"It really has gotten quite late."

Teal thrust the hand holding the crumpled map into the air in a hurrah motion. Rouge-tinged fingerprints rubbed the edges from her blood-stained hands.

"We'll find again the key
To set your shadows free
And return you to where you belong.
But keep your hood wide
Room for a pixie to hide.
Because you can bet, I'll be tagging along."

And with that, she gave us a big, needle-toothed smile and darted to the other door across the hall.

I moved to open the door for her, as she was only a foot or so tall, but she thrust her other little arm out and blue sparks blasted out from her palm, thumping against the door. It shot open wide, revealing a similar room that she flew off into before the door swung back shut from sheer force.

I stared, mouth wide, at the door the pixie just went through before I was tugged back in by the ties. Kaderyn closed the door and proceeded to walk over to the bed, pulling me with him. If he had any idea he was dragging me around, he didn't show it.

I felt bad enough that I had tied him to me, so I said nothing. "Can all pixies do that?" I asked as he started removing the clasps and buttons on his shirt.

"For the most part," he said as he worked on the sleeve of the arm I hadn't tied to myself.

Teal's pixie magic smelled differently before. "It smelled different in Iradown Tavern," I said absently, rocking on my heels—my gaze avoiding the bed entirely.

Kaderyn stopped undoing a button near his chest, and there were a lot of buttons on his chest.

I trailed them down and stopped abruptly when my eyes reached the buckle of his pants.

"That was something else altogether." And before I could ask any more questions on it, he said, "Teal feels she needs to help me get . . . on my travels and as such has taken it upon herself to be resident cartographer."

"And tea maker," I added.

"Yes," he said with a small smile.

I froze. It was the first time he'd shown me any reaction other than disdain.

"Who's Oir?" I turned away as he shimmied out of his black shirt.

He pushed it down to dangle on the Caterina del Aamod ties between us. My fingertips brushed the still-warm fabric and my cheeks flushed. What was I *doing*? I was acting like a tittering faeling. I shook my head once, trying to clear it.

"She's Shadowfae. Lives back in Auris, the capital of Shadow Court. She's my advisor, of sorts." He seemed to feel that was explanation enough and flopped down to the bed behind me, tugging roughly at the ties.

My calves bumped into the soft sides of the bed.

"She had a map of Eadha hanging in Auris' library. But it was found one morning shredded apart under mysterious circumstances. The mystery being how Teal has managed to elude my questioning on the matter entirely," he continued.

"And yet, you know it was her?"

"Small, pixie-sized bite marks through the entire thing. And she declared—while standing on the shredded drawing—her intentions on my travels. Would you rather I take the floor?" he asked, because I was still standing at the edge of the bed, facing away from Kaderyn's shirtless body.

But I couldn't get to the other side without climbing over him. So I mumbled something incoherent like a well-put-together Summerfae and raised my leg over his large body. And as my thigh touched his bare side, I ignored the silver eyes intently watching me and the tingle of the shadows against my smooth, bare skin.

I needed a distraction. "Teal mentioned crewmate?" I asked, as I quickly flung myself down on the other side.

He watched my every move.

"Did you travel by sea around the island?"

He cleared his throat. "No. Teal has a thing for ships, much to Jairek's disappointment."

"Oh, he's not a fan?"

"Not in the least."

And he surprised me when he chuckled. So much so that I was nervous about what to do with the silence that stretched on. I wanted to hear his laughter again. It was much more welcome than the displeasure.

"For what it's worth, I'm sorry. For this," I said as I lifted my wrist and it pulled tight on his.

He sucked in a breath. "You did what you had to to survive. But I have a feeling you will not like where we're headed."

"Your chest is in the Narrows between Autumn and Winter?" I pulled the covers up over my shoulders.

He closed his eyes. "The key to the chest is stuck in the riverbed on the other side of the Narrows. The first chest is in a cave in Spring Court."

"How do you know this?" I tried hard not to ask why he didn't have the key and his shadows back already. I felt that hardening in my chest and footsteps outside the door.

"It's Jairek," Kaderyn answered as if I asked a question. "And I know this because I'd already tried to release my shadows from the first chest in Spring Court."

I chewed my lip. He really didn't want me to ask questions. But it was becoming painful not to.

He sighed as we heard Jairek go into the room with Teal. "You're not going to let this go, are you?"

"I just feel like I should know where we are going. Unless you know of a way to release the ties before then."

His face shot to mine so quickly I froze. "Oh, I know of a way to get a Caterina del Aamod tie to release itself." My stomach dropped, and he looked away. "I can hear your heart beating faster. Relax, Valentina. I might be from the Underworld, but I'm not a monster. I'll never force you to do anything."

He *was* from the Underworld. He could have cut off my arm within seconds of me leashing him. Or worse, made the scarf release itself the way it was meant to—through intensely gratifying sex. And I wanted to squeak out a thank you. Or an acknowledgment that I recognized the position I inadvertently put him in. But I could do none of it with the lump swelling in my throat. I was so far from the safety of the theater.

He must have seen the reaction on my face because he sighed and changed the subject. "I don't suppose you can touch iron, can you?"

And I still didn't trust myself to speak, so I shook my head.

He shifted slightly to retrieve something from the back pocket of his pants. He smoothed a beautiful pouch flat in his hands. It shimmered, like the scarf that bound us but in veins of blue and silver. Like the sea.

"This is called Faebric. This will allow me to hold iron—which the key and both chests are made of. Iron is the reason my shadows are trapped. Iron is the reason I dropped the key when it burnt my hand"—he held up his hand as the fae glamour faded from his skin, showing an angry red scar on his palm—"the first time I got to the chest in Spring. And because I have no more luck than a flea on an ogre, it fell into the Brinnalone River, which starts in the caves and ends at Embee Lake. In Winter *fucking* Court."

"It's beautiful."

"It was a part of the bargain for saving the pixies."

"And saving Jairek?" I asked, yawning. But as I glanced up at Kaderyn, red puckered marks—like streaks across his chest—caught my attention.

"That—" he said, shifting, tucking the Faebric back into his pocket and returning his hand to its usual flawless skin with fae magic. I blinked at his chest as the scars that were there faded, too, as he continued, "—is a story for another day. Get some rest."

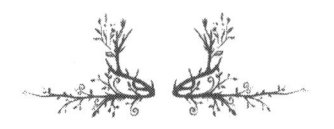

AND, by the gods, the next morning came far too fast. The inn's bed paled in comparison to our furniture in Elaria, but we were also able to wield magic. I had a feeling Autumn Court gave nothing in return when they came looking for the metals mined in the Yegevani Mountains.

I ran at Kaderyn's side across a snow-covered street as we basked in the morning light and braved the dying storm. Jairek and Teal were already up, getting the horses ready. We'd be eating breakfast on the go, much to my dismay.

The soft lights of a shop called The Rusty Anvil welcomed us in. A tired old faeless sat behind a counter with a pair of glasses hanging off his nose. He peered over them at us and dropped a heavy pen to the counter with a thud. Charge us double, indeed.

But something was different the minute I entered. Something flowing and familiar.

Kaderyn stopped at a wall of fur-clad boots, but I couldn't shake the feeling. I glanced around. The golden eyes of the merchant seller met mine. No magic flowed off him. Faeless, I knew.

But there, just around a rack of auburn cloaks, was the back of a head I recognized. I'd seen his midnight-black hair running from a magog's fist more times than I could count.

"Roshan!" I yelped, trying to step forward, but the ties held me back.

And sure enough, upon hearing his name, Roshan swiveled

to face me. Tears pooled in my eyes as a weight lifted off my chest. I pulled a reluctant Kaderyn along, the ties digging in, as Roshan ran to me.

He wrapped me up in a hug.

A hug of warmth and water. A hug of Summer.

Roshan's mouth was muffled against my neck. "Val, I've been looking for you everywhere."

Soft traces of inky shadows trailed into my vision above Roshan's head as if trying to remind me the Lord of Shadows was there. Like I could forget as I stood there, arm outstretched behind me, held back by the blessed golden ties that bound me to him.

"How'd you find me?" I stepped away to look at my friend.

"Lord Grigory might not know how to trade and bargain with other fae. But I can." His eyes reached Kaderyn behind me, then traced his arm down to the ties attached to me. Recognition and horror blanketed his face. He stepped closer to Kaderyn, furious. "What have you done?"

And I felt it. My water magic was back. Flowing through my veins, easing my anxiety. Drops of lush clear water slipped off my fingertips onto the swept-clean floor. But I saw Kaderyn's shadowsword materializing, and I would have to bask in my magic returning later.

I stepped between them, pushing my palms against Roshan's broad chest. "Roshan, it was me. I leashed him with it. I was trying to . . . to survive somewhere else."

I didn't look at Kaderyn, but by the way Roshan was, I could tell he wasn't helping me calm matters down. "Please, Roshan. I need to know. Is everyone at the theater okay?"

He looked down at me. Intense brown eyes sharp, as he sucked in a breath. "The theater's fine. Sisaria is okay though her neck will be scarred for a bit. The tall skinny one you talk to tried getting permission to come, but Daria said no."

I felt my shoulders sink as they released their worry. Sisaria could hide the scars with her glamour if she chose to. "Is Daria okay?" I asked.

His stare turned hard. "Sisaria told me what you've been doing. For Daria and the theater."

I froze, heat prickled my skin.

He continued, "Valentina, why didn't you tell me? I could have helped you get away."

But confusion racked through me because I *was* the help. I didn't need helping. At least not then.

And when I said nothing, he continued, "She was using you! For your—"

"Stop," I interrupted because Daria was using my ability to take away pain, yes, but she also kept me safe in the theater. Gave me a place to sleep and food to eat. She took me in when my father was murdered.

But also, because Kaderyn had no business knowing about my ability to take the pain of others. Cillian was right. The less who knew, the better. And it seemed the entire Otti Theater now knew about it, thanks to Avril's declaration to General Mohr.

Roshan ran an angry hand through his short hair. His eyes darted up to Kaderyn. "And you can't get out of this?"

It came out far more condescending than I thought Kaderyn would tolerate, and I found myself grimacing.

"Seemed to have left my god's sexual-scarf-breaking sword at home," Kaderyn drawled, and I shot him a hard stare.

"Okay." Roshan nodded, not finding Kaderyn funny as he came to some sort of conclusion. "I'll stay with you. I'll stay by your side until we find a way to get it off."

Worry pierced me through at Mohr's threat against Elaria. His threat against Sisaria and bringing her to the Fortress. "No, Roshan. You need to go back. Protect the theater until I can get there. It was my fault . . ." I choked, thinking of the dead magog on the stage, Sisaria's neck, and Avril being let out into the desert. "It's my fault they got hurt. Can you get Lord Grigory involved?"

Roshan nodded. "He must *do* something."

Kaderyn scoffed at the mention of Lord Grigory, but we both ignored him. Because I had something else to ask.

"Roshan"—but I was nervous—"does Cillian know I've been taken?"

Roshan met my stare with the cool compassion waterfae had, and it made me want to cry again because I felt so stupid. "I don't know. I asked some Spring Court soldiers I passed on my way into Autumn Court if they'd seen him, but it was all I could do to get away with my head on my shoulders.

"Everyone is tense, Val. I had to mention I was a regular at Otti Theater just to get them to let me pass through." And Roshan *was* a regular, just not the paying kind.

"Valentina, time to go," Kaderyn ground out.

Roshan looked back up to Kaderyn, venom in his words. "And you're going to keep her safe until I can get her unleashed from you."

Kaderyn's silver eyes met Roshan's and the shadows moved menacingly slow. I gave the Summerfae a tight hug before moving to Kaderyn's side, lest something bad happen to Roshan.

But it hurt, leaving him there as we walked out into the uneven ground covered in ice chunks and frosty snow and I looked back to my friend more times than I could count until we were away and around the corner to the stables. We met Jairek there with Teal plopped on his shoulder. The horses stood side by side, fully geared and ready to go.

Jairek frowned, interrupting something Teal was peppering on about as he said, "No boots?"

I looked down to my feet, ripped black lace on cold cobblestone. I forgot.

"Fuck," Kaderyn shouted.

So had he, apparently.

"Get the cheeses and bread I ordered from inside. I'll get the boots and a coat," Jairek said, already tying the reins up once more.

And I thought about arguing, just to see Roshan once more, but Kaderyn was fuming mad. I didn't want to push it.

And with that, we were off, through the faeless town in minutes with a warm, rich-brown coat covering Autumn Court's small outfit and warm matching boots on my feet.

"I didn't buy you new . . . under-things." Jair's face contorted. "Afraid it's out of my area of expertise."

I grinned at him, and I let out a sigh I didn't know I'd been keeping. It didn't matter. Because this was it. Elaria was safe. The theater was okay. Roshan would get Lord Grigory of Summer Court involved. And there was a chance Cillian was off looking for me. He'd know what to do about the scarf.

This was going to be a really good day.

17

KADERYN

This was the worst fucking day ever.

We riders in the Wild Hunt couldn't feel compassion or fear or love. And what I would do to give this all up and go back to that state of mind. To relinquish the weaknesses being fae gave me.

Hunters protected their own.

Their horses, their hounds, and each other.

And the longer she was by my side, the harder time I was having calling her a stranger.

I woke this morning exhausted. Anytime I moved in the night, Valentina would stir at my side and her face would draw down into itself as if she was in pain. Dreams or memories—I had no idea what she fought while she slept. By the third time, I had contorted myself into an unnatural position in an attempt to keep still. But lying immobile sent my mind racing and my fucking back aching. Why did I care if I disrupted her sleep? Fuck, it'd been ages since I laid with a female.

Just this morning I'd accidentally pulled her too hard with the ties, and she flung forward into my chest. And as I caught her around the waist, I opened my mouth to apologize, but nothing came out. Because it was easier to be mad at her for the golden ties around my wrist. It was easier to keep her at a distance because I wasn't entirely sure I could get my shadows back and keep her from harm. Not with what lay in the Spring Court cave I avoided telling her about. So I pushed her away without a word. One thing at a time, and first on my list was the key.

But maybe I could slow my gait, take smaller steps.

Maybe, I could do that.

By the time we saw her friend from Elaria in the merchant shop, I wanted to run my Hunters through the town and pull anyone that ran into my grasp. Because that Summerfae she called Roshan actually thought the sex ties were my bright fucking idea. He was going to find out how little Lord Grigory really cared about the fae of his court. And in all that, I forgot to get her warmer clothes. How the fuck was I going to get any of us out of this alive?

The saving grace was that the weather had warmed and by midday we'd stopped only twice to rest the horses.

The ridges of the Yegevani Mountains rose like warring giants on either side as we traveled the Kenevik Narrows between them. The wide path, too big to be blamed on wildlife, was well worn, which made me nervous. But Valentina looked in awe at the mountains on our sides and I found myself biting my tongue when I thought to tell her the Sidina Mountains between The Court of Shadows and the Courtless were far more majestic.

At one point, she stiffened in my arms, and I looked around quickly to see what startled her. My shadows felt no danger, but I circled the horses once just to make sure. She mumbled a sorry and shoved her hands into the large coat Jair got her and we carried on.

"Which way is Embee Lake?" which was the tenth question from her that hour.

I pointed ahead to the right, towards Silvermere City, in Winter Court. A path we were not, under any circumstances, taking.

"But your shadows are leading us the opposite way?" She nodded towards the trail of shadows I sent out, looking for the iron key.

"Yes," I said, sucking in a breath as she shifted against my chest. I was going to have to tell her everything at this rate. "The key is made of iron. Iron is easy to find on Eadha because there is so very little of it. It burns my nose and stings my shadows. For whatever reason, the key did not make it to Embee Lake."

"You can't tell why?"

By my hounds, give me patience. "I can feel with my shadows, not see. At least, in this state. Once I open the chest and regain them, that should change."

"I like them."

And I had no fucking clue what she was talking about. My eyes shot to the rowan trees surrounding us. Fed by the same glacier water Kyrrahalyn prided themselves on. Finally, and I shouldn't have, and I don't know why I needed to know, but I asked, "What is it you like?"

"The shadows."

For the past two days they'd been curled through her hair, searching the coarse furs, eager to lie against her skin.

I choked back the words. *They like you, too.*

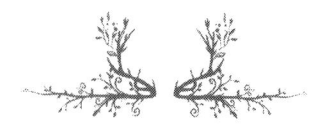

It was early evening when we reached the far side of the Narrows. The horses were quick, happy things as it was a straight shot on even ground in cool weather. My shadows curled and danced around at a spot forty feet ahead. But an uneasiness prickled my skin, and I looked up to the sides of the mountains. We were going to lose the cover of the dense trees, as the river we needed to reach was technically flowing into Winter Court.

"Woah," I said as I eased Malvasia to a standstill and Jairek followed suit.

We met each other's stare, and though his gaze was steady and calm as ever, he felt it too. This wasn't going to be the easy retrieval I'd dreamt it would be.

Teal shivered from where she sat inside his hood with her little hands tucked under her armpits. Valentina absently pulled a rowan berry from a branch on the tree beside us.

"You two stay here with the horses. Valentina, for obvious reasons, will come with me to see what, pray tell, has the key stuck," I said.

Jair sniffed once, defiant. "Till the end, Kaderyn." He rolled his shoulders and looked north into Winter Court. "Frost is flowing on the breeze. Let's make this quick."

"Teal?" I checked. This was the out if she wanted it. To stay by the horses under the cover of the branches.

"O-onward we ride
I'll s-stay by your side." She shivered through her words.

Valentina was watching us, wide-eyed and staring with an unreadable look on her face. I didn't bother asking her if she wanted to go. Unfortunately for her, she didn't have a choice. I jumped down from Malvasia and the ties pulled tight. I lifted Valentina down as Jairek tied up the mare beside Malvasia under the cover of the forest.

"Let's go see what has got my key," I said, moving into the clearing towards my swirling shadows.

"You're rhyming like Teal," Valentina whispered from where she stayed by my side as we walked closer.

I could sense the iron was there, but I couldn't see what was wrong. The Brinnalone River flowed out of Spring Court, right across Winter Court into Embee Lake. So what was the key stuck on?

We were a little too far away to tell . . .

"She tends to have that effect." I squinted ahead. "Oh, no."

Jairek swore with a humorless laugh. He realized it, too.

"What?" Valentina asked, eyes darting around.

I sighed, tugging her ahead. "It's not stuck *on* something. It's stuck *in* something. The fucking river is frozen."

"You can't get it out?" she asked, trotting at my side—her naivety was killing me.

We were ten feet away from the river's edge. A frozen white slate greeted us. "Yeah, I'll just go borrow a pickaxe from the Yegevani mines."

Which she didn't appreciate because she said, "I really don't think you've planned out this expedition."

I looked down at her. "Your mouth is getting awfully bold."

We reached where my shadows were furiously swirling, and it grated my bones that the ice held our weight. Not a good sign when I wanted to break through it.

Jairek kept watch and kept his nose in the air.

Valentina squirmed. "I just feel . . . in my chest . . . I feel . . ."

"Brave-hearted?" I offered, glancing up at her from where I knelt. I brushed the snow off the top layer of ice. Here we go. I could see the dark outline of the key that vexed me so. I looked back at her when she didn't answer and the look she gave me pinned me still.

Desperation and shock ran across her face with a vulnerability it hurt my heart to focus on. Damn fae emotions. And I was going to slaughter the one responsible for dragging me down to this island, making me feel this bullshit in my chest. I didn't want to read into it because, for some stupid reason, my heartbeat picked up at the sight of her.

"How do you know?" she whispered.

"Because sometimes your heartbeat beats in unison with Jairek's. Now step back, little lion."

And she asked me something after that, but my key was so close, and I needed it back.

I materialized my sword from the shadows. I'd have to use my right hand, unfortunately, unless I wanted to swing Valentina into the ice as well. I crashed the sword down onto the surface of the ice. The resounding sound echoed off the hillsides. This was going to be as stealthy as Iradown Tavern.

Bang! I thrust at the ice again, pulling hard on the strength the shadows gave me. They swirled around me faster and I willed them to avoid Valentina. Her skin was becoming a distraction to me and them.

Bang! I lunged again, my sword into the thick, clear ice. Shards flew off, which spurred me on. Again and again, my sword smashed into the ice, chipping away chunks.

Soon, I was halfway there.

"Kaderyn." Jair gave a warning, but I was so close. Too close.

I tossed down my sword, and it disappeared the way it came, into shadows and darkness.

I smashed at the ice with my fist. I came all this way. I scaled the Anduat Mountains. I dragged a Shifterfae across a court destined to hunt him. I blew up an Autumn Court tavern. I got leashed to a Summerfae being chased by a general.

"Kaderyn!" Jair roared.

I smashed my fist down and down again. I wasn't leaving until I got the key. I grabbed the Faebric from my back pocket and with one last punch the ice gave way and my knuckle stung where it touched iron. I scooped it out with the Faebric pouch, breathing heavily as Valentina screamed and all thoughts scattered. I shot my head up as Jairek crashed into my back.

And there, to the north, was a band of gold and blue armored fae; Winter's soldiers, led by a small white-haired female in all black. Her bow arm was outstretched, its string loose from just being released. The soldiers at her side held their arrows tight, waiting for her command.

Helle, the leader of Lord Aborys' army, and his daughter, stared at us. Calm and cool, like she hadn't just shot my friend.

Valentina was screaming, Teal was squealing, and Jairek let out a roar that shook the mountains far louder than the echo of my sword had.

In a fury, I shot up a wall of shadows between us, impenetrable but temporary.

Jairek lay panting on the ground, blood soaking the snow from the white-wooded arrow sticking out of his stomach.

"It's my fault! He jumped in front of me." Valentina was kneeling beside us as I held Jairek's head and chest. His body was under my legs.

I shook my head, refusing to believe this was happening, and my stomach dropped. I was going to get everyone killed for this. Regret coated my body in a cold sweat, and it soaked my tongue like burnt toast.

Jair's body rocked in my hands. "Jair, hold on, don't shift yet." I didn't know why they weren't raining arrows down against the shadows, and I didn't have time to look. "Teal! To the cover of the trees!" I was a much bigger target than her. Hiding in my hood was not a good place to be.

I heaved Jairek and I up.

Valentina tried to help, but Jairek was big and if he shifted, he was going to get even bigger. I leaned him against my shoulders, and we hobbled back to the brown horses under cover of the rowan trees. We tripped over each other as Jairek's body convulsed, wanting to shift under my hands. My mouth turned ashen dry.

If he—if Jair died . . .

I brought the wall of shadows back with us, but I could tell the warring group was gone. Going up against Autumn soldiers was one thing. I could outsmart them. But Helle was a different thing entirely.

We reached the cover of the trees as Jairek stumbled to the ground and rolled to his side. His face contorted in pain.

I was going to have to get the arrow out.

Valentina shoved into my side, her face wet with tears and her nose dripping. "Why didn't you stop? Why did you have to keep going? They were coming!"

And I ran a hand down my face and swore because she was right.

Teal was hugging her little arms around Jair's sweating head. The bronze metal arrowhead had gone straight through him and lodged itself five inches out of his back. The same metal coerced from Kyrrahalyn's faeless.

"Help me get it out," I said to Valentina, but I didn't meet her eyes. I didn't want to see what they held, so I knelt beside my friend as Valentina dropped hard beside me.

"She's got a hard shot for someone so little," Jair cursed, speaking about Helle. His words slurred as he held steady the arrow shaft in his abdomen.

My throat was constricted as I said, "I'm going to pull it out and you shift immediately after. You'll heal faster." I pushed his hands away and grabbed the white-wooded arrow fletched with black feathers as big as my hand at his chest, snapping the end off. The jostling caused Jair to growl. "Teal, back up."

The arrow was going to have to go through, thanks to the jagged barbs on its tip. I had to be quick. He didn't want to wait to change.

"Tell me what to do," Valentina urged.

"When I pull this arrow out, get out of the way," I said, a hand on Jair's shoulder and the other gripping what little I could of the arrowhead. "One, two . . ." And I pulled.

Valentina covered her ears as Jair roared into the mountainsides.

As soon as it was free, I dropped it to the ground and grabbed her around the waist, pulling her back as Jair shuddered atop a thin layer of snow. His muscles pulled and released under his skin like mice under a blanket. *By my hounds*, it never looked this painful.

I pulled Valentina back farther.

"Deep breath, Jair," I shouted, over his groaning.

I watched his nostrils flare as he did as I asked. He needed to relax, though I didn't think he'd react well if I told him that. As soon as he let out the breath he was holding, his face tightened with concentration. The shift started and was over in a matter of seconds.

Valentina gasped at my side. "He's a . . ." Her voice trailed out.

"Jairek is a lionshifter. Heir to the Courtless throne."

"A king?" she asked, not looking away from Jairek's tawny lion form lying below the drooping rowan berries.

He was panting into the snowy ground. Teal flew down to nuzzle in his mane, and I pulled Valentina closer to him. I needed to compress the wound. Shifted or not, he was still prone to infection, unlike fae, who were immune to such things.

"If he chooses to be," I said as we reached his side. "I need to clean the wound. Now would be a good time to have some water, Valentina."

But she stood there, face crumpling in on itself. "I can't."

Anger pierced me through. I knew she wasn't faeless. I could feel the magic coursing through her, but more and more evidence was adding up to the contrary. I grabbed her shoulders, making her face me. "You're Summerfae and can't wield water?"

"Get off me," she bit back, her hands in fists. Her hands . . .

I scrunched my brows. *Oh, no.* I pulled the Faebric pouch out from my back pocket. The one I put the key into. The one that was now empty with a large rip down the side. I looked back to the iron key that now lay bare in Valentina's hands.

"Oh." I laughed, humorlessly. "Of course, the gods tied me to a faeless. You're touching iron, Valentina. That's all the proof I need."

Her gaze shot down to her hand. Her very healthy, not burnt hand. "I—I don't know what's happening. I'm Summerfae. I'm not faeless."

"Your life expectancy just got reduced to nil," I mumbled, holding the bag out for her to put it in, careful to pinch closed the rip. No fucking idea how to fix it. I needed to talk to Deryn, the one who gave it to me.

"You're an asshole!" she yelled, but her fingers traced her

palm where the key was. More to herself she mumbled, "I saw it fall, and I just grabbed it—"

"Perhaps, but it doesn't make me less right." I shoved the pouch back into my back pocket. Hoping it stayed covered. Not that I didn't deserve my ass being singed. "Come on, we need to get the canteen off the horses."

I trudged, dragging her along to the next couple of trees over where Malvasia and the mare stood. Malvasia's ears flicked as we approached, and I rubbed a hand down her nose.

"I sent Jairek, not only into a den of firefae who actively hunt his kind, but I sent him within mere feet of his brother's lion pelt as it lay at the entrance to Autumn's Fortress," I said as I leaned my head against Malvasia's nose. Soothing me more than her. I could feel Valentina's wide eyes on me, and I didn't have the strength to look. "He was the former King of the Courtless, and Autumn has his skin laying as a doormat to their festivals.

"For both our sakes, Jairek was able to let it be. He didn't attempt to take it back as he rightfully should have. Like I *would* have. And now," I said as I pulled away and grabbed the water canteen from the side bag, "and now I have Jairek Sanguis bleeding out in the same fucking court."

On our way back, Valentina snatched the water from my hands. I was too angry to open my mouth again. The next likely thing I'd do with it was gnaw my own arm off of these fucking ties. And I cursed myself even more because it was my fault. The evidence of dragging this group on my quest was the pool of blood running down Jairek's lion form.

We reached him, and I directed her to pour water down the wound as I held Jair down with a hand on his head. Valentina laid one of her small hands down near the wound, tentatively, like she was nervous to touch him. And with her other hand, which was shaking now, she poured water out of the canteen and cleaned the wound.

I leaned my full weight into Jairek's muzzle, expecting him to thrash. But his body shuddered once, and his eyes softly closed as if he'd fallen asleep. I shot up off him and thrust my hand near his chest, feeling for a pulse as I leaned into his snout. Soft deep breaths blew across my face, and though the wound still leaked blood, I could hear his steady heartbeat.

So whose heartbeat was beating as fast as the Wild Hunt's Hunters could run through the sky? I looked up into Valentina's face as she tried to turn away—but not before I saw her pained face.

"Valentina?" I leaned across Jair's body and grabbed her by the shoulders. What the fuck was happening?

"I'm fine," she whispered. "I'm fine."

She seemed anything but *fine*. Maybe she couldn't handle blood? She nudged the canteen to me with shaking hands and fell back against Jair's back, our hands locked in the ties across him.

Teal flew beside my head with clean bandages. I looked back at the wound. It looked clean enough.

"There is no safety in the Narrows
From the rain of Winter's hollywood arrows," Teal
chirped as she purchased herself on my shoulder. Like a
talking ten-pound rock.

I rubbed a hand down my face. Fuck, none of them deserved me.

"We won't leave the cover of the trees until Jair can move. As long as there's no infection, he'll heal as fast as any fae. Once he wakes, we will move to the horses and set up camp for the night."

Jair's golden fur and my swirling black shadows did nothing to camouflage us. I dropped to my butt, put pressure on Jair's wound, and gauged the amount of shit we were in. Not that I had much of a choice in changing our situation. I hadn't been able to change much of anything in almost two centuries.

The horses stood, hungry and tired, farther in the forest. While Malvasia had learned to be calm around Jair's shifted form, the other mare scared easily. Any jostling on a horse would prolong his healing.

We were stuck.

18

VALENTINA

I'VE FELT DAYS-OLD KNIFE WOUNDS. I've felt scorched lungs, melted skin, and broken bones. I've felt migraines strong enough to cripple an army and, thanks to Mohr, the pain of a wound by a god's sword that would never heal. But an arrow to the gut?

I didn't think I'd survive this one.

Or the shock that Jairek could shift into a lion. A part of me knew it was a large animal and only Kaderyn calling me 'little lion' minutes earlier gave me any sort of clue. But seeing the transformation? One minute he was fae and the next—with Kaderyn calming him—he was a massive lion.

Bleeding out in front of me.

I flinched as I tried shifting my weight. Visitors of Otti Theater were usually healed enough to make the trek to us, but this fresh wound was dragging me under.

The white-haired Winterfae was so fast I didn't see her grab an arrow, let alone let loose it. But I knew her piercing, sky-blue gaze was on me when she did it. I felt the chill of Winter I'd only felt once before. When my town was being slaughtered, frozen solid by Winter Court.

And all Kaderyn cared about was the stupid key. A stupid key made of iron that I could touch. Which was more confusing than ever. And I wanted to go home, to Elaria, to the theater. To Petri's tight hugs and warm Summer air. Where my water magic flowed easily, and I knew what I was.

Teal and Kaderyn had decided that we were to stay under the cover of the trees tonight and all I could do was grunt in response when Kaderyn asked if I understood.

Not just because I had taken Jairek's pain into me or that I still couldn't use water magic but because when that Winterfae was shooting her arrow, ice magic rose from my hands in a cloud of frozen mist.

By the middle of the night, the wound had stopped gushing and Jairek woke up with clouded eyes. Kaderyn and I leaned against opposite sides of the trunk of a tree when Jairek grunted to four paws. He was shaky, like when I watched a baby deer stand outside the theater when I was leaving thistle seeds out on the courtyard's ledge for the birds.

Kaderyn told him no. But when Jairek just turned his face and growled at him, Kaderyn used his shadows to guide him to the trees the horses were under. There was safety in numbers, and the horses were all we had.

But frustration at Kaderyn's lack of caring about anything but the shadows had worn me thin.

"Why didn't you just do that earlier?" I snapped, as I watched his shadows practically lift Jairek up.

"I can give you a wall of shadows that no arrow can penetrate. No matter the hollywood kiln-hardened arrows of Winter Court. Or I can use them to guide a lionshifter to the horses. Take your pick."

"I thought you'd be stronger," I muttered, fuming as I walked a step ahead of him, following a floating lion deeper into the small forest.

The ties on my wrist snapped tight, pulling me to a standstill.

"Beg your pardon?" Kaderyn gritted out, moving into my face. Silver eyes, deadly angry.

But so was I. And it wasn't any Autumnfae heat. This anger, this irritation at how careless he had been, was all me. What I would give to go back to my friends in Elaria and make sure they were okay. And Kaderyn couldn't look up from his desire to get the key.

If he had just let the key go, Jairek wouldn't have gotten hurt.

"Get off me." I shoved him. Or at least I went to, but he grabbed my hands and held them hostage.

Shadows licked around us, incredibly slow.

"Oh, I'd love to, but someone, that's *you*, has chained someone, that's *me*, with an ancient Caterina del Aamod scarf, in case you've forgotten. Like it or not Valentina, you are stuck with me until we find a way to break the magic, which, *thanks for asking*"—I didn't ask. I didn't dare speak as his shadows rolled off him like the waves in Autumn Court's oceans, powerful strokes turning in on itself—"is a magic older than this island itself. Or I fuck you so well and hard that you and your naive soul are satisfied enough that the gods release the charm. *Which I can*," he added softly, looking down at my lips as a heat coursed through me. "If you so choose it."

And I did the only proper thing I could think to do.

I spit in his face.

Pure blackness erupted in tendrils whipping wildly from him. I recoiled painfully, twisting as far as my arm and the ties would allow me to go.

Out of the darkness, he shouted, "Or I could cut off your arm and be done with it all!"

Blue sparks ignited the shadows between us, and I ducked before looking over to see little Teal with her arm outstretched.

"Though you deserved spit in your face
This is no proper place
To be yelling, announcing our keep.
Kaderyn, set up the tent
Circumvent the resent
Until we've all had decent sleep."

My cheeks heated in embarrassment. "Sorry, Teal," I muttered, but she rounded on me, and I wished I'd said nothing at all.

"You're not off the hook
Don't give me that look
I saw Winter's ice on your hands.
But first, we heal Jair
Then, you clear the air
Until then, this crew's in MY command."

The shadows retreated into Kade, except for one that lingered around my ankles, but his silver eyes stayed locked on me. If Kaderyn had questions, he didn't ask them.

He swirled his hands absently in the air, as the shadows got the tent from the back of Malvasia, and they worked on setting it up. We moved together, reluctantly. Neither one willing to apologize, though I could feel it on the tip of my tongue. He could be rude and careless all he wanted but I had stooped to his level of brooding and that was on me.

Hours later, sometime in the night, we sat around the small fire we made to keep the warmth in our bodies. The ties pulled tight against my wrist as we sat as far apart as we could. Which was still far too close for comfort. Jair breathed softly and would occasionally wake up, look at each of us, then lay his head back down.

I could hear Teal snoring from the tent.

Kaderyn had a needle and thread and was trying to fix the Faebric. By his third attempt at patching the hole, and his shadows swirling slowly, which I was learning was never a good sign, I held out my hand to him. He stared for a minute before sighing and handing it over.

And because maybe I'm more like Teal than I realized, I needed to break the silence. "I lived . . . I live," I corrected, "in a theater in Elaria. It's a small town bordering the desert."

I looked to him, and he nodded once in recognition. I thought back to Teal's map and wondered if I would find it on there.

He stayed silent as I did a whip stitch right down the side, so I continued, "I've stitched up a lot of dresses. But only with the silks and cottons from Summer. This Faebric is beautiful. It feels more like the ties—"

"Valentina," he interrupted. "What are you?"

My hands froze and my heart beat wildly out of control. His eyes flicked to my chest and back up to my face, I knew he heard it. I finished the last stitch, looping it around itself, and pulled tight.

If I could talk, I'd tell him he needed stronger thread. But my throat choked up. I picked up the key from the grass-covered ground at his feet. Its weight, still surprising, and the cold of the iron still startled me. There was no iron in Elaria, or at least at the theater, and I always assumed, being able to work water magic, that touching it would cripple me. We both looked at it before he met my eyes. Because fae weren't supposed to be able to touch iron at all.

"I don't know," I whispered.

19

VALENTINA

JAIREK HAD FLOPPED himself into the tent not long after and we followed, crashing to the padding and cloth. We were all careful not to ruffle the little seething pixie.

The tent protected us from the worst of the chill of the Narrows between the courts, but I woke to find my arm draped across Kaderyn's bare chest.

And my leg sprawled across both of his.

I folded into myself quickly, hoping he didn't wake, but missed his warmth when I did.

I was getting used to the riding and the food and being bound to Kaderyn—but the icy air? No. I didn't think I'd ever get used to that.

"Ready to get up?" Kaderyn asked so softly that I froze beside him. I thought he was asleep.

I nodded avoiding his gaze, praying he didn't know that I had flung myself on him in the night.

"Good because you and I are going hunting."

"What?" I shrieked and Teal snorted near my head.

I couldn't hunt.

The theater was a product of fae magic. The ingredients for meals came and went whenever Daria wanted them to. I asked her once why she couldn't just make the magic clean the dishes and, with a scolding, she made me clean them by myself that night. I tried another time to clean them with my own magic, but I was so exhausted afterward that I crumpled in on myself on my chair hours later, not moving well until the theater had cleared out. I never tried it again.

"I can't hunt," I whispered, but he was already shrugging on his shirt.

"Either we hunt, or we starve. We don't have the room to bring more food, so we must hunt every few days."

I clamped my mouth shut. Could I kill an animal? I looked down to my warm, lined coat from Kyrrahalyn and frowned. Even with it, I wasn't used to this chill. I was going to freeze. "Can we wait until the sun is higher in the sky?"

"Nope. You may crave its light, but it'll send other animals off to hide." He stood over top of me with a hand outstretched as I tried to think of another reason we couldn't, *shouldn't*, go.

"Will we get warm tea afterward?" I grumbled when I had no good reason to let us starve.

"I'll make it myself, let's go."

Two hours later I scanned the muddy bog once more as I shivered next to Kaderyn under a large oak tree that still had its leaves. Nothing but squirrels and crows came by to taunt Kaderyn with their chittering and cawing. His shadows licked slowly around us, and I knew he was displeased at the racket they were creating. I rewarded them by throwing their cute little paws some acorns from the surrounding base of the old oak. Just because we might run out of food didn't mean they had to.

"How much longer?" I whispered as my teeth chattered. I pulled apart a piece of bark, keeping the warmth in my fingers, as I listened to the chirps of chipmunks as they chased each other through the forest. No amount of distraction was pulling me from the fear of the cold.

"It depends how much racket you and your new friends are deciding to make."

I huffed and turned away from him but just as I did, something small bounced into view. I froze still as a large, white-furred hare stuck its nose in the air, wiggled it around, then jumped once more, closer to our spot. Its tall, sprawling ears flicked both ways before it leaned down to nibble on a patch of grass. It occasionally shot its head up, looked around, and then went back to munching. It was adorable and delicate, and we were witnessing such a peaceful moment that I didn't notice Kaderyn beside me until the shadows quickened pace. I turned my head slightly to see him, arms outstretched with a solid-black bow pulled tight with an arrow nocked, ready to shoot.

He was going to shoot the bunny.

Without thinking I immediately shot out my hand and slapped the shadow bow to the side. The arrow whizzed far wide and clipped three trees before it was lost to the leaf litter on the ground. The shadow arrow lost its form and slunk through the air back to Kaderyn, returning to his ever-present shadows. The bunny, upon hearing the mess of the arrow and Kaderyn's swear words, leapt quickly back the way he came.

"By my fucking hounds, Valentina—"

"It was a tiny bunny. I'm sure we can find something bigger. Meaner. Uglier," I said to the tree trunk. I was far too nervous to look at Kaderyn.

"It was a full-grown hare. Do you have an ounce of self-preservation in you at all?" he snapped.

I recoiled as shame flushed my skin, and I turned away, even as I saw his face soften. Self-preservation? He had no idea what I'd done to survive. As a faeling and now.

Maybe I was too soft to let him kill the hare but this accusation from him rocked me to my core. I was sitting, frozen and scared, next to a heatless oak tree and a Shadow Lord that didn't care.

"Look, I'm sorry," he mumbled but I didn't want to talk about it.

"Can we grab more blankets at least?" If this was going to go on much longer, I needed out of this cold, or it didn't matter if an entire drove of hares ran by, I was going to lose my mind.

Kaderyn stilled for a moment as he watched my face. Before, much to my surprise, in one fluid motion, he sat back and heaved me across him to sit in between his legs. He wrapped his arms around me as he scooted in close to my back. It felt far too affectionate for two fae who almost killed each other yesterday.

"Are you going to tell me why you hate the cold so much?" he said, much softer, into my ear.

"Are you going to tell me what you needed the coast for when we were at the Fortress?"

I heard his breath catch.

I thought so. "Keep your secrets, Kaderyn, and I'll keep mine, too."

Though, his back blocked much of the wind and almost instantly I felt warmth flow through my core again, I wasn't ready to talk about that horror. I wasn't ready to tell him why I feared Winter.

A few hours later, though I was warm, I was getting far too comfortable with his body locked around mine, and just when I was about to ask to try again in a few hours, a tree moved ahead of us.

No, not a tree, but big enough to look like one. I'd never seen a moose before, but I was sure this was the biggest moose in all of Eadha's forests. Its antlers, which were far taller than I was, sat curved and forked on its head. The moose ambled slowly through the shallow waters heading our way. Its legs easily cleared the brambles that lined the bog, and it was snorting, in a way that had me pressing myself into Kaderyn.

I felt Kaderyn still, unnaturally so, at my back with his legs on either side of me. The shadows quickened again and formed a bow in his hands, arrow already nocked. He slowly, ever so slowly, lifted until he had sighted the moose properly. It sunk its head down to eat whatever it was eating again and I swear I didn't breathe. And when it lumbered closer again, my heart raced in my chest. I knew moose only ate plants, but I prayed to Angus it didn't come any closer. His black bow and arrow sat less than a foot from my face as I was trapped between his arms.

"Can I shoot this one," he whispered so close to my head that I felt his lips against the curve of my ear.

I nodded. *Oh, yes please.*

I turned into his shoulder as the swoosh of the arrow leaving the bow echoed close to my ear. I didn't think I could watch.

I felt Kaderyn relax around me as his arms fell to my lap, shadowbow, gone.

"It's done, Valentina. But you're not going to like this next part."

And he was right. It was horrible. I sent many prayers to Angus for the poor creature who died so we could survive.

MANY DAYS LATER, Jairek was up on his feet, rotating some strips of meat over a low, smoldering fire as I bristled at the falling hail in the Narrows. I was unsure if it was in Winter or Autumn Court boundaries.

"How are you feeling?" I asked as Kaderyn dragged me along to Jairek's side.

To my surprise, Kaderyn pulled him into a quick hug. They clapped each other's backs—in the way only males could—before releasing.

Jairek looked down to me, eyes bright as he said, "Much better." But he absently rubbed the spot the arrow had pierced, and I found myself doing the same.

"Good, because it's time to move. Winter's been kind enough to leave us alone, though it terrifies me why," Kaderyn said.

Jairek moved a step or two away, rustling the leaves on the ground with his foot. "We're ten feet into Autumn Court lines. Likely they realized we aren't a threat to them. I've been up smoking and salting our last bit of meat. It'll last for a day or two, then we'll need to hunt."

"I don't suppose we can eat these berries, can we?" I asked, pointing to the plump red berries on the trees we huddled under. They looked like the cranberries we had in Summer Court.

My stomach soured—what I would do for some fruit. Something lighter than salty meat and cheese and breads. My mouth watered thinking about the dripping delectable honey pastries.

Jair picked up a small jar with ruby-red jelly filled to its brim. "I boiled a batch down this morning. It would be fine on bread if you can beat Teal to it."

"Where is Teal?" Kaderyn asked, looking around.

"She's been hugging my face all morning, so I sent her and that damn map to the top of the tree to keep a lookout. She filled me in on what happened."

Kaderyn cleared his throat and looked at me like he wished I would disappear. "Listen, I'm sorry, Jair."

"There's nothing to be sorry for. We were successful." His eyes flicked back to me. "Besides, an arrow to the gut was surprisingly not that bad."

My skin heated despite the cold, and I cleared my throat. "Is Teal safe up there?"

He grimaced. "I'll smell Winter's general coming before Teal sees her."

Don't ask. Don't say anything. I willed myself to stay silent.

"Because you're a lionshifter?" I blurted.

"Because I am a lionshifter," Jairek repeated, eyes shining, smiling down at me.

Kaderyn sniffed sharply, and I noticed his shadows taking down the tent and packing it up. A stray one curled around my face playfully. "You're well enough to ride?"

"Well enough to get away from Winter's borders," Jair said.

I looked up into the trees to see a shadow swirl up to its top. Movement, loud and noisy, followed it on its way back down.

"But Teal rides with you," he added.

20

VALENTINA

It was two days following the edge of the Yegevani's western ridge towards Spring Court. Tall, white-barked birch trees marked the edges of Lady of the Woods far ahead. At least those few still standing. The forest was first thin and then thicker as it went on westward. Stumps littered Autumn's dirt ground like broken limbs off a body.

I peeked behind at Kaderyn when I could. There was a stillness to him I was seeing, a markedness to him. Like he didn't walk among the trees like us. No, more like the ground rose to meet him. Like he came first, before the golden sun dropped onto the island of Eadha, heating it from its frozen slumber and nature knew it. The trees groaned as he moved past, the grasses pulled away, not because it wanted to but because his resolve gave it no choice but to listen, all as if bowing to the Hunter I'd attached myself to.

"Are you going to fight when the War of Many boils over?" I asked as I sat in front of him on Malvasia.

He grunted. "I will do no such thing. With any luck, and I

do hope it finds me soon, I'll be reunited with the Wild Hunt and off this fucking soil before that happens."

"You're abandoning your court?" I twisted around in the saddle.

He looked down his nose at me with squinting eyes. "They will be protected."

"How did it happen? How did you fall? Did you get pulled out of the night's sky?"

"I was lulled by a song."

My mouth twitched. "That was it?"

"It was enough. No more questions."

I sucked in a sharp breath as we passed a particularly tree-leveled spot.

"Autumn uses birchwood for their forges, to make those daggers you treasure so much," Kaderyn said in my ear.

I could hear the faint chirping of birds. Not unlike the canaries I'd trained sitting atop Otti's courtyard wall, coaxing them from Spring's borders. The reminder was comforting and blindingly painful all at once.

"They're destroying the woodland
Creating a sight sore wasteland," Teal squeaked from
my shoulder.

She had been telling me about a ship raised from the bottom of the Galeairy Strait beyond The Court of Shadows. About its moss-covered mast and the sea mollusks that made it their home.

Kaderyn grunted, "Birchwood burns hot for forging. Spring would do it too if they had the mines on their side of the mountain." He paused. "And if they had fire magic. But Summer Court uses the alderwood for its dyes and Winter uses the hollywood for its arrows. Don't pretend they are the only court using the land for what it gives."

But he didn't mention his court.

"And Gillies Forest?" I prodded, daring another personal question to the Hunter. I knew enough to know it bordered Summer, but we never dared venture in. Summerfae who went into its thick purple-black shadows and fog never came out. And I thought for sure he'd ignore me. That he'd feel it was too personal, like most of my questions before.

His voice was soft in my ear as he chose his words carefully, "Gillies Forest is far too valuable to be tearing down her trees."

Kaderyn spent the rest of the afternoon singing a crude song, a vile parody, something about a virgin and a cliffside. I had turned to Jair and asked, "How do you put up with this from him?"

Jair only laughed a big belly laugh as Kaderyn took it upon himself to reply, "And who do you think I learned it from?"

That night, we came up to the edge of the woods where Spring met Autumn, and for whatever reason, I thought Spring and Autumn would blend together seamlessly. But they didn't mesh at all. Spring sent a musty smell over, which Autumn blew my hair in my face to send back. The only good thing to come of the two warring courts was the birch forest, Lady of the Woods. Sprawling tall, white-wooded trees gave way to purple wild violets and yellow dogwood flowers at their roots. Vibrant, frazzled ferns grew in large patches. Autumn's side was razed, but Spring's was dense and thick.

Teal told me about the sacrifice of the silver birch. The first to grow and the first to die, making way for the taller trees to take root, which was the silver birch's role in nature.

"A song in transition
From chorus to verse
We take Winter's prelude
Back into reverse.
A balance between
Night's ashes and day.
The Vernal season
Is my court's mainstay."

"It's beautiful Teal," I said, looking to the vibrant lime-green buds on the trees as we walked through the edge of the forest. We were giving Malvasia a break from our combined weight.

Small fireflies lit up the underbelly of an uprooted tree. Its once-white bark was broken, and new life sprung from its soft composted wood.

"Don't be fooled." Kaderyn thumped his foot against a massive fallen log. It rolled over, crushing a patch of yellow dandelions. "Spring hides its death from sight, but beneath, it's full of deceit." A smell wafted up from the carcass of what might have been a fox.

Teal growled, much like a young pup, and she leaned over my shoulder to better yell at him.

"The island requires balance
To keep everything moving forward.
Life and death stuck in a dance
A never-ending caress
Don't pretend it's different
In The Shadows or the Courtless."

Kaderyn smiled a wicked smile I couldn't look away from

and I was starting to get the feeling he enjoyed seeing Teal in a tizzy.

Teal seemed to do everything more. Her anger racked her entire little body into seething convulsions. Her joy brought her saucer-large eyes to tears. Her laugh, infectious as any faeling, had us all beaming from ear to ear. Her rhythmic chatter in my ear, where she sat on my shoulder, became second nature. And I felt bare when she chose Jair or Kaderyn to entertain.

My eyes got stuck on the small indentation in Kaderyn's cheeks I'd never noticed before. Dimples pressed into his cheeks above a sharp and strong jawline. *Were they always there before?* Shadows swirled up, licking his hair of the same color.

As my cheeks heated, I asked, "Is there life where you're from?"

Instantly he looked down and the smile washed away. And I regretted opening my stupid mouth, wishing we could go back to watching Teal fume.

He pressed his lips together and guided Malvasia around a denser patch of forest, tugging me along with him, before he spoke, "The Underworld has life not unlike The Court of Shadows." His eyes flicked down at me. Those silver eyes speaking more than his words did. "But not everywhere. Not where those go who are destined to reside in its depths."

My throat choked as I tried hard to swallow. I thought back to the magog who died because of a secret I told. To the Autumn soldier who perished and was left behind in the Glenora Desert because Mohr was desperate for revenge. I wondered how much more blood would be on my hands once I could get home. "And," I said as I shuffled at his side, "what exactly does one have to do to be destined to the depths?"

His laugh startled my panic but did nothing to calm it and I bristled under its weight. "Little lion, there is nothing you could do in this lifetime or the next to warrant my hounds to drag you to the Underworld. Your moral compass points due north and you have the naivety of a faeling."

I grimaced at his words. It was painfully obvious I'd never had the experiences the lot of them had.

"Except when you're angry." He nudged my arm playfully. He was smiling again and there was comfort in that.

I'd known two towns my entire life. In the last few weeks, I'd been thrust across an entire court and dragged back and forth across court lines. There was no experience in Otti Theater to prepare me for this.

The sun stayed high in the sky, allowing us to travel farther during the day than in Autumn Court but right now it was taking its leisurely time setting low and, my gods, it was beautiful. I was closer to Summer Court, I could feel it.

I sucked in a deep breath of lilac and lilies and fresh, clean air. A familiar reminder tickled my memory at the scent. And to my horror, it took a minute to register as Cillian. Oh gods, the jasmine reminded me of Cillian. Who I had not thought about at all even though we'd crossed into his court.

Before I could think more about it, Jairek came sauntering up in fae form from the north trees. Shoeless. He'd gone off searching for food and shelter for the night. A deer lay slung across his shoulders, teeth marks on its neck.

Teal squealed and squeezed her little hands together.

"There's a clearing half a mile north of here. Old smells of predators but no dens to worry about." He looked to me. "And a couple of crabapple trees that Valentina might enjoy."

I straightened as my mouth watered. I desperately needed to sink my teeth into something juicy and sweet. In Summer we'd suck the nectar right out from the honeysuckle flowers. Or Petri would climb the mango trees outside the theater's walls and toss them over the courtyard wall. The first bite would send shivers from my tongue to my toes.

And it was me pulling Kaderyn now as I trudged behind the Shifterfae, eyes sharp, searching for a hint of glossy, ruby-red fruit through the trees.

We reached the clearing not long after and I dragged a laughing Kaderyn to the first stubby apple tree I found. I pulled an apple from the branch and went to brush the skin, only slightly pockmarked, on my clothes and frowned. I was still wearing Autumn Court furs. It didn't feel right rubbing the fruit clean on it.

Kaderyn grabbed the small, mottled apple from my hands and proceeded to rub its sides on the sleeve of his soft obsidian shirt. I stared at him.

Not just because he was being kind or that he was smiling again—a sight I was never getting used to because it stole the air from my lungs. *Was he always this gorgeous?* But as his shadows swirled, clashing with Spring's rose-gold setting sun, it dawned on me that Kaderyn, the leader of the Wild Hunt, was cleaning *my* crabapple.

Malvasia, who I'd so selfishly dragged over, was trying to pluck the apple from his fingers. Kaderyn pulled her head away with a laugh and held it out to me. His tanned skin looked golden against the shined red fruit, and his eyes were wide and unguarded. There was a vulnerability he was showing me that worried me.

Because the more he relented, the more I craved more of him. I took the apple, careful not to touch his fingers because they weren't just the Lord of Shadows, leader of the Wild Hunt's fingers anymore. No, I noticed they were thick, and scar-marked, and some edges were mottled red from where they had been burned on an iron key. *Was he dropping his glamour for me?* And how much I wished to have been there to take his pain. Kaderyn's pain.

I noticed his throat as he swallowed and how his brows

furrowed when I stood there staring. I noticed the careful guardedness that hardened around him when I said nothing. His shadows quickened and slowed and did it again before I snapped out of it.

Whether he was shadows or fae, he hadn't had an easy run of things. And I found myself wanting to know who dragged him down to Eadha. I wanted to know if it hurt. I wanted to know if it would have been better if I had been there.

I wanted to know if I could have helped.

And that scared me. Because I had a theater who needed my help first.

I held out the buffed apple to a pulling Malvasia who greedily gobbled it down. I plucked another two from the tree and handed one to Kaderyn, avoiding his eyes, and took a bite straight from the other. He followed suit, but I could feel his eyes on my back as we moved to the clearing where Teal was gathering twigs for a fire and Jairek was cleaning the animal. I tied Malvasia up beside the other mare, a knot Kaderyn had taught me two nights prior while Kaderyn set up the tent I was beginning to find comfort in.

But some anxiety was settling over my skin, and I curled it in on myself. Because I wasn't supposed to feel comfortable here. Or crave the tea that Teal was pouring into three mugs, the smell already permanently etched into my senses. I wasn't supposed to still find joy in watching her pull a smaller mug, one no bigger than Kaderyn's thumb—whose size I was aware of now—and dunking it into a larger steaming mug of tea, pulling out a mugful for herself.

We ate without talking and I feared it was because of me. Jair passed a plate of barely cooked meat, and I knew it was for Kaderyn. The pinker piece for me came later and the heart and liver went to Teal. I didn't have to look to know he kept a piece of the haunch for himself.

By the time we were done eating, my anxiety was a palpable growing thing, and I could feel it infecting the atmosphere. Jairek raised an eyebrow to Kaderyn, but I didn't look to see what he did in return. I didn't want to talk about any of it.

After a moment, Jairek cleared his throat and stretched. "Teal, it's safe. Grab the instruments."

I looked to the fluttering, blue-skinned pixie who dropped the chunk of meat she was holding to the plate below. It landed with a squelch and a splatter. She took off towards the tent so fast Malvasia snorted from where she stood, dozing.

Teal flew back quickly, tent flaps wavering as blue sparks trailed out in her wake. She had two sticks in her hand that looked much like bamboo shoots and gave the longer one to Jairek before settling on his shoulder.

He gave her a thanks and an affectionate glance before bringing the instrument to his lips. The most delicate sound came out.

Peaceful light music drifted over the clearing as Teal joined in with her smaller reed. They moved their fingers up and down, covering and lifting their fingers off holes in the wood in sync with each other. Teal's little wings fluttered behind her excitedly when the tempo had picked up. And after a new terror settled in my chest, at making noise in an unknown wood, I swayed along to the sound, as it eased my nervousness.

It was lighter than music in Summer and miles happier than music in Autumn. Much like Spring's breeze, it was a joyful, pleasing tune. Teal, fingers still whirling over the instrument, flew to Kaderyn and bumped into his shoulder, over and over.

"I won't. Give it a rest," he said from where he sat, leaning against a fallen tree beside me.

I looked at him quizzically, but he refused to meet my eyes completely.

Jairek moved the reed from his lips and sighed. He got up

from the log he'd been sitting on and placed the reed down behind him. "Carry the tune, Teal," he said as he came over to where we sat. "Valentina, dance with me."

And with the vigor of a lionshifter and the boldness I felt in my chest, I only hesitated a moment. Movement always settled me. I brushed my hands against each other and rose to greet Jair's outstretched hand. Only to be pulled tight by the Caterina del Aamod ties and the stubborn Shadowfae at my feet refusing to move. Jairek and I looked down at Kaderyn.

He swore some words I wouldn't dare repeat before standing up in a huff, and held out his arm, giving me more space to move. "Go on, then."

Jairek grabbed my hand and put his other on my waist as he guided us to the music. And I found myself smiling—laughing even. The movement was needed, it kept my mind from focusing on any one thing. On my magic, or lack thereof, of touching iron and of how comfortable this was all becoming. Dancing was easing my mind and soul.

And if there was a power to Kaderyn, there was a lightheartedness to Jairek. The bees made lazy trails around his head on afternoons we'd stop to eat. The chipmunks would scramble across his splayed-out feet. Pure life exuded from the Courtless Shifterfae more than the summer sun heated Summer's crusted earth. But he was secretive.

Watching him was like watching behind the curtain at the theater. Seeing what the audience wasn't allowed to see. And when Jair would catch me looking, trying to figure him out, he'd just smile. He certainly didn't have this charm when he snapped that Autumnfae's neck.

And there Kaderyn stood, grumbling, leaning against the tree trunk of a strong silver birch, not unlike his eyes, as Jairek and I danced to Teal's reed instrument.

Jair spun me and caught me, both of us laughing as he untangled the twisted ties.

"Why do you ride with Kaderyn?" I asked, wiping away tears of laughter.

Jairek moved us to the beat of the music and looked over at the Shadowfae, still moping beside us. But he picked his words gradually, carefully. "The grounds shift under our feet, slowly, achingly. The dead have not rested. Shifterfae are a little different from the rest of Eadha, and we can tell nature is not happy. Our dead, no matter where they are destined to go, deserve to move on from this plane and into the other."

He moved us again and I found myself looking at Kaderyn, whose silver eyes locked on mine. I hadn't realized how it was affecting the island. The Hunt had been gone for so many years.

"*And,*" Jairek continued, "he saved me from being a giant's punching bag a few decades ago."

"A what?" I cried, stopping us both.

"A debt he's paid a thousand times over. You owe me nothing, Jair," Kaderyn growled like it was a conversation they'd often had.

Jair's kind eyes turned to me. "That's a story for another time."

And with that, Jairek turned away to throw another log on the fire and I found myself breathless and calm at Kaderyn's side with shadows tickling my hands.

"Feel better, little lion?" he murmured, pulling some birch seeds apart.

I looked to Teal, softly playing to herself, and Jair fanning flames for the fire to grow, and to Kaderyn, who was so careful not to meet my eyes. But his shadows gave him away as they moved, skintight over areas of me the furs left bare.

He'd saved Jair and Teal in some incident that seemed to have changed them all and banded them together. I huffed out a breath. Maybe he wasn't as selfish about his stupid shadows as I thought.

But grumpy he still was, and I didn't want to explain my revelation to him, so I said, "Come on. We are on dish duty. I know we passed a stream a bit back."

BY THE TIME dishes were done, we found Jair by the crackling fire and learned Teal had gone to bed. When I asked if all pixies needed as much sleep, Kaderyn squirmed and said, "Teal is not quite like other pixies."

But the two of them got to talking about the travels ahead, and I found myself yawning. I draped the coat over me as I laid down against a fallen log Kaderyn had dragged back after washing dishes.

Kaderyn interrupted something Jair was saying to look down to me. His voice hitched low as he asked, "Did you want to go to bed?"

I blinked up at him because though my body was tired, I didn't want to interrupt them. I didn't want to impose more than the Caterina del Aamod ties and I warranted. And I didn't know why I cared. "No, no. I'm okay for a while yet."

But I must have been more tired than I thought and found myself dozing off to the sounds of the male fae talking and the sweet-smelling air of Spring Court.

Things were different.

Changing.

21

VALENTINA

Things lived in these woods.
Things I didn't want to meet. I was learning to sense it now.

Dew fell from the moss-green leaves of some closely packed aspen trees as we made our way through the northern reaches of Lady of the Woods.

Kaderyn, tight, close to my back, kept his eyes ahead, tracing his shadows as they led us to where the chest remained.

In Autumn, the songbirds sang long, loud melodies high above our trails, like odes to warmer days. But here? The birds all fought with each other to be heard. Like squabbling lovers trying to get the last word. Bugs chirped from their hiding places under the leaf litter. Ravens crowed from high above us in the frothy green of silver birches. The wind rustled the leaves, causing them to dance to the songbird's chaotic tune.

And here, the wind moved on its own, pulling and pushing, stirring more like a living thing than a natural breeze. But I watched the frogs jump out of the way of Malvasia's feet and the ravens hop from tree to tree behind us. An odd behavior I frowned at. It caused my skin to prickle.

Because it was a noisy forest.

Until it wasn't.

Jairek, with his head tilted, was listening as he shushed Teal on his shoulder. Kade called for Malvasia to halt, pulling on the reins. I looked back to the ravens, staring at us from where they perched, watching with their black eyes, unabashed. Canaries of Summer never stayed where monsters were. They flew away at the first sign of predators. If there was danger, I'd expect the birds to fly off. *Why weren't the ravens flying?*

I was counting on the ravens.

I finally caught Kade's inquisitive eye over my shoulder.

"Why are they staring at me?" I asked.

"They wait to pick clean the bones of the prey."

I swallowed. "I don't want to be the prey."

Kade clicked Malvasia forward, but her ears twitched back. I couldn't tell if she wanted to charge off ahead or go back the way we came. "We're half a mile too late for that."

I looked to the treetops. Something lived in this forest; something I did not want to meet. "Can we double back around?" I asked.

Just then, something whizzed by our heads and thunked into the tree to my left. My instincts started screaming. A black-wooded arrow fletched with long brown feathers stuck out of a tree.

Kaderyn wasted no time urging Malvasia into a gallop.

More arrows flew as Malvasia danced around the forest trees, dodging roots.

"Afraid not," Jair answered as he charged the mare alongside. "Seems to be a pissed-off general behind us."

"Go!" Kade yelled, jutting his boots into Malvasia's sides. "Get farther into Spring Court."

The arrows lodged into trees or skittered to the ground around us. I was going to risk a look behind, but a bellow echoed through the trees and instead, I tucked down into Malvasia's neck.

"Valentina!" Mohr roared.

A different fear shot down my spine. "Will he come into Spring?"

"If he's desperate enough," Kade said. His forearms tightened around me as he gripped the reins. I refused to look up at his face, though I could feel it was on mine. He wanted to know why Mohr was chasing me down. A seemingly faeless from Summer Court.

In one swift move, Kade grunted, then reached behind him, grabbing an arrow out of the air that was coming for his head. He snapped it in half and threw it to the ground.

"Enough of this," Kade growled, pulling Malvasia to a halt. He swung off her in one go, grabbing me off as he went.

My feet thumped on solid ground as I looked back through the haze of shadows that Kaderyn sent out, acting as shields, and saw the rich reds and browns of fur clothing just beyond them. My stomach wanted to leap out of my body as fear made me curl in under Kade. Mohr was here.

Kaderyn's shadows lingered mere feet away from Mohr's boots, halting at the edge of Lady of the Woods as Mohr's stare bore into me.

"Why aren't you attacking?" I asked, desperate.

"If I attack him in his court, he'll wage a war on mine. He holds the same risks I do if he comes into Spring. Difference is, Spring and Autumn have been at war for centuries. We're merely shadows passing through. But if I kill an Autumnfae on their court lines, I'm bringing that fucking fae spat—"

"The War of Many," I corrected.

"—to The Court of Shadows' doorstep."

Mohr's severe mouth twitched. I looked around at the silver birches. The ravens flapped their wings in anticipation.

"Sir, they're coming," came a shaky voice from a soldier to Mohr's right.

The firefae soldiers around Mohr shared an uneasy look and backed up farther into their razed lands. The wind rustled through the leaves and through the ends of my hair as Teal peeked her little face out of my hood.

"Aw fuck," Kade swore. "Jair?"

"I smell them," Jair answered, but his gaze was down, looking towards the base of the tree trunks.

"Take the horses. Back them up against something solid. They'll try to take out our way of escaping first."

"Teal, with me." Jair's nostrils flared before his lips pursed in contemplation. He turned Malvasia around quickly as Teal shot from my hood to his shoulder. "They don't usually roam up this far. Autumn must have really done a number on the forest farther south."

"What's coming?" My voice came out as a whisper as the shadows laced through the trees along the court lines.

"Aim for the Hunter or I'll give you to the hounds myself!" Mohr shouted to his soldiers, and suddenly we were inundated with another onslaught of arrows.

Kade grunted as his shadows blocked the assault. "Birch hounds. They protect Lady of the Woods. Valentina, walk backward slowly. My shadows will keep Mohr back, but he seems to have a death wish trying to get to you."

But my muscles were locked tight, and I wanted to run. I tried to remember any passing mention of what birch hounds were from my days at the theater, but I couldn't get Mohr and his endless fire out of my mind. "Will he risk the birch hounds and a war to come into Spring?"

But before Kade could answer, a throaty growl sounded

from farther into the woods where Jair and Teal had gone. I prayed to Angus it was the growl of a lionshifter.

"Are they going to be all right?"

"Birch hounds viciously protect what's theirs. Lucky for us, so does Jairek."

My hands shook uncontrollably from where I gripped Kade's one hand in mine as we dodged thick roots and fallen branches. We walked backward until Mohr and his soldiers had faded into the burnt colors of Autumn's lands. Until Mohr's shouts were a faint whisper; until the arrows stopped skittering to our feet. But we weren't out of danger yet.

"How big are the hounds?" I asked. With Mohr out of sight and us farther into Lady of the Woods, I searched the trees for courage, but every leaf looked menacing; every log looked like it held ill will. I squinted into the base of a particularly strong, white-barked tree when—

That couldn't be right. It was growing. Moving.

"We can compare sizes later, let's—"

Kade was cut off as, out of the tree, launched a massive white and black creature. It crashed straight into me, toppling me to the ground. I fought to find my bearings as the bark on its front legs gouged against my forearm and its jowls loomed over my head. Instinct wanted me to go for my daggers, but I caught sight of its emerald-green eyes—the same color as the walls in Otti Theater—and I froze.

Kade let out a strong-footed kick square into the birch hound's side. A puff of air left the hound as it was tossed off of me. But it righted itself quickly and leapt for Kade's face as I scrambled to my feet. Its teeth immediately went for Kaderyn's neck, which he fought back with one hand braced on each side of its massive muzzle.

But I really *looked* at it. This wasn't a monster. This was a creature of Lady of the Woods. Instead of fur, it had a coat of white and black-speckled bark that curled up at the edges much the same way as the surrounding trees. Its pointed ears and long winding tail were made of the same birch-colored hair, finely twisted in dozens of braids no different than the ones I'd find near the nape of my neck when Teal would leave my shoulder.

That same tail I was admiring snaked along the ground before it lifted, reached out in front and wrapped around Kade's neck. Kade let out a strangled gasp as one hand went briefly to his throat before he rose it in the air and between his fingers materialized his shadowsword.

"Wait!" I shrieked at the struggling hound and the Hunter.

I rose my hands in the air and stepped between—in the very small space between—Kaderyn and the birch hound's chomping teeth. Much like I did with Roshan and the magogs so long ago.

The birch hound shifted its head and eyed me, pulling back slightly. Because, while it was busy snapping at Kade, I noticed its teeth were blunt. Good for chewing leaves and not so good for fae bones. This wasn't a monster, and I didn't need my water magic to calm myself before this hound.

"Valentina." Kade struggled to talk as I showed him the back of my head. "You don't have your—"

"Magic? I know," I muttered. "Kaderyn, drop your sword. He's just trying to protect what's his."

"So am I." Kade's voice was gravel in my ears, reverberating through his chest and straight through to mine.

"Drop it, Kade," I urged. "We aren't the monsters here."

Reluctantly, Kade's shadowsword disappeared into smoke at our sides. Warm air from the birch hound's nose puffed against my upturned hands. He huffed once more before tucking his head to his chest slightly and I took it upon myself to decide this was a good enough time as any to try and release Kade's neck. I reached up behind me and dug my fingers between its thickly braided tail and Kaderyn's warm skin.

"Easy there. We don't want to hurt you. Or your woods." I wondered if he believed me, as I stood there in Autumn's clothing. "We mean passage, not malice."

His eyes met mine again, and it sent a pang straight through my heart. He was this sacred forest's protector, and around him, every day, it was getting destroyed. At the theater, surrounded by emerald-green walls, *I* was the help. And Mohr had threatened my theater—my home—too.

I ran a soothing hand down the hound's head and slowly, ever so slowly, his thick tail released from Kade's neck and retreated to brush against the fallen leaves behind him.

Kade shifted on his feet and cleared his throat.

The hound backed up and stood tall and proud, sniffing the air as its long, braided tail continued to flick across the ground in methodical waves. I couldn't hurt this creature without becoming something I hated. And I wouldn't let Kade do it either. I didn't need my magic to understand this creature or to be helpful. And I knew that whatever happened, even without my water magic, I was going to be all right. Because I was still *me* and this island would not take away my compassion—no matter how hard it tried.

An awful howl echoed through the trees around us—the soul-crushing sound of something dying. The birch hound before us crouched low, startled into a self-defense position. Kade slunk his hand around my waist and pulled me behind him. But the hound took off running towards the nearest base of a silver birch and disappeared into its roots like it had come.

"We have to find Teal and Jair," I said, brushing the leaves out of my hair, hauling Kade onwards.

"Valentina, you're bleeding." Kade's hand held me still by the elbow and I followed his gaze to my arm. Sure enough, thin streams of blood ran down my forearm and dripped through my fingers.

"I'm fine," I said, shaking Kade off. The birch hound's bark hide must have scratched me more than I thought.

"I have a tonic in my bag on Malvasia that can help with the pain. I gave most of it to Jair in the Narrows, but there is still some left."

"Oh, *this* pain is nothing," I answered, absently. If only he knew.

But more blood dripped onto the ground at our feet and Kade's face drew down into concern. "What does a fae from a theater in Elaria know of pain?"

I wanted to stop and laugh, but we didn't know what that dreadful cry was, and I feared for Jairek and Teal. I wrapped it as best I could in the coat Jair had got in Kyrrahalyn and ignored Kaderyn's question. How was I to begin to explain it?

"Also, I was talking about your daggers before. You stepped between the hound and I, unarmed." He gave me a knowing look. "It's curious you don't have magic and yet you say you're not faeless."

But I didn't know if I was ready to talk about that loss yet, so I said, "I don't need water magic to be helpful."

"Clearly," he said as we jogged through the woods. Faster now, without Mohr's arrows raining down on us.

"I didn't want to harm the hound if we didn't have to. Its teeth didn't look like the type to shred us to death."

"More of a problem when those long-reaching tails—perfect for whipping and winding around their enemy—pull you into the trunks of their silver birches. Disappearing in one and coming out another. Well, they come out. You would not. Though it's true, they might not be monsters, you should fear them all the same."

But before I could defend myself some more, the unmistakable trail of Teal's blue pixie sparks caught my attention through the trees and we ran the rest of the way into an open clearing at the base of Spring's Yegevani Mountains.

"Teal . . ." I started, but my voice trailed off when I caught sight of what lay on the ground in the middle of the clearing. My breath caught in my throat.

22

VALENTINA

A LARGE WHITE birch hound lay motionless on the ground and a distraught Jair knelt over top. His thick hands tended to the dead hound with surprising care as he spoke soft words into the sweet-smelling air. Teal fluttered from the horses, where they were tied up just inside a cavernous hole in the mountain's side, to Jair and back again. She didn't seem to know what to do, either.

"I have to bury it, Kade," Jair said, looking up at us through heavy eyelids.

I didn't know if he had more of a connection to the creatures of Eadha than the rest of us, but there was no way I was letting anyone say no to his request. "I'll help," I said, but a wicked, awful smell overcame me as I tried to step forward and I recoiled. "Ugh," I gasped. *By all the gods, why was I tasting it?*

"Oh, that's all right, Valentina. You have bigger problems. Mainly," Jair said, pointing towards the cave where the horses were tied up in its mouth, "that way. And they tend to look as good as they smell."

"What is it?" I rubbed my nose, wishing I could go back to smelling the lilacs and lilies. I turned and buried my nose into Kaderyn's vanilla and wood-smoke shirt, hiding the tears for the birch hound at Jair's feet.

"Nuckelavees," Kade said.

I stilled, hand half rubbing my nose, as though a weight was being pressed down on my chest, and looked up at him. "They're not supposed to live inland."

"Well, the six up ahead in that cave guarding my chest of shadows never got that message."

"What?"

"Did I not mention that part?" Kade asked, refusing to look at me.

"No," I shouted to the suddenly quiet air.

The skin on my neck rose because this was a different matter entirely.

Teal shot into Kade's hood beside me, but he coaxed her out with gentle hands. Her poor wide eyes looked vacantly at the cave mouth.

"Not this time, Teal." Kaderyn's voice turned quiet and solemn as he turned to Jair and asked, "Can you hold them off?"

"Don't be having any tea parties in there, and Teal and I should be fine," Jair said, neck flexing, but that barrier was back up, and I didn't want to leave him. "They are just protectors, Kade. I don't want to kill any more of them if I don't have to."

Panic was also settling into my bones. "Why? Where are you going?" I asked Kade. "Does he mean the nuckelavees?"

"*We*, Valentina. *We* are going in there." Kaderyn pointed forward, past the horses, as we crossed the small clearing to the mouth of the cave on the other side.

Drops of water fell from the cave roof into puddles at our

feet as that smell, that rotten, molding smell blew across our faces. It was no more welcoming than the trunks of the trees around us now.

"Teal will stay with Jairek out here in case the birch hounds decide on retribution. Besides, I'm not making her enter any caves ever again," he added.

Teal buzzed to Kade, bopped her forehead into his in a weird affectionate move, then turned to me to do the same as a screech rang out from the cave. We both froze, our faces inches apart and looked at the opening. My shoulders clenched so hard they ached.

"Watch out for their teeth
And their long-reaching arms
A nasty beast
With very little charms.
I'll stay out here
Teach these old dogs a new trick
Not to mess with my pixie fire
Or my sidekick, Jairek," Teal said as she chomped her needle-pointed teeth together in a mock show.

"Whose teeth? Teal, come back here!" I whipped my head around looking for the pixie, but she had fluttered off to Jair's shoulder.

Kaderyn grabbed my hand, sucked in a deep breath, and brought us past the horses and deeper into the mouth of the cave. When he tried to pull me forward more, the ties and my stubbornness held him back.

I shook my head. I couldn't go up against nuckelavees. They weren't creatures like birch hounds. They were true monsters of Eadha. Sea beasts that were supposed to be locked into the waterways around the northern islands. I didn't realize I was pacing until Kaderyn pulled me to a standstill.

His gaze was fierce as it held mine, capturing it, and I couldn't look away. His voice had turned as dark as the cave around us. "Stop pacing, Valentina."

"I'm not moving until you tell me what nuckelavee mess we're running into," I hissed as I pointed a finger at the gods-awful-smelling cave.

He stood up straighter, no doubt finding patience. "Some time ago, around the same time fae across the island went missing, the nuckelavees in this cave found a way inland. They became encircled by a ring of fresh water which they cannot touch, leaving my chest trapped in the middle of the entire mess."

He tried once more to move us on through the ominous cave, but my brain was having trouble processing. We were too far from Jair now, any bravery he leant me had dissipated; any lion-hearted steadiness was gone. I was running from one monster, no doubt it being Mohr, and into the home of another. And I couldn't breathe.

"Kade, I can't do this."

The dead were stuck in the soil of Eadha, not able to move on. This was a bigger problem than just me, but there were far more qualified fae to be by Kaderyn's side. Especially against nuckelavees. I didn't think any plea of upturned hands would be enough to calm the monsters they were rumored to be. Kaderyn needed the help of a warrior trained in combat, not some fae who lost her magic. It was one thing to coax canaries from Spring, calm birch hounds, and negotiate with magogs, it was another to purposefully enter a monster's den.

Panic had now seized me whole.

He turned to me with startling concern and placed both his

hands on my forearms, careful to stay away from the gash of the birch hound.

I expected his anger. I expected his impatience. I half expected him to drag me onwards, towards a monster I'd never paid much attention to, as I was never supposed to be anywhere near where they were. Instead, he leaned his forehead into mine, and I inhaled the smell of him again before he pulled his head back.

His thumbs brushed up and down my skin, which now had me thinking about his dimples again, and I wanted to run from it all. He opened his mouth like he was going to say something but when he said nothing, I fluttered my eyes closed and sent a wish for bravery up to Angus.

"Hey, look at me."

I looked up into his silver eyes, but they were now wrought with an emotion I was too consumed by my own to decipher.

"You don't have to fight them. But I do need you to come with me." I watched his throat swallow and followed it down to where his shirt met his chest of solid muscle, as he choked on the words, which was odd since, of course I did. I was tied to him. He pulled me into a hug, warm and tight, and this closeness was different than riding with him. "They won't come near you, I promise," he whispered into my ear.

I sucked in a breath. I knew he needed this. He'd traversed the entire island and here he was, not forty feet from his chest, finally with the cloth that would allow him to touch iron. And I was holding him back. I pulled my daggers out. I might not have wanted to fight, but I had a feeling I was going to have to. The cut on my forearm stung as I flexed my hands against the cool metal. Even I could smell the dried blood on my damp skin. Damn.

I looked up at Kade, our faces close, but his eyes were

cautious. There was a part inside me that desperately wanted to help, wanted him—even as cantankerous as he was—to get his shadows back. But I was so far out of my comfort zone.

So I nodded once, briefly.

Because what choice did I have?

23

VALENTINA

There was only one path through the cave and, except for the alcove at the beginning, the cave tunnel stayed fairly straight. If I had the eyesight as any good hound, I might have been able to see the far side from where I was. But it was dark, and the smell had me nervous to look too closely.

"And you've been here before? You've tried to get to the chest before, right?" I whispered over the drip, drip of water from somewhere up ahead, trying in vain to distract myself.

He glanced at me, silver eyes shining like stars against a moonless sky in the darkness of the tunnel. He rose an eyebrow. "Let's hope my supplies are right where I left them."

I let my wrist graze against his and took comfort in the closeness.

He grunted. It was considerably darker now, so if he looked at me, I couldn't see it as he continued, "Nuckelavees survive in salt water only." Which explained the burning of salt water in my nose. "Let's hope my boat is still . . . *ah*, here it is."

Something wasn't right, I thought as Kaderyn pulled me faster into the recesses of the cave. Its dark-brown jagged edges were wet with moisture, but a yellow rock occasionally glistened as we walked by. I pulled at the furs; it was far hotter in here without Spring's breeze.

As we moved to the far cave wall, it slowly grew brighter, and I looked up, searching for the light source. There was a hole in the cave roof, circular like a ring, where afternoon light shone down and hanging vines drooped from the ledge.

Kade pushed aside thick moss and vines and lifted a small, haphazardly built wooden boat before setting it carefully in the first ring of water. The small amount of light allowed me to read its name—*Sea Barrel*—as it was scrawled on the boat's side.

This circular stream was only ten feet across and surrounded a ring of cave floor that was onyx black in color. It, itself, was only five feet across before falling into black bubbling ooze that I wanted to go nowhere near. And beyond that, in the center of this alternating ring of lakes and lands, was a bigger chunk of solid cave ground with stalagmites growing up. It looked like a target. My nerves bubbled in my gut, and I hated that this was where Kade was leading us.

Kade helped me into the small wobbly boat after pleading with me again to keep moving forward. I'd never been on anything but solid ground, and I wasn't sure this was something I'd want to get used to. The vulnerability I felt in the boat did not trump the worry I had for the nuckelavees, and though I feared I'd topple out entirely if I didn't hold on to the sides, I kept my daggers in my hands.

He reached behind him and pushed off the rock ledge.

I yelped, falling backward as we jutted forward, straight into the short side of the next ring of cave floor.

But before we crashed into it, he leaned over me and grabbed the land, arms flexing, holding us steady next to it.

"Sorry," he mumbled into my ear. "I left the paddles in Auris. These waters below are made by the runoff from the mountain. They feed into Embee Lake. The nuckelavees can't cross it."

"That's comforting."

"Too bad we're going passed it."

But whatever incoherent thing I muttered was drowned out by a loud screech from up ahead.

Kaderyn's jaw twitched, and his face hardened. We quickly got out onto the five-foot platform, and he lifted the crudely made boat to place it in the oozing water on the other side.

The sickening smell of nuckelavee and brackish water burned my nose. Oh gods, this was where they lived, these exact waters where Kade was settling in the boat.

I looked back at the ring of water we just pulled the boat from. That must have been the water Kaderyn dropped the key into—the river that flowed to Embee Lake in Winter Court.

If we crossed to the middle, we would be surrounded by this sludge. Kade waved a hand for me to get in. I looked ahead to the platform we were destined for, and I hesitated.

"Please." He tilted his head from where he leaned over the side. His shadows licked off him—anxious or excited, I didn't know.

I blew out a breath and sat low in the boat, not wanting to be anywhere near the sludge that plagued the water.

He pushed off slower this time, not causing such a large wake, and we hit the end with a small thud.

This time I didn't hesitate to scramble out. The idea of nuckelavees under me had my head pounding with adrenaline. I looked around as all sides of this platform dropped into the salt-water sludge. We were surrounded by it.

Kade beckoned one of my daggers and jabbed it into the hard ground before tying the short boat rope to it.

I looked back at the dagger Cillian gave me—insignia and all

—sticking up from the cave floor. "You don't think I'll be needing that?"

"We lose the boat and the next song I teach you will be our funeral tune."

Before I could say something else, Kade inhaled so sharply I looked at him. But his stare was one of awe as I followed it to its source.

There, at the base of the biggest stalagmite, was a black and silver chest. It was intricately molded in the shapes and curves of smoke and curling, swirling shadows. And like a heartbeat, it seemed to give off a life of its own. An empty hook protruded from the stalagmite above the chest.

"Is that where the key was?" I whispered.

"Before it burnt my hand, and I threw the fucking thing? Yes," he answered. "Then I spent half a century trying to find a way to touch iron, regain the key and unlock the chest. Which I did, only to be tied to an apparent faeless, no offense, who can touch iron anyway."

"You're very unlucky," I muttered as I waited for him to move.

"You have no idea." But before he could step forward, because gods know I wasn't going first, the water to our right rippled.

"Can't you use your shadows? Make us invisible or something?" I whispered.

"No, no, no," he cooed. "Magic in a nuckelavee cave is a very bad idea. It rebounds funny. Something about the ooze secretions, I'd imagine."

"Ew," I said under my breath. I gripped empty air with the hand tied to Kaderyn. I desperately missed the security of having a dagger in both.

He looked down at me and raised an eyebrow when I

bumped into him again. "You can hold my hand if you wish to."

"You're being far too kind and far too funny," I said, my skin still warm from his hug and the humid air. I refused to blink, and my eyes burned from watching the ripples in the deep black waters too closely.

"It doesn't give me pleasure dragging you into here, Valentina. If I had it my way, you'd be waiting for me at the cave entrance."

I frowned at his back. "You wouldn't wish me back home in Elaria?"

His eyes shot to mine and an unreadable expression crossed his face, but movement from the water stole our attention.

Something black, slick, and oval was slowly rising. At first it looked like a slimy rock protruding from the oozing seawater, but it kept rising until horror shook me still, because it was a head. And I knew nuckelavees didn't have eyes, but it didn't stop me from looking for them, anyway.

"Maybe they won't remember you," I said, trying to instill confidence and slow my pounding heart.

The nuckelavee had grey skin so paper thin that I could see its black bones underneath. It had an oblong head attached to a barrel chest, a gaping smile with a lipless mouth and teeth as big as Teal's arm, though pointed much the same way as hers.

It rose from the water slowly, head jutted into the air in different directions, like it was using the holes in its face to smell where we were. I knew nuckelavees were half-horse creatures, but I stumbled back a step once its lower body rose and there was the bottom half of a horse with skin just as translucent as its upper half.

"Keep moving," Kade ground out, low.

I shuffled my feet as it lifted its endless arms, ones long

enough to drag on the ground, out of the water. It grated its claws against the rock face between us.

"Teal said nothing about its claws," I whispered, horrified.

"You mean the ones as long as she is? Must have slipped her mind."

Which was a ridiculous thing to say. I'd never forget them as long as I'd live. Which was looking shorter and shorter with each passing minute.

"What happened last time you were here with the nuckelavees?" I asked as its skeletal body grew larger and angrier.

"We had communication issues . . . hey, there's my dagger," Kade said.

Sure enough, sticking straight out of the bones in its back was a black-shadowed blade and a bronze-handled knife. Kaderyn materialized his long shadowsword, twirling it once in his hand. The nuckelavee shrieked an awful noise.

"Get to the chest," he shouted as he stood between the grotesque screeching beast and myself.

I gripped my dagger harder and willed my feet to move, pulling at the back of Kade's shirt with my tied hand, trying to keep him close. Even if I had both my daggers, I'd doubt I'd be able to fight with it tied so close to Kade.

The moisture in the cave made the floor slippery. At least, I hoped it was humid air and not that foul-smelling ooze I was slipping on. I picked up my pace, tugging Kaderyn along to the black iron chest. Out of the corner of my eye, I watched the beast's front hooves reach the platform we were on, its arms dragged closer on the ground, its claws reached farther across the stone floor.

"Where's the key?" I shouted, adrenaline making it far louder than necessary. My voice bounced around the cave in a taunting echo.

"Back pocket. Make it quick, there're more coming."

Kaderyn's shadows swirled quickly as another torso appeared on the other side of the plateau and Kade shifted his feet to accommodate.

I felt his pants for the key but as I went to grab it, he lunged forward, blocking the long-reaching arms of the first nuckelavee, pulling away from me. My scream echoed around the cave louder, causing a screech back from a different one I hadn't seen before.

Kade's sword sliced down but didn't cut through the beast's claws. Whatever they were made of, they combated a shadowsword. Kade's back flexed and I realized it was like fighting with one hand tied behind his back.

"The key, little lion," Kade said, over his shoulder, calm as could be.

And I thanked the gods for it because he was the only thing grounding me.

I reached for it again and did not hesitate to pull the silky soft Faebric from his pocket. But the coldness and heaviness that lingered when my fingers touched the iron key sent my already irregular heart beat sporadic.

"Take your time," Kade said, slashing down at the front legs of the nuckelavee before swiveling and protecting our backs against a second one that ducked closer.

I turned to the chest and reached but we were still too far away. I could sense his shadows swirling faster than I'd ever seen them. Desperate. I pulled farther away from him, the ties tight against my wrist, but another nuckelavee slashed down, and I ducked.

I swiped my dagger at its lingering arm, and it squealed backward. Their claws might have be tough, but their skin was not. I grabbed Kade's free hand, warm in mine, and pulled us back to the chest.

"Come on!" I yelled over the screeching. I slipped on the

sludge that seeped off the nearest nuckelavee and steadied myself with Kade's hand.

Kade fought hard at my back, grunting low, but I didn't dare turn around and see how many of them there now were.

Once I was close enough, I dropped sharply to my knees at the base of the chest. But I had one hand, so I had to let go of my dagger and trust him—as much as he had to trust me to unleash his shadows.

I ran a hand against the cold, metal chest. Smelling of Kaderyn and . . . and something I didn't know. But this was no time to be cautious. I jammed the key into its opening and turned it quickly.

Kade's shadows swirled faster, occasionally pitching me into darkness as I dug for the edges of the top.

I tried to lift the heavy lid; tried to pry my cut fingers between the top and body of the chest but time and humidity had sealed it shut. I picked up my dagger and smashed the butt of it into the top, cursing something fierce. We finally made it! We were right here for this *stupid* chest and . . .

And it cracked open. I thrust it open the rest of the way and fell backward as inky black shadows exploded from it, swirling in a tornado around Kaderyn. The nuckelavees screeched and tripped over themselves to back away, retreating to the waters they slunk from, thrashing their faces as the eddying of shadows grew big enough to swallow the cave.

Kaderyn tossed his head back into the air as his shadows dove in and out of him like living things, happy to be home. Power swelled in the little cave and occasionally a tendril of shadows would skirt across my body. His normal silver eyes had become pools of inky blackness. Kade's hair twirled wildly through the shadows, and I didn't know how long I'd been watching them reunite with him when he turned above me and looked down into the chest.

Like on a command, the swirling darkness settled down and I noticed what he was staring at. Something was glowing from the bottom of the chest I leaned against.

I crawled to my feet at his side, and we stared down into the chest together. A few lazy shadows lingered, but nothing could hide the vibrancy of the two daggers that lay across each other in the bottom of the chest. One was a muted red and the other a vibrant yellow, like Sisaria's golden hair in the sun. Both were intricately engraved with trailing vines of ivy up their grips.

Kade let out a throaty laugh at my side, but his voice was darker, spitting more gravel than before. "Quickly, Val. The nuckelavees will be back."

He wanted me to pick them up?

"Those aren't mine." But even as I said as much, there was an otherness, a soft, deadly promise in my gut that was pulling me to them. Not a promise of peace, but a promise of justice.

"I promise you, the gods would never grant me access to their weapons. Besides, I much prefer the length of my sword." He lifted his shadowsword to rest on his broad shoulder.

He warned once more, saying my name sharply and without humor before I leaned down and wrapped my hand around one of their hilts. I was vaguely aware of Kaderyn taking Cillian's insignia-marked dagger from the ground at my feet. Its twin was still holding our makeshift boat in place.

"Gods' daggers?" I choked, pulling the yellow one out, and my blood hummed through my veins. "They're beautiful."

"Pointy end that way, please. One touch, no matter how small, and you'll find yourself leashed to a rather dead Hunter."

I quickly pointed them down and grabbed the other from the chest. So, they were deadly. "Is that all they can do?"

Kaderyn met my eyes and gave me a hard look before turning away. "Let's go."

We moved back to the boat, now bobbing in the saltwater's

wake and the creatures under it. Kade stepped in and reached back to lift me in. I rested the gods' daggers in the boat's bottom and reached back to pull Cillian's dagger from the cave floor we were tied to.

I chewed my lip as anxiety about being above the creatures threatened to choke me.

It wasn't lost on me that I now had four daggers and two hands. The gods' daggers were beautiful, but Cillian's were familiar. Kade reached behind me to push off and I kept Cillian's daggers, the ones I was used to, in my hands. Besides, I was a dishwasher from Elaria; gods' weapons had nothing to do with me.

Kade pushed and sat back down on his side quickly, scanning the water. I watched his shadows swell thicker than before, menacing even, as they moved around us. His once silver eyes, now black, ringed with white as strength and confidence flowed off him in waves, in a rush of sheer power that had my skin prickling. He must have felt me looking because his dark eyes darted to me and held me still as the shadows curled around my face and caressed my cheek. The boat thudded into the other side of the short waterway, and it took far too much concentration to clear my throat at their smoky touch as I stood to get out of the rocking boat.

I lifted my foot to move closer to him as Kade's eyes widened. Something hard crashed into the side of the boat, and we tipped halfway over on its side. He reached for me, but I was already falling.

I hit the black seawater in a panic, thrashing through the oozing slime I couldn't see through. It took far too long to find which way was up, but eventually, I looked up to where Kaderyn leaned over the boat. His hands wrapped around the ties that bound us but before he could pull me up, something curled around my leg. Strong, boney fingers and claws curled around my foot, tugging me down farther. My empty hand curled around ooze and water, and my heart stopped. I'd already lost one of Cillian's daggers. A sob bubbled in my throat.

Kade's grunting was muffled but I could hear him shouting something above the water as I became a doll he fought over between a nuckelavee. My joints screamed as Kade held tight to the Caterina del Aamod ties and an awful laughing came from the nuckelavee below me, trying to pull me into the darkness. It echoed through the sludge, consuming my thoughts. I tried to pull up my leg. I tried to swipe the last of Cillian's daggers that I had at the nuckelavee's arm, but it was too far away.

A scream chased the laughing nuckelavee voice out of my head, but I choked as black slurry washed through my mouth. It was me; I was screaming.

I was being pulled far too tight. The last of my air escaped my mouth in bubbles, clouding the view I had of Kaderyn. But I could see well enough he had a shining gods' dagger in his hand. His hand gripping mine tightened before the realization hit me.

He had his shadows.

He was done here.

He didn't need to be playing tug of war with a nuckelavee. Oh gods, I was far too vulnerable as the only way out of this for him was to cut it off entirely. And the nuckelavee seemed to realize this too as that awful laugh rang through the goo again. Wretched, long claws dragged up my leg in a show of possession, cutting into flesh. My mouth bobbed open like a fish, but no bubbles came out.

In one motion I threw Cillian's dagger at the nuckelavee below me, blade first, wishing it was the gods' dagger I left on the boat. If only one nick could kill.

The dagger bounced off the nuckelavee's boney chest and I cried out. Out of breath, out of ideas, and out of daggers. I looked back up to Kade, his face distorted in the water's rippling as his mouth moved out the words, the unmistakable words, 'I'm sorry.'

I was out of air.

I stopped struggling as my tears mixed with the salty sludge. He was going to cut me loose. He was going to cut my arm off. Free himself once and for all.

And as Kaderyn's hand went in the air and thrust down into the water, I slammed my eyes shut, wishing I wasn't here, tasting nuckelavee secretions and choking on salt water, with my vision fading into blackness.

I wished I was home, enjoying my lazy summer days around a dusty theater.

Power, strong and quick, danced down my body and smacked into the nuckelavee below us. The screech of the beast that followed had me wishing I could cover my ears as it echoed through the water like a lightning bolt in a riverbed. The claws loosened around my leg and with all my strength I kicked out, shaking free as warm air hit my face and I sucked in a deep breath. Kaderyn lugged me back into the boat and we tumbled to the bottom in a mess of limbs and black ooze.

I coughed and gagged, strangling for air. He held me to him as the hand still tied to mine by the scarf desperately tried to pull my thick hair away from my face.

"Oh, Valentina," he mumbled as I pressed my face into his chest, snot bubbling out of my nose. But he just kept pulling me back and looking me over, his eyes racked with torment.

"Kaderyn," I tried to choke out between heaving breaths as his hands patted down my body. They reached my lower back and pressed down the curve of my butt before I swatted him away. "What are you doing?"

"Checking to see if you grew a tail," he ground out,

sounding gutted. His eyes flicked over me quickly—looking for what? I had no idea.

Finally, once he was satisfied, he smushed me to his chest and tucked my head under his chin. "Magic does funny things in a nuckelavee cave," he reminded.

With his other hand, he leaned over the edge of the boat and, with powerful strokes, paddled us to the far edge of the ledge.

I grabbed the yellow and red daggers that lay on the boat floor and holstered them at my sides where Cillian's daggers had been before huddling back into the bottom of the boat. I didn't want to look at my leg that was stinging and pulsing with every beat of my heart. I curled into a ball of chilly salt brine, praying I never had to board a boat again.

The boat jostled once as it smacked into something hard, and I felt Kade scoop me up from under my arms and legs as he stepped out. He had the boat in the freshwater that was trapping the nuckelavees in the cave and had us to the other side within minutes.

I risked a look back in the cave and wished I hadn't. Three nuckelavees twice as tall as me, hooves hammering the cold, hard rock floor, reached out their arms for us, screeching wildly like writhing beasts. One lay near their thumping hooves, one arm completely missing as its teeth thrashed at the air. Two others, or pieces of others littered the rock platform.

And I wanted to mourn the daggers I'd left behind. Something about it made my stomach drop. These daggers, now locked at my sides, were more powerful, but Cillian's impending disappointment still curled through my mind.

Kaderyn trotted through the straight cave tunnel with me in his arms towards the light beyond.

I prayed little Teal and Jair were okay.

He skidded to a halt at the alcove where we left the horses, but it was empty.

"Where are the horses?" I asked. My heart fell as I thought of Malvasia and the mare trapped, no better than me, between two monsters of Eadha.

We rounded the last edge, and the sunlight blinded me in painful strokes. I lifted a hand to block the light as the other curled around Kaderyn's neck. His hair stuck to my sludge-covered face. The next breath I sucked in had me hardening my chest. I recognized that feeling.

Jair was nearby.

I pulled my hand away as Kade slowed to a walk.

There, in front of us, was Jair holding tight to the reins of two horses and Teal chirping away on his shoulder. My heart swelled and tears flooded my eyes at seeing everyone alive. Kade placed me on the ground in front of them and I would have hugged them all if I wasn't caked in goo.

"How'd it go out here?" I asked and it was then I noticed the large patch of upturned dirt just inside the tree line of Lady of the Woods. I looked at the swaying birches moaning in the breeze as gunk fell from my shoulders. Though I knew the birch hounds were just doing their duty, the forest seemed meddlesome now.

"By the looks of it, much better than in there," Jair said, looking at the slime that covered me. He looked up to Kade, whose shadows were swirling thicker than ever, before nodding. "How's it feel?"

Kade flexed his arms and rolled his neck as I moved to pull a linen cloth from the bag at Malvasia's side to wipe my face and finally look at the gashes on my leg.

"Everything from here on out is going to be a piece of cake," he said.

"Ugh, Kaderyn," Teal squeaked from where she flew near me as I wiped the sludge off my eyebrows.

But he ignored her. "Better tent, better food, better drink—"

"Dear leader of mine
Don't press your luck.
There's a time to celebrate
And a time to—"

Just then something large and black flew out of the cave, crashing into a boasting Kaderyn, knocking him to the ground, pulling our ties tight.

An almost rueful screech rang out from the nuckelavee cave.

"—duck," Teal finished.

24

KADERYN

IT WAS FINALLY DONE.

I'd reached the first chest, regained part of my shadows, and again found myself traveling Spring Court's upper valley.

Nothing was more important than re-claiming my shadows but Val at my side challenged that thought. We woke up two nights ago tangled in each other's limbs. My shadows were slow, lying against her, and it took more control than I'd ever admit to keep them from tracing her skin every waking moment.

Val was a distraction, the most beautiful, damned distraction I'd ever seen. Her curiosity and wonder hit me in the chest like a crashing wave, swallowing me whole. Every inch of traveling this island was like seeing it for the first time through her eyes.

Where I saw Lady of the Woods' decaying underbrush, she saw a lush forest waking in Spring. Regrowing, renewing, and it was intoxicating. It made me want to slay its beasts for her to continue to see the world like that. She'd once asked me how a soul gets destined for the Underworld, how one gets pulled up into the Wild Hunt, and it was like watching a doe plead with a hunter. I used to shuttle the damned souls to the Underworld, riding through the lands with my five Hunters. There was never a sense of right or wrong before becoming fae, but I was seeing it now with her.

And I was the asshole that just dragged her into a nuckelavee cave.

As we wandered through Lady of the Woods, reaching the point where it met with Kinswood Forest, all my thoughts led to the truth I was holding back.

I didn't tell Valentina those very daggers she found in the chest could cut the Caterina del Aamod ties that linked us together. That, and I was stuck focusing on the rank smell coming from her hair where she sat on Malvasia in front of me.

But the daggers were Angus's daggers. And the fact that the God of Love's daggers showed themselves to her in her time of need had me thinking she was more Summer Court than I originally thought.

What was supposed to be a monumental moment was overshadowed by the fear that if the ties were broken, she'd leave. And what was worse was why I felt this way. I rubbed the back of my neck for what felt like the sixth time that hour because something else bothered me more.

I used magic in a nuckelavee cave.

Oir, my most trusted advisor, and the oldest of our Shadowfae, was clear. Don't use magic in a nuckelavee cave. Slice them with swords, crush them with boulders, burn them with fresh water, but no magic near their sludge. But Valentina was drowning, and that damn skeleton had a grip so strong that if I pulled any harder, I'd be burying the half a body I ripped apart instead of being mounted on the horse behind her now.

But now, there was a tapping inside my head like a mouse at

a cat's door that had nothing to do with the voices of the souls trapped in the ground. And I wasn't going anywhere near that fucking noise in my head until I had a better idea of what it was.

"Kaderyn?" Valentina asked as her fingers played in my shadows surrounding us. "Say we don't get these ties off"—tension hung in the air, there was a *very clear* way to get the ties off—"and I go back to Auris with you. Is there, perhaps, a library? Maybe someplace with knowledge of the island?"

"Auris has a library. Curated by Shadowfae."

"And what about in the Underworld?"

I looked down at her then. "Biggest and oldest library there ever has been. Artos, one of my Hunters, often makes a mess of it." I pressed my lips together, refusing to say more. Not because of her, but because of how it was making me feel. And I didn't tell her it was Malek who often cleaned the library up. I cleared my throat and asked, "You're searching for information?"

She stilled before me. "I am."

Her stomach rumbled under my hand, and only then did I realize we had forgone a meal. By the time we got out of the cave, Jair and Teal had chased off the rest of the birch hounds, with the exception of the one Jair found under his teeth. He gave him a proper burial.

Shortly after, adrenaline had us moving forward, heading towards the passage up to Winter and the towns nearby to regain supplies. If we were lucky, we could make it to Arnprior in two days' time. But my body was fucking aching and I could just imagine how Valentina was feeling.

"Jair," I called up to him and Teal as they rode the mare ahead. "Curve to the right, I can hear water runoff. We can stop for food." My eyes shot to the top of Valentina's crusted hair. "And a bath."

She looked back up to me in a move that had my heart

racing, those blue eyes piercing me still as ever. "A bath? And how's that going to work?"

I had to look away before my body reacted, before my body thought too long about her naked and instead focused on the dried black sticky sludge in her hair. "With soap and my eyes closed."

That tapping continued, louder even, and I shook my head once, trying to clear it.

Jair guided the mare down a game trail towards the water that I heard, and that I knew he could smell.

I sent a trail of shadows off, searching for any reason why it wasn't a good idea to set up camp there for the afternoon. I sighed. I had regained half my shadows, and I knew the general idea of where the other chest was. I felt better knowing I could linger near the apex of the courts for an afternoon.

With her.

I scratched the back of my head. For fuck's sake, I should just tell her right now. I should tell her to use the daggers on the ties.

And yet...

We breached the small clearing in front of the mountain base to find a small waterfall trickling off the rock face. Insects buzzed around, stopping in for a drink and flying off to do what they do in spring, make homes and offspring. But I was seeing it now, the differences in the courts. The way Autumn Court prepared, with weapons and filling up on heavy food as they prepared for a season that may never come. Or Spring, and the abundant life force that drove it onwards. I was seeing the beauty even before Valentina gasped in awe, but pride filled my chest that I was the one to show it to her.

And I feared it entirely. This fact that I was caring about someone else on this damn island I was so close to leaving.

"Kade, it's beautiful," Valentina said, tapping my arm as if to get my attention when all of it was now always on her.

I looked down at her. Her deep red lips had parted, and her cheeks were flushed from traveling Spring Court in Autumn furs. Her small body sat curved against mine and I mumbled into her hair, "I've been noticing."

Teal squealed from up ahead, flew up in the air in a flip and a flutter, and curled up in a ball before splashing into the small spring water. I dismounted and pulled a laughing Valentina off after me. We tied Malvasia to the same tree near the mare, Valentina doing the knot herself with a little guidance before we moved to the water's edge.

Jairek raised his head from the water, and flicked his blond hair to the side before spitting out a mouthful of water at Teal. I started working on the buckles of my shirt, wondering if I should warn Valentina that Jair wasn't wearing any clothes.

"How am I to . . . Kade?" Her innocent eyes looked up to mine, and I wanted to light Mohr on fire with his own fucking fire magic for ever hurting such a beautiful being. Her eyes flicked to my shadows, which lingered slowly around us. Did she know what she was doing to me?

I cleared my throat, trying to clear my head.

"Get in the water, then take them off." I dropped a spare shirt on the nearest rock face. The only other shirt I brought. "You can wear mine when you get out and we'll get you different clothes at Blackwater Junction before we head to the southern pass."

She stilled along the spring's edge, half a leg in the water when she snapped her head up to me. "Blackwater Junction?"

"The closest town to here before we reach the city of Arnprior before the pass," I explained. "We'll stop and get you better clothes and some more food. Maybe a back sheath for these new daggers. So these ones are farther away from stabbing me in the . . . leg."

And if she had more questions about it, she kept them to herself.

I reached for her hands and slowly nestled her into the water on a rock ledge. She winced as her leg, the one scratched up from the nuckelavees, touched the tepid water. But eventually, she closed her eyes and sighed in a way that made it hard not to look back at her mouth.

I shucked off my shirt as far as I could with the ties—it was likely to get wet anyway—before working on my pants.

Valentina saw what I was doing, and spun around quickly, creating a wake in the water. *She* might hold modesty dear, but exhilaration ran through me as I now had half my shadows back.

I slunk in after her into the warm spring water, and I dipped my head under, running my fingers against my scalp. It'd been so long since I had a bath. It had been so long since I stopped to enjoy anything.

"Heads up." Jair threw me the bar of soap we kept in the pack from where he sat under the waterfall.

Lingering pain from the previous battle shot down my arm as I caught it, but Jairek's hair covered half his face and I found myself smiling. It was good to see my friend at ease.

I passed the soap over Valentina's shoulder as she, for some reason, refused to turn around. She cleared her throat and thanked me, but the ties were too tight for both of us to wash up properly, and I held my hand close to her head to allow her space to move. On her third pass of missing the back of her head, I stilled the soap and her hand against her scalp and watched goosebumps rise against the nape of her neck.

"Let me do it, you're missing globs of nuckelavee secretions," I said, laughing.

She scrunched up her nose. "Well, when you put it that way."

"Take off the furs while you're at it. They'll smell like wet fox when you get out, which I can't say is an improvement to this hair," I said, lathering up her hair between my fingers.

Her eyes reached back to mine. Her face was unreadable as her hands moved to undo the clasp for the top. "It'll be stuck on the ties."

I materialized a small shadowknife, one of the perks to having half my shadows back, and brushed up the straps of her top and sliced through it without force. It sprung free from her body and her hands snapped up to cover her chest.

I looked away, as promised, and went back to washing her hair, curving my fingers around her pointed ears, gathering all of her hair in my hands. I ran its length through my fingers, scooping water on the worst spots, and trying to undo the braids Teal had a habit of making. It was a complete mess if I was being honest.

And I loved every second of it.

Eventually, she got brave enough to take off the bottoms, and it took far too much to still my shadows from dipping under the water like they wanted to. Curious things they were, not unlike Valentina.

Jair sat out of the water, half-clothed, tying sticks together with some reeds he must have found. Teal flitted in and out of the water, here and there, lost in a world of her own play.

"Okay, lean back," I said, gently pulling her head down to rinse out the soap.

She pensively put her head back in the water, and I sent my shadows to cover her chest in an attempt to make her more comfortable. Her wide eyes stared up at me as she trusted me to do this for her. I swirled my hands through her hair, rinsing the long length of it out. And eventually, she lay back in my arms completely as I massaged her scalp.

She helped me get my shadows—and no matter how much I tried to deny how I was feeling about her—I had to accept that I would always be grateful for her. I didn't rightly know how long we stayed like that before Jair's voice broke the silence.

"Here, Teal. Come try this out," he said, pushing a little twig and green-reeded boat out onto the water.

Teal let out a chirp at a decibel only the birch hounds could understand, shot up in the air, and landed on the small structure as it bobbed in the water. He'd made her a small pirate ship out of water reeds and blades of vanilla grasses.

Valentina had leaned up and was laughing beside me, her body covered in my shadows, as we watched Teal tell an invisible crew to hoist the sails and scrub the deck. Valentina's hair was still in my hands, and I gave it a playful tug.

She turned to me in the middle of Teal's performance. "My turn." She held out her hand for the soap and before I knew it, she had moved behind me and her fingers were lacing their way through my hair.

And thank fuck the water was dark and my shadows darker as I used them to hide my obvious growing arousal.

Her calf touched my side and stilled against me as she used me to brace herself against the flowing current. I couldn't see where the pool emptied into, but it was a good enough guess what fueled the ring of fresh water around the cave we'd left. I slowly ran my hand tenderly across her leg from the knee down. Once, in an asking and when she didn't pull away but pressed harder into me, did I grip her even closer, still. Pulling her tight against my back. The tapping grew fierce in my head, and I wished to the gods I didn't trust to make it stop and not ruin this moment of her warm dewy skin against mine.

Her breath came hot and fast on my ear that threatened to

undo me completely when she cleared her throat and said, "You're all done."

"Good, hold your breath," I said, giving her a moment before pulling her tight across my back and dunked us down into the water.

I needed to cool down and clear my head, and break this moment during which, if I had it my way, I'd be leaning her over the edge of the pool and soaping up every possible crevice of her I could find. Or of turning around, burying myself between her legs, and nestling my face in her neck.

We rose from the water, gasping.

Her arms around my neck were tight from surprise. But she was laughing, and I focused on Jair, whose knowing look was doing wonders to kill my erection.

He raised an eyebrow. "Time for food?"

Which I knew well enough was code for, *need help?* And I did. Fuck, I really did because I was finding myself thinking about Valentina more than my shadows. Centuries on Eadha and I was unraveling at her hands in weeks.

"Time for food," I confirmed.

25

KADERYN

WE LAZED BY the waterside, drying off, easing our aches, and eating the last of our meats. I wrapped Valentina's cut leg with some of my black linen. It was already healing, which just confused me more on what her magic was. Teal had scampered off to find a patch of raspberry vines and she brought back as much as she could stuff into the magical little place all pixies had.

She may have been able to fit more if it wasn't for what Deryn Ironside, an isolated faeless on the Mainland, had given us. The same stuff that had exploded in the tavern the day I found Valentina under the hands of Mohr. Effectively drawing Valentina to me in ways I could not even imagine. And I wondered if I'd ever need to tell her of our plans in The Court of Shadows and the Courtless.

But I wanted to. And that was dangerous.

"Kaderyn?" she asked about an hour into our ride to Blackwater Junction.

"Hmm," I answered, still thinking about the dangers of

telling her what exactly exploded in Iradown Tavern, and confessing our plans when this was all over.

"How did you become fae? I mean, I've heard rumors, but how did it happen?"

I clenched my jaw. "I was bit by a vampfae in a cave northwest of Auris, the main city in my court, back before it was anything but a desolate wasteland."

I heard her inhale sharply. "I didn't know vampfae still existed."

"They don't anymore," I growled.

"Kaderyn, true to his form
Hunted every clan, pack, and swarm.
Because of the bite of those creatures
It turned most of his features
From Wild Hunt leader to fae
Now roaming Eadha Island, he's forced to stay," Teal said from my shoulder, and I could feel the braids she'd already woven under my ear.

"Bivanna, the vampfae in the cave that day, likely intended to kill, but no Hunter of the Wild Hunt had ever been bitten by a vampfae before. I woke days later with fae blood running through my newly formed veins. But splitting my shadows? Nah, she couldn't do that. I don't care how strong a vampfae she was. That work reeks of the gods. Or magic. I haven't found out which."

"You don't know who was responsible?" Valentina asked.

"Not yet. But I will." I promised, thinking back to that day in the cave. I told her about the footsteps—calm, cool, and collected footsteps. The ones I heard right before my shadows exploded, smothering that wasteland and any faeless who were unlucky enough to be hiding out in it. Effectively turning them Shadowfae.

She hesitated. "So they aren't of your blood? They were not your faelings? The Shadowfae."

I choked on a swig of Solanci Ipsum, an alcohol I made in Shadow Court, which I had brought down from my lips as Teal cackled beside me.

"Kaderyn does not keep female's company
His mood only stretches from angry to grumpy.
He might be the original Shadowfae
But he's not sired any faelings yet to this day."

Valentina's silence stretched on so long I could hear Jair laughing up ahead of us. And because Teal had no way to stop, she kept going.

"Although there was that bout
With many females in and out
Of the—"

"Teal! Stop! For the love of my hounds, go entertain Jair," I fussed, shaking the pixie off my shoulder.

Valentina was laughing against my chest and the sound soothed any worry I kept. But I had a question of my own. I rubbed a thumb down against the softness of my linen shirt against her stomach. And I didn't want to fucking know, but *not* knowing was so much worse.

"Is there anyone waiting for you? I mean, is that why you want to get back to Elaria?"

Her laughing stopped abruptly, and her gaze lingered ahead. "In Elaria? No."

And she told me about Mohr and his threat against burning

the town down if she disobeyed him. She told me about a male dancer named Petri and how he taught her to fight. Which explained why it felt like a dance before. She told me about Sisaria, the bleeding heart of the whole theater.

This island seemed to want to gain our attention, Valentina's, and mine. For what reason? I didn't know. Valentina was getting a crash course in the island's horrors and the harder I tried to ignore its plights the more of it that disturbed my days. It seemed we had this in common, we both had someplace to be and a thousand obstacles in our way. I looked down to her, small as she was in front of me, and gripped her tighter. The longer we rode the harder it was to call her stranger; the harder it was to leave her to her naive devices. And maybe that's why I tried to save her in the Fortress.

But then she mentioned a name I didn't want to fucking hear. One she mentioned back with Roshan in Kyrrahalyn. "Cillian, I mean General Cillian of Spring, is my . . . he's probably out looking for me."

"We've been in Spring Court for a while now. He's not searching very hard," I said with more attitude than I meant to.

"The furthest reaches inland, sure. But we've been keeping to ourselves."

"I'm not hiding, Valentina. Cillian can come," I said, but a challenge marked my voice and I wished to scrub it out. As if I didn't have enough problems already.

That tapping in my head became stronger than ever, like a water drip churning into a steady stream.

"He's just busy," she said after a while.

I kept my mouth shut when I wanted to tell her I'd rain down black shadows through every soul on Eadha to get her back if she was mine. I would have driven my sword through the belly of Mohr if he managed to touch a hair on her head again. Better yet, I never would have let her get taken in the first place.

If she was mine.

But these thoughts were far too dangerous. Because I was the leader of the Wild Hunt and there was exactly one place I was supposed to be trying to get back to. The Underworld.

My Underworld.

So I closed my eyes and sucked in a deep breath, willing my thoughts to clear. I stopped short of telling her she might not like what would greet us in Blackwater.

Then I focused on the steady knocking in my head. And though it didn't seem malicious, it was currently smelling like soap and fresh water. Like Valentina in front of me, and she always reminded me of home.

"How do I remind you of home?" Valentina asked, flicking her hair over her shoulder into my chest.

I shot my eyes open. "What did you just say?"

"You said I reminded you of home. I'm asking how?" she asked as if she hadn't just read my mind. "I can't read your mind Kaderyn, that's ridiculous."

I pulled Malvasia's reins tight, and she snorted once before complying. What the fuck was happening? "Look at my mouth, Valentina."

She swiveled towards me, but I grabbed her chin in my hand to make sure she was paying really close fucking attention here. In my head, I started singing the song she hated so much.

Once upon a time there was a virgin on a cliffside
Who had large breasts and an even bigger backside—

She swatted me with her hand. "I hate that song."

I pulled her soft, small hand to my mouth where it lay motionless as I thought, *I'm not speaking, Valentina.*

Her eyes flew wide. "I can read your thoughts? No, no, no. Can you read mine? Oh, this is not good."

Her anxiety was thumping through my head like a constant chatter like I stuck my head inside a ringing bell. "Shhh . . . maybe if you concentrate, you can close me out. But not with all those thoughts flying around."

But her brows furrowed. "The magic? In the nuckelavee cave?"

"The gods truly hate me and unfortunately you've found yourself leashed to my side," I said, urging Malvasia on, catching up to Jair and Teal. I was going to have to watch my thoughts and figure out how to close that damn buzzing door to her mind.

Trying to reach my shadows and keep everyone in one piece was like asking the heaven-roaming stars to bend. I looked around at my friends, my family.

Maybe, if I was smart about it, I could get us all out of here alive.

Maybe, I could do that.

26

VALENTINA

BEING THERE TO help Kade get his shadows back sparked something in me. An ability to be helpful without having to take another's pain into me; to not sacrifice myself on the way. Even with everything that happened, I wondered if that was a future I could see for myself. A future that did not involve huddling in the corner of a theater on a broken chair.

I didn't know why I lost my magic, or to what purpose it could possibly have been meant for. A new sympathy towards the faeless had found a home in my gut. I couldn't shake it and I didn't know if I wanted to.

And Kade . . .

Kade had become the dark embodied, a black hole demanding attention. With part of his shadows back, his steps now echoed through the trees like those loud drums in Autumn. He pulled shadows from the forest harder than before, like he could command them all at once. If this was how it felt being near him now, I wondered how it would feel when he had regained them all.

I thought of Kade's hard body behind me where it pressed into mine. It took concentration, blocking him from my thoughts and I prayed to Angus that he didn't hear what I was thinking in the hot springs. How I had wished the shadows that draped across my chest were his hands.

Crawling, pressing, gripping into my skin.

He grunted once behind me, and I felt it rumble through his chest. I hoped it was in answer to what Jair had said and not my stray thoughts trailing through to him.

I sighed and sunk deep in the saddle against his chest in his warm linen shirt that smelled like Kade. That smelled like the shadows that twirled around us, thicker than before. His shirt hung off me like a blanket and we had to cut the right sleeve apart to get it on with the ties. His arms tightened around me, and I felt the slightest nestle of his head into mine. Shadows consumed me every which way I turned, and yet I still craved more.

I wanted to see this through, see him rise back to his rightful place in the Wild Hunt, where he was meant to be.

"We can stop here for the night," he said close to my ear.

"You don't want to push on to the nearest"—I swallowed—"town?"

He'd said it was Blackwater Junction. The town that sparked *everything* back in Elaria. What was in that town that had everyone on edge? Cillian said they were faeless, and I didn't think much of it then, but I couldn't understand how a town like Kyrrahalyn could be troublesome. They were very much the victims in this mess.

He was silent so long I twisted in the saddle to see his face.

"One more day before Blackwater couldn't hurt. The dead

aren't going anywhere." The sharpness of his jaw when he smiled had me sucking in a breath.

A lingering cloud snuffed out the last of the sunlight and we stopped in Spring's evening mist along the edge of Kinswood Forest.

Kade and I now moved as one, no longer at odds with the ties. His shadows set up the tent as we, together, built a roaring fire. But he was full of an energy I could sense, like a hound needing a run or a cat needing to scratch, so I let him do the cooking of the deer Jair had caught.

Though my body was sore and cut, my spirit was alight. I felt the heat of the adrenaline from our battle in my cheeks. A new purpose was firing through me.

Jair passed me a plate full of raspberries from earlier, a small piece of meat, and the soft inside of a crusted bun. Teal had made the tea as one of her self-assigned duties, and I pulled out the reed instruments when we sat down to eat. But now I stared down at the plate before me. Full of everything I liked, and none of what I didn't. Without even noticing it, I'd become one of them. And I wondered how I could possibly feel at ease so far from home.

Home. A term I was now questioning.

Only when we were stuffed and had enough meat curing for the rest of our travels, did Jair pick up his flute. He played a soft melody that had me leaning against Kade. I was being lulled into the safety and comfort of the leader of the Wild Hunt beside me, the lionshifter before me and the blue-skinned pixie who, perched on my shoulder, was weaving small tight braids beside my ear.

By my third yawn, I looked longingly over at the tent.

Kade interrupted a hawk's cry and said, "Come on, let's head inside. The bed is calling to you like a lover."

But the very mention of me having a lover on Kaderyn's lips had my cheeks heating.

"Jair, are you coming?" I asked as we stood to retreat for the night.

Jair flicked his blond hair back and stretched out against the misty ground. "Shortly."

"Shadows will be on guard tonight. Get some rest, Jairek. Who knows what troubles will find us tomorrow," Kade said.

The inside of the tent had me gasping in awe. The once-short bed was raised tall and far larger than it used to be. It was overflowing with black sheets and billowing with deep amethyst-colored pillows. And now an inky, black, feather-filled duvet was draped across the entire thing. Kade was right. It had called to me like a lover. Teal's velvet pillow was larger, now a deeper purple, and had a black button in the middle that puckered the fabric down and in. It sat on the far top corner of the bed.

Shadows danced in and out of the candlelight, flickering through the glowing light of the dozens of candles strewn across the tent floor, which was now a thick, deep-onyx pulled carpet.

I was in such a daze as I took in the new tent that I hadn't noticed Kade had taken off his shirt until he stood half-naked beside me. I tried hard to think about boring things like basins for dishes and horrific things like the teeth marks in the bones Teal picked clean. And tried not to focus on the steady, firm muscles of Kaderyn as they flexed, flowed across his back and arms as he lowered himself to the glorious bed. I bounced onto the bed beside him and only when his dark eyes widened slightly did I realize I was beaming from ear to ear. *Oh gods, it is even better than our beds in Summer Court,* I thought, nestling down.

"I love what your shadows can do," I said absently, twisting my hand in curling shadows above my head as I tucked in closer to his side.

Memories of them pressing into my skin rose again, and Kade spun his head to me sharply.

I froze, and wondered if I left the connection between us down. But if I thought he'd shun me, I was wrong. Instead, he pulled my hand, linked by the gold and silver ties, across his chest and curled his strong, warm fingers through mine. With his other hand, he pulled my leg up across both of his and left his hand tucked in tight behind my knee.

"Get some sleep, Valentina," he growled softly with sleepy eyes looking down at me. "Tomorrow, we go to Blackwater—"

"And after, your shadows," I finished.

READ ON FOR THE FIRST CHAPTER IN BOOK 2: SHADOWS OF SOLACE BY HJ REESE

SHADOWS OF SOLACE (THE WILD HUNT: BOOK 2)

KADERYN

Once upon a time there was a virgin on a cliffside
Who had large breasts and an even bigger backside
She held their gaze, and the fire blazed
With a heat the males mistook
And when they tried to have their way
They met her strong right hook

I THREW MY HEAD BACK AND LAUGHED. "That's not how it goes. I distinctly remember it being far viler than that," I said into Valentina's hair from where she sat before me on Malvasia, my horse.

She had modified Jairek's song and had just used our mind-speak, our newfound ability to communicate mind to mind, to share her version.

"I guess you haven't figured out how to close your mind to me yet," she said, turning to look at me as a delectable smirk crossed her face.

"Maybe it's impossible to keep you from my thoughts."

The sun was low in the sky by the time Valentina, Jair, Teal, and I reached the road to Blackwater Junction. The soft pattering of rain on birch leaves rang out before the sky opened up and unleashed herself fully. Then every step forward was like walking through a wall of water.

So much for drying our clothes back at the waterfall.

But I had finally done it. I'd regained a part of my shadows that had been locked for centuries in an iron chest hidden in a nuckelavee cave in Spring Court's Yegevani Mountains. I splayed my hand on Valentina's belly and pulled her closer to my chest, tugging her further under the cloak I had fished out of one of the bags at my thigh.

General Mohr from Autumn Court was chasing her down across Eadha Island. But unfortunately for him, she had tied herself to me with a Caterina del Aamod scarf in Autumn's Fortress. The Caterina del Aamod ties were relics from the gods, sexual ties meant for lovers and only found in Summer Court.

Valentina and I had gone back and forth trying many different ways to close the mindspeak that my magic in the nuckelavee cave must have opened. I wondered if it had to do with the ties around our wrists, like some magic of the gods, or if it was just terrible fucking luck blasting a hole in a nuckelavee —a sea beast that found its way into Spring Court—to save her. And when Valentina would answer my mindspoken questions out loud, I knew I hadn't figured out how to close the door between our minds yet. So, we kept trying.

But the rain smelled funny, and it had me tensing up—in a familiar sort of way, in a way that I didn't want her in my head for. So, I hastily pictured shadows clouding the connection of the mindspeak we shared.

And the rain continued to tumble down.

"Hey," she shouted over the downpour. "You did it. I can't hear your thoughts anymore."

Relief tried to settle in, but there was something in the air. "I blocked it with shadows. Jair!" I called up ahead.

Jair turned around; his golden hair was matted to his head. He looked as miserable as a wet cat. "I smell it. Let's keep moving."

Teal, the one-foot-tall, blue-skinned pixie, was tucked, grumbling, inside his hood. Her little pointed hat drooped low over her large eyes.

"Where's your balance, Teal?" I shouted up to her.

"It's unnatural
This rain that we're in.
Cities are not supposed to swim.
I'd be less concerned
But it smells like . . . him," Teal growled.

Blackwater Junction was a sleepy faeless town at the apex of the three northern courts. I'd come this way long ago, the first time I tried to get to the chest. After learning Kyrrahalyn was still standing after coercion from Winter, I wondered what Blackwater had given up for its sovereignty.

Lord Aborys was trying to wipe out the faeless, a magicless group of fae on Eadha. To what end? I did not know. I'd never considered the faeless a threat, but from what Oir Winnetiren, my advisor back in Shadow Court said, faeless could reproduce quicker than the fae and live just as long. Oir did not know what sparked a faeling—a term for all fae younger than eighteen—to be born without magic; just that it did not discriminate. Two full fae parents could birth a faeless and two faeless parents could birth a fae; along with any combination between. Magic skipped generations, and I never cared enough to ask why. I would have said luck was involved, but I knew better; I knew how the gods worked.

The road led us to a courtyard shrouded in fog, and in the middle sat a large fountain, moss covered after years of unuse. Murky water poured over its basin sides as I watched the rainfall pool into soft streams along some worn, eroded cobblestone. It washed downhill until it flowed into a river that I didn't remember being there before.

Bags of grains were stacked against the rushing river, acting as a makeshift wall, holding it back from taking over the town. The smell of mold rose over the smell of the sea and that damn demigod. I groaned. I couldn't think of what value it was to Adrian, the son of a sea god, to be involved with the faeless town of Blackwater Junction. What could he possibly want with such a town?

Jair guided us on, following the fuzzy lights of the shops along the road to the tavern and adjacent inn where we were hoping to stay.

And still, it rained, soft but steady like an afterthought to a thunderstorm.

We tied the horses to a swollen rail under a covered awning and made our way through the drizzle to the door.

"Think she'll welcome us?" I asked Jair, shoving the Caterina del Aamod ties under my shirt sleeve.

He heaved the door open an inch, needing a little more arm strength to pull it past the waterlogged door jambs. "With a drink and a song, Kade. We'll stop here for a day. Two at most, resupply, and head north. All will be fine." Jair gave a lopsided smile and threw the door open to a noisy tavern smelling of warm food and damp corners.

"Avika!" he called, launching his arms wide in a greeting to the faeless behind the bar.

Frown lines marked her deep brown skin, the color like red oakwood, and fury lit her light gray eyes. "Get out, all of you."

Avika slapped a damp rag onto the bar top. It landed with a squelch.

The rest of Blackwater Tavern's patrons grew quiet and stilled as they shifted in their seats. Valentina tucked closer to my arm and instinct had me stepping sideways to shelter her from view. I didn't think firefae would come to this town, but Mohr was bullheaded, and anything was possible.

"We were hoping for warm food and a place to get dry. But I fear we were drier in the river," I said, pushing off my hood as Avika came to the doorway.

She was small-boned, almost hungry looking, though her baggy clothes suited her well. Damn, I'd forgotten how much she looked like her sister. But she carried an air about her, one of confidence and control even if she didn't have a single magic bone in her body. The faeless before us dropped her hands onto her hips. If anyone knew why this town reeked of a demigod, it was going to be Avika.

"One meal, one night, and one drink," she said, holding up a finger like we were too stupid to know how to count, *really* driving home how happy she was to see us.

"I'll concede on the first two, but we've had a nightmare of a trip and could use more than one drink," I said.

"Well, come on, close the door. You're letting the river in." She led us to a booth. "I don't carry that vile Solanci Ipsum you make in the Shadows, Kaderyn."

I pulled the bottle out from under my cloak. The obsidian liquid sloshed inside. "Quite fine, I've brought my own."

I guided Valentina to sit down first, and I slid in beside her.

"I'll send Sloane over. Let her know what you'd like," Avika said, leaning her calloused hands on the table, glaring with a ferocity to compete with Autumn Court's tempers. "Keep your heads down and don't cause any trouble."

"You won't even know we're here," I answered, trying to

give an innocent smile, but her glare continued. I was going to have to work on it.

Teal took it upon herself to tell everyone what to order. My roasted lamb came with a side of cooked cinnamon apples, which I unthinkingly passed to Valentina's plate even as she pushed half of her meat and steamed beets onto mine.

Sloane was a friendly little light-haired faeless with skin as fair as the silver birches we'd passed coming through. She beamed at us with almost sleepy, hooded eyes. Val gave her a warm smile once we had finished scarfing down our food and she returned to grab the last of the dishes. I would need more information before I could ever close my eyes in a town that smelled so strongly of a trickster god.

But I was fae—at least some form of it—and like it or not, I couldn't lie. And I couldn't think of a single fucking way to bring up Adrian without calling him the prick he was.

"Avika tells me you'll be staying the night. I'll clear this and go make up your rooms shortly," Sloane said with a sweet smile as I drummed my fingers on the table and swished my drink between my cheeks.

And thank my hounds that Jair had more control over the situation. "You're not afraid to have the Shadows and the Courtless in your tavern?"

"Oh no, we are protected." She looked out adoringly at the rain. "The noble god, Adrian, has been shielding our town."

I choked on the Solanci I was guzzling as she continued, "I know you mean us no ill will. The rain he gifts us with protects us from those who mean us harm."

"You mean Winter Court?" Valentina asked, leaning forward.

She nodded. "And the firefae to the east. They cannot step foot in the rain without shriveling up like vines of grapes left in the sun," she said with a vulnerability and an innocence that rivaled Valentina's.

And I wanted to warn her that Adrian was an absolute piece of shit, but Avika had a backbone stronger than most fae and she'd kick us out before I got the words out. I should have just risked the trip to Arnprior. If we'd done that, we'd have bypassed this fucking town entirely.

"Adrian just . . . protects you . . . out of the"—I leaned forward and cleared my throat, trying to get these words out—"goodness of his heart?"

She nodded, her hooded eyes dazed as she said, "He loves us."

I took another pull of the bottle because, *fuck's sake*, that couldn't be it. Adrian liked three things: his wine, his appearance, and causing others misery. I grumbled into my deep onyx drink; we were going to get nowhere with Sloane. Clearly delusional.

That's not nice, came Valentina through the mindspeak.

Neither is Adrian, I answered the same way.

Who is he? she asked.

A giant pain in my ass.

Sloane walked toward the kitchens with our empty plates. Teal followed close behind as the two chatted about everything Teal'd been missing in Spring. I knew she was eager to catch up with the stories of her home court before she'd found herself in an ogre's cage.

"Well, I see a pile of dimas with my name on it," Jair said as he heaved himself up and sauntered toward a table of faeless males playing cards and a stack of dimas, Eadha's currency, in the middle.

They greeted him well enough, but I wondered how much of it was out of fear. Jair, as beings of Eadha go, was a calm creature. Unless he was mad. Then even I stayed out of the lion-shifter's way.

Valentina yawned into my arm as I took another drink of Solanci.

"What is that?" she asked. "It smells like oranges and vanilla, but it looks like the night's sky."

She was right, the drink was black with small white sparkles running through it.

"It's called Solanci Ipsum. You smell blood oranges grown under shadows and the ash of vanilla bark harvested in Gillies Forest. There may also be a touch or two of rice alcohol," I said. I halted the bottle halfway to my lips as the memories of my Hunters crashed into my thoughts. Quieter, I added, "It's the closest drink I could make like it is back home."

"In The Court of Shadows?"

I swallowed down the Solanci and the damn pain in my chest that sprang up whenever I spoke of this. "In the Underworld."

I looked down at her as her eyes closed against my shoulder. By my hounds, she was beautiful. In deflection to thinking about her or the Underworld, I cleared my throat. "Let's get you to bed."

"Mmhm."

Later that evening, Sloane led us to our room, and I steered far clear of any more conversations with her. I was bound to put my hand through the nearest wall if I heard any more of her delusional opinions about Adrian.

Avika would love that.

I shucked off my shirt and lay in the middle of the bed, giving Valentina plenty of arm's length to get herself ready on the other side. My mind was rattling as I watched her lay her red and yellow daggers on the side table. The gods' daggers that I damn well knew could cut the ties between us. But I feared she would leave, so instead of being an honest fae and telling her the truth, that with one swipe of those daggers she could be free of me for good, I watched her in silence.

Water from her damp hair dripped a path down her chest. It trailed past a crude watermark tattoo on her clavicle and soaked into my black Court of Shadows' shirt she wore that was three sizes too big. I looked farther down at the fox-fur Autumn . . . underthings—as far as I was concerned—she was wearing. She looked like an enigma, a mash-up of the courts, and I didn't have to wonder if she felt like she fit in on this island. I knew what it was like to be different. The difference was, I had a feeling she cared.

"We can go in the morning and get you some proper-fitting clothes," I said.

She looked down at herself with a startled expression. I tried to pry inside her mind to see what had her so preoccupied, but she'd learned—clever creature—to keep me out.

"Are there faeless in The Court of Shadows?" she asked, ignoring what I said, and I dragged a hand down my face. Where, pray tell, was she going with this?

"No."

She turned to me and rubbed her fingertips over her full lips, contemplating something. Her eyes were blue and wide as the sea, and they were doing funny things to my insides. "Do you think the faeless will survive Lord Aborys?"

I yawned, sprawling out further onto the bed, wondering how much truth I should tell her. I settled on honesty. "With the lords and ladies of the courts doing nothing about it? No."

"And yet, *this* town still stands," she argued.

I threw an extra pillow to her side and eyed her cautiously. "Please don't mistake whatever Adrian is doing as kindness."

She huffed and crossed her arms. No matter my actions, I

couldn't coax her to the bed. "Do you think so highly of everyone?"

I stilled and looked up at her face—her absolutely pissed-off face. What the fuck was going on? I raised an eyebrow as I tried to open our mindspeak again, but she was closed off entirely. Fuck.

I swung my legs over the edge of her side of the bed and pulled her to me. I trapped her between my knees, holding her still, with no more intention than to drive home the understanding of what I was about to say.

"When my shadows exploded across the wastelands, turning those faeless who were roaming there—exiled by their own courts—into Shadowfae, we needed supplies. Food and shelter. And we were turned away. Every time, for far too long. It wasn't until our numbers grew and we began to make our own concoctions from Gillies Forest did they want anything to do with us. And it all stopped again when the fae went missing."

Her features softened. "Even the Courtless?"

"Their heir to the throne was missing. They kept to themselves until I returned him to them."

"Jair?"

I nodded.

She rubbed her bottom lip with her fingertips again, contemplating what I told her.

I traced the subtle movement with my eyes, like a pendulum, ever curious to know what those lips felt like. That impulsive brush of a kiss I gave her in the Fortress had only served to tease me. So I did what any noble fae would do; I tried a third time to forcibly pry inside her head to see where she was going with this. I was met with a thick black wall; she had barred me out completely and wasn't giving in. Which was probably a good thing, considering the direction of my thoughts.

And like a cold bath, those piercing eyes shot back to me as she said, "So you'll do nothing? About Lord Aborys' attacks against the faeless or if The War of Many finally comes crashing down?"

Ah. Here it is. My mouth twitched. "When I get my shadows back, and I will, I will protect my court and the Courtless as best I can. But the other courts? They can squabble and steal and rip themselves apart for all I care."

She looked down as if she wished to not see me, and my skin prickled at her reaction.

I was becoming increasingly aware that I cared what she thought of me. I was letting her down, and something inside me was *hurting* with this knowledge. "You don't like my answer?"

She pursed her lips. "When my water magic left me . . . I felt —I feel, helpless. And I hate it. But that's how these faeless in Kyrrahalyn and Blackwater and across the island feel every day. And you sit here with all this power. These shadows," she said, gesturing to them as they trailed up her legs, "are pulsing in waves I can feel through my entire being."

She was doing bad things to my ego.

Keep going, I urged through mindspeak.

Her eyes locked with mine again. "And yet, you do nothing."

Ouch.

I tugged her toward me, pulling her off her feet. I wanted to coax her out of her misery. She relented and landed on my chest with a huff. I tucked her into the curve of my body, spooning her. And I wanted to tell her to sleep and enjoy the soft bed we had for the night. To leave the problems of the island for the morning. But I knew her mind was whirling like spokes on a spinning wheel.

And the worst part? She had me thinking, too. Thinking about how she was infinitely better than anything else on this fucking island and how selfish I was to want her to stay with me while I trekked Winter, got my shadows back, and left, possibly forever.

I looked over at the traitorous gods' daggers on the bedside table. The ones that would cut this magical gold-and-silver tie that bound us to each other. She'd be free to go. And I feared it more than ever, that if she wasn't tied to me, she'd leave. Because what in me was there worth her staying for?

I sighed. "What is it you'd have me do? If I were to get involved?"

"Help, Kaderyn. I'd ask you to help them."

AUTHORS NOTE

Thank you, dear reader, for taking the time to finish Dancing With Darkness. This was a labor of love (andpainandhurtandtearsandblood). I wanted to take a minute to draw attention to its themes and the personal reasons I had in writing it. Though in fantasy, I am at liberty to make up quite a bit of its content (looking at you, Teal), Valentina's deep-seated desire to help is one I feel on a personal level.

I started Dancing With Darkness prior to 2018 when I was working in healthcare (both hospital and community) and throughout its creation, it has morphed in many ways. Though oddly enough, Teal and Adrian (who you'll meet in Shadows of Solace: The Wild Hunt book 2 if you haven't already in Skies of Onyx: Wild Hunt Short Story or Haven of Feathers and Ore) have demanded *loudly* not to be touched. But it has not morphed like a butterfly. No. It has completely changed shapes, species, forms, worlds.

At the time, I was trying to navigate—to be strong for—a scared world in a profession that was constantly under-appreciated. Those higher up the food chain swore we were 'all in this together' as they sat in velour high-backed chairs in front of a computer screen while we maintained frontline care for a panicking world. And the dance, the tightrope-walking tango I was attempting to do, between putting aside self-care, my family's best interest, and my profession, came crashing down when my own little faeling of three-years-old went through a medical crisis I wish on no other parent.

His heart was being fixed as mine was shattering.

What do you do? When you can't be in three places at once?

The tightrope snaps and you fall, and you have no choice but to pick up the pieces and try to shove them together. Some pieces will fit, and some get left behind.

Like Kaderyn trying to return home, to his old way of existing, I tried returning to my tightrope. (Now, with frayed ends tied haphazardly back together; like a child trying to tie their shoes—seventy knots of nonsense a light touch unravels.) And guess what? My tightrope disintegrated through my fingers into nothingness. But it left me with a story and a wish.

The story you've already started.

The wish: please don't feel alone. If your life has smashed into a million pieces, look down at the shards, see something beautiful in the remains, and always keep going.

ALSO BY H J REESE

Dancing With Darkness

Shadows of Solace

Rise of a Huntress

King of the Courtless
Coming soon

[Short Stories on Eadha Island](www.hjreese.com/newsletter/)
(Available for free if you're on my newsletter) Sign up for my newsletter at www.hjreese.com/newsletter/

Haven of Feathers and Ore

Skies of Onyx

Origins of Shadowfae

ABOUT THE AUTHOR

H J Reese is a left-handed, second-born, Sagittarius, who often falls into all the stereotypes these represent. She lives in a small town in Ontario, Canada but her dreams take her around the world. She is the author of the Wild Hunt books. Visit her website at www.hjreese.com for more information.